To Annabel — With warmest wishes
and a hope that
this as much as —
     Lorraine ·

GW01072097

Mary Darling

Mary Darling

L M D'Mello

Matador
9 Priory Business Park,
Wistow Road, Kibworth Beauchamp,
Leicestershire. LE8 0RX
Tel: 0116 279 2299
Email: books@troubador.co.uk
Web: www.troubador.co.uk/matador
Twitter: @matadorbooks

ISBN 978 1788035 453

British Library Cataloguing in Publication Data.
A catalogue record for this book is available from the British Library.

Printed and bound by CPI Group (UK) Ltd, Croydon, CR0 4YY
Typeset in 11pt Aldine401 BT by Troubador Publishing Ltd, Leicester, UK

Matador is an imprint of Troubador Publishing Ltd

For my brother Henry
without whom this novel would not have become a reality.

PROLOGUE

Oh no… Here it was again… She held her breath, waiting for the usual pattern. The single bell-like tone followed by the silence stretching into minutes, it seemed. And then the whistle…

The way she saw it, whistles could be encoded. All sorts of intentions could travel by way of a whistle – signals, instructions, promises, even feelings. This one, it seemed, heralded things to come. It was an alert call – wake up! Take notice! The question still needing an answer after all this time was – take notice of what?

Now the colours were on their way…

By degrees, the familiar cloud of luminous lavender, cornflower, gold, was massing, misting the air. And, once again, the temperature had plummeted. Again, it was an ice chamber. How odd that no one else seemed to notice. The tones next. Unearthly, haunting… A minute or two later would come the cry.

She waited, listening. Different times, different places but always the same sequence. Unfailingly. The music the prelude, the whistle the signal – for everything that followed.

A year of this with no explanation. How she wished she knew where it was all leading. And when she would find out.

ONE

Bored out of her skull, she was staring out of the window when it came. As usual, it blocked out everything else. Maths, of course, was especially easy to block. Sooo boring. Not only for her either. Half the class were messing with things far removed from the quadratic equations that Lasher was scribbling frantically on the board.

The cry would come next. A wild creature, very likely… But what and where? And so sad! Always the same. This time she just *had* to find out. The pattern, so familiar now, always tailed off with a cry. Lately it had sounded too often to ignore. She *had* to know. An animal or a bird? It had to be. Hurt? Maybe. Frightened? Almost certainly. Separated from its mother, perhaps? Hmm…

BANG! She didn't see the heavy book coming. It slammed down on the desk accompanied by the usual bellow – 'Mary Darling! Maths your last concern as usual, I see. Where were you this time? Mars?'

Unmistakable, the loud, grating voice. She

grimaced. Lasher! All the subtlety of a sledgehammer. The source of the nickname bestowed on him by every First Year entry at Milton Upper.

'Is there the remotest chance, do you think, that we might have the privilege of your company today, Mary Darling, or are you above all this?'

Heavy sarcasm. His speciality.

Titters rippling around, open sniggers from the Fellowes bunch. Loathsome creep! And his breath was vile. Must know she hated him; loathed being the object of all eyes. If only she could escape this! But it seemed to happen every day now. Trouble was, the distractions were always tons more interesting than anything going on in mathematics. A small bird last week, desperate to get in, the gleaming emerald-black beetle crawling across her desk on Friday and, last lesson, a brilliant, jaunty Monarch butterfly fluttering up the window. All mesmerising. Really, though, any wild creature was enough. Far more appealing than mind-numbing maths. And certainly the cry – *that* was absolutely irresistible.

Lashley was nothing but a bully. He picked on anyone who didn't see maths as the centre of the universe, tormenting those he disliked and terrorising the weaker ones, exposing them to everyone. Crud!

He disliked her particularly, she knew. Her obvious lack of interest in his lessons galled him, her defiance even worse. He knew he didn't intimidate her; what he didn't know was that Mary had picked up something else, something extraordinary, a deep-seated ugliness that seeped from his every pore whenever he looked at her. Hatred and contempt, of course. But something worse too, something foul, diseased, something that couldn't be concealed… She shuddered inwardly. Now he was swelling with importance.

'Well, Mary Darling? Do we have you with us today – or not?'

Hanging over her, his bony finger stabbing her shoulder, he oozed satisfaction. Faugh! Garlic again! He was coming even closer – agghh! The ugly thing, the darkness, it was there, right up close… She recoiled. And then relief – the bell. End of ordeal. And just as Lasher was distracted by the mass exodus, the Head was at the door beckoning to him. Well, Lasher couldn't ignore *him*, could he? Her chance had come.

She grabbed her books and bag, leapt up and ran. There was no option but to burst past Staddon and fly down the corridor into the school grounds, looking and listening to see if she could trace that cry. It had sounded so desperate. Where had it been coming from?

Just then – oh damn – snorts of derision from behind. Fellowes and her cronies with the usual sneers. Mary never knew what to expect but, as always, the physical odds weren't in her favour. With a deep breath, she drew herself up and stood like stone, surveying them with scorn. The usual status symbols flashed at her. Ugh! From day one, her indifference to the designer accessories had rankled with all three. Now, her face gave her away yet again; she could feel her contempt rushing to the surface – the bullies would not miss it.

Lana (*Lay*-na, she insisted) Fellowes, the only child of wealthy parents, had gathered cronies around her from similar backgrounds. Pure sycophants, they simply followed where *Layna* led, all three and their hangers-on lording it over the more impressionable amongst their classmates.

Mary had been an enigma from the start. Their initial whispered curiosity behind the curtains of immaculately-groomed hair and perfectly-manicured hands had soon become simmering antagonism. Squalls progressed to open hostility and, by the end of her first month at Milton Upper, she had been branded inferior, alien, a fair target for persecution.

Now, taller and heavier, they surrounded her, relishing the intimidation of physical menace in their favour. Her face, expressionless, betrayed little hint of inner tension. Only her hands were revealing. The brown skin was pale and stretched tightly across even paler knuckles as she stared back at them, fists bunched at her sides. As she did so, she felt the extraordinary sensation that was becoming familiar, starting up again inside her: a tidal sweep of energy surging from her feet by degrees, up through her limbs, back and chest.

Her breathing was slowing automatically yet, despite the churning in her stomach, there was quietness in her head. With each second, the odd force was taking possession of her. Somehow, she felt in her skin and yet not in her skin. How could this be? She shivered. So weird. One day, a little voice in her head began repeating, *things will be different*. One day, it would be in her power to dispatch not only these but any other bullies fool enough to stand in her way. One day…

Her tormentors fell back at the odd look in Mary's eyes, hardening now to the colour of steel, signalling somehow – against all the odds – her command of the situation. And something in that frozen, unearthly expression unsettled them.

The unknown strength continued to increase as she awaited the usual barrage of unimaginative taunts.

'Lost something, freaky?'

'Forget it, Paula, she's dumb.'

'Mental, more like!' Bagley muttered, sidling back.

They nudged each other uneasily. 'Watch it, she could be a witch.'

'Yeah. Black magic.'

'Or voodoo.'

'Or an alien…'

'Nooo. Retard, most likely. No wonder she was dumped – mum ran off with her gipsy mates.'

Whatever it was inside her was rising still, higher and higher. In desperation, she clenched her fists. What would happen if she couldn't contain it? Would she implode? Oh no! The blood beginning to pound in her ears, a hideous urge was sweeping over her, a compulsion to open her mouth and send out a high-pitched howl before disgorging whatever it was inside her all over them. Bizarre!

Yet suddenly that seemed absolutely applicable. For though the bullies looked outwardly stylish and shiny, the ugly, foul energy they were exuding clashed with their appearance. It needed exterminating. And, strangely, it seemed as if the force inside her carried a vigilante element, powered to destroy any toxic matter confronting it. She felt like its keeper, tasked with preventing it from bursting out because, unchecked, it would cause too much grief.

Her heart was hammering in a way she had not experienced before. Her tongue was glued to the roof of her mouth. With a gargantuan effort, she tightened her stomach muscles and, jaw clamped rigid, dug her nails into her hands. Perhaps the pain would check the flow within her! Her three tormentors, unaware of the intense internal battle before them, but realising something was going on, exchanged looks warily.

Just then, a spirited voice sounded behind them. 'Back off, you lot!' All three swung round. The girl facing them was a different proposition. Not quite as tall as Lana but strong and well-built, she was not only everyone's equal in sport but superior academically. Just as important, Lizzie Paige was not short of confidence. Knowing she could run rings round most of their year and had the general respect of all her peers, she was intimidated by no one. She stared them steadily in the eyes.

'Beat it!' she ordered. 'You're just yellow-bellied bullies. Fine all together – wimps on your own. Clear off or I'll let Staddon know your lousy game.' She moved forward, pushed through, stood by Mary and confronted them determinedly. The three hesitated, glanced uneasily at each other, then, tossing their heads carelessly, disappeared slowly through the school door with 'Gippo lover!' as a parting taunt.

'Thanks,' said Mary quietly.

'No probs.' Lizzie stared at her thoughtfully. 'Look, I don't know what's going on here but I do know that people – especially that bunch – tend to kick at anyone different they don't understand. And you *are* different – aren't you?'

Mary was silent.

'They're scared of you,' Lizzie continued. 'They've decided you're an alien because you're not like anyone else, really. You don't make the right noises.'

Her face betrayed her amusement. 'You don't admire their designer gear or even seem to notice it, come to that. You don't show the slightest interest in them and you don't bother to hide that either, so they can't get through to you.'

'So, if I'm so alien, why doesn't it put you off?'

'Because my folks have taught us, my brothers and me, not to judge people 'til we really know them. So it doesn't bother me who or what you are, I'll wait to find out. For now, until you show me something I *don't* like, you're okay. But I'd watch your back with that lot – they're a nasty bunch of bullies. Me, I hate bullies. Always have done.'

'Me too and I know you're right but I don't know what I should do,' said Mary, feeling the need to respond to this unexpected honesty from Lizzie.

'Stand up to them, that's what. They're pathetic. In a pack, they think they're so strong but singly, they're weak and if you get in first – go for the jugular, my father says – they'll back down. Honestly. You don't have to use your fists, don't think that'd work anyway,' she grinned as she looked Mary over, 'but you could try wit or sarcasm or even just laugh at them maybe. Bullies never expect that sort of reaction – it's a bit too advanced for them. It could be more powerful than you think. But whatever, you should do *something* to show them they can't intimidate you. That's just the way it goes – there won't always be help around, you know.'

Mary nodded. 'Mmm, I know, but it isn't as easy as that. I need to make sure first where it's going.'

Lizzie was right, this bunch *were* all yellow bellies and she could have put the wind up them easily. They'd probably have peed their pants at the first sign of a real threat, especially from someone who didn't look like she could frighten a fly. But she'd had some good teachers in the past and they'd taught her only too well.

Still, the time for trouble like that wasn't now. There'd come a time when she wouldn't need physical strength at all. This power growing inside her would change everything. One day. Awesome. She didn't yet know how, except that it would be hers to command at some point. The strange energy, and whatever difference it was going to make, had receded for the time being, but when it didn't, she'd have to be ready. Oh boy, would she!

As this all flashed through her head, she studied Lizzie carefully. How great to have a friend like this. Cool, the way she'd just waded in. No hesitation, no wavering. Yeah, stupid cool. But it looked like Lizzie Paige walked alone too, so maybe she didn't need – or want – any friends.

'Yeah, well, whatever…' said Lizzie, her voice tailing off as she turned to go.

Alone again, Mary weighed Lizzie's words. She was anything but unaware of the malevolence involved here. The "source" within her had made the stakes only too clear, the message explicit: the time would come when the need for her to act, to dispatch bullies, tyrants of all kinds – all classes, ages, races – would be unavoidable. That time might be coming earlier than anticipated. The temptation was already intense. She hated Fellowes and her cronies passionately – like all the bullies she'd met. Even at this stage, she could not only give them something to remember her by: if she wanted, she could stop them in their tracks completely. But there had to be other ways, solutions less direct – there had to be.

She mused. Spontaneous combustion, now… She'd read about that. People bursting into flames for no obvious reason – and *she* could make fires happen. She'd tried it in the Home once, focused really hard on some paper in a waste bin, and it had worked. Bit scary, but she could do it. Better if she could just wish it on them from afar, though, then no one could connect it with her. Maybe she'd start practising.

Meanwhile, there was the matter of the cry. She listened again. Nothing. Slowly she made her way to her favourite spot at the bottom of the lower playing field where she felt at peace, especially at this time of year.

Spring colours were beginning to cloak the poplars edging the field and the wind whispering through the leaves mingled with intermittent birdsong. Despite the pale sunshine, though, a chill lingered and the school canteen would have been a warmer option, but Mary preferred to eat her lunch outside, alone with nature and her thoughts. The grass felt like part of her and everything – trees, plants, birds, even the air whispering across her skin – felt natural.

Still thinking about the strange events, she reflected on that cry and how something like it had sounded at intervals even before she'd arrived at Milton Upper. Now things seemed to be moving on – she'd heard it every day this week. Although she'd accepted them, her unusual gifts had baffled her from an early age. There'd been those people, in clothes from a bygone age, who came and went at the Home: two women, then the old couple and then some children. Never stayed long, any of them, only minutes each time, never spoke, just smiled at her before fading away. Weird. All of it.

She'd begun to sense things about people, too, could often read their minds and "see" how their thoughts didn't always match their words. Finding that purse that had gone missing had been another uncanny business. The Voice just telling her where to look. Life at the Home had become more difficult after that until – no great surprise – she'd been moved on, fast. And the mysterious things had carried on happening, the things that she could do, hear and see, developing.

The telepathic ability. Now, that was really far out. Starting up without warning and still growing, though somewhat erratically, whilst other powers – like the pyrokinesis and this disturbing energy within her – seemed to be moving faster all the time. None of it was comfortable.

Tom and Susan Darling, her adoptive parents, found her odd, as well. They couldn't understand why, in all her years with them, she still preferred her own company – or nature and wildlife – to the company of other girls.

Mary sighed. She was fond of the Darlings and wished she could have been less of a disappointment to them. She couldn't have been more different from their own pink and white daughter. Photographs of Abbie, killed in a hit-and-run accident when only four years old, showed a sunny smile, an open, guileless expression. Mary's gipsy colouring and the naturally closed expression that faced her in the mirror every day, said the direct opposite.

Suddenly, in the midst of her reverie, there was a rustle in the bushes. *What was that?* She waited, listened. Nothing. A minute or two passed. Then – there! A definite movement. *Something, some creature, was in there!* Mary held her breath. Tense seconds passed. She crawled forward silently, watchful. The rustling continued. A short distance from the bushes she sat back on her heels, completely still, waiting. Minutes later, the leaves suddenly began to flutter, the bush to move. By degrees, a timid nose poked through. Gradually, the nose was followed by a long, pointed muzzle and then the head followed – the head of a *fox* – staring right at her! Their eyes met, locked, as Mary held her breath, gazing at it in wonder.

For what seemed like forever, the two stared at each other and then the strangest thing! She picked up a voice. *My leg is bleeding. Please… can you help me?* She looked around her. Where had that come from? Again it came. *It's really painful… please?* With no one else around, it had to be the creature!

Peering in amazement, Mary shook her head to clear it. Was it her imagination? Was she hearing things? No, there it was again – *Please, please… My leg is cut… Will you help me?* She stared at it incredulously. Then, slowly, the entire body of the animal appeared – and its leg really *was* cut and bleeding quite profusely. Barbed wire, no doubt – or some sort of trap – and yes, it did need help, fast. Poor thing.

Without any further hesitation, she stooped, scooped up her bag and the animal – it came without a struggle – and ran. Through the school gates and down the hillside, she raced, along the lane and across the busy High Street, with only one thought in her mind. *Freedom Fields!* She would take this poor creature to the best sanctuary she knew – to Annie…

Her mind flew ahead to the welcome in store. Annie would be delighted to see her, even happier to see her patient. The stock of valuable herbs and potions would be raided immediately and before long, that ugly wound would be a mere memory. The little animal would be in matchless hands. She did her best, breathlessly, to reassure the fox trembling in her arms.

I'm taking you to someone very special, so don't worry. You'll be just fine.

TWO

Tucked away at the end of the lane on one edge of the small town, *Freedom Fields* cottage was a sanctuary to all comers but mainly to wildlife. The trees behind it fringed a lazy river with fields and meadows housing hedgerows and rich undergrowth stretching into the distance, all of it the ideal habitat for a wealth of wild creatures and an abundance of plant life.

Mary, arms full of fox and well used to her friend's ways, kicked the bottom of the door to announce her arrival. Within seconds, it opened and Annie stood facing her, her own arms heaped with vegetation. She took in the situation at a glance.

Annie Towers. Ageless, wiry, with a face resembling creased parchment, she was a weaver of miracles: nothing and no one that came to her wounded remained so for long. Herbs, plants and flowers from the hedgerows were Annie's medicines and, backed by the knowledge of centuries, her use of them was powerful. Another potent skill had given her instant recognition of Mary's fledgling gifts – especially the one she knew it was her mission to encourage and develop – as well as a clear vision of the girl's future. And there were many times when this skill would operate spontaneously, when Mary would arrive unannounced – and yet expected.

So had the girl become her protégé. Her lack of friends and aura of isolation had made the wise woman determined to help in whatever way she could. Mary's own nature had done the rest. Touched by her sensitivity and her love of the natural world, Annie had decided swiftly to teach Mary all that she, herself, knew and more, aware that the time would come for the girl to need every ounce of that knowledge.

Now, she didn't waste time on words. Taking the injured animal immediately, she carried it to her large, old-fashioned, wooden kitchen table, at the end of which resided a colourful collection of tins, bottles and jars filled with creams and potions. Quickly she examined the leg then, taking a wedge of cotton wool, dipped it into the contents of one of the wide-necked jars before gently but expertly swabbing the wound clean.

'Nasty cut,' she commented, 'caused by one o' them trap things. See the edges, girl? It's metal wot done that, serrated too. Bustards!' Annie's language was colourful at the best of times. Now she didn't hesitate to voice her opinion of those who laid out traps for creatures in the wild. In her experience, *all* wildlife was infinitely superior to human beings. Mary, well used to hearing what Annie thought, nodded her agreement. She watched with interest and respectful attention as the old woman set about repairing the damage to the little animal.

'Will you need to dress it?' she asked quietly, 'or will it heal if you just leave it open?'

'The cream going on now, lass, be strong enough to heal the cut in a flash but we'll bandage 'im up just for today to make sure it kicks in. Don't worry, we won't let this little one out 'til I can see for meself that it's done the trick!'

Fascinated by the old woman's work and longing to be able to do the same, Mary felt her own hands beginning to throb. She tucked them behind her back, flexed her fingers now pulsating oddly, and ran her right hand idly back and forth along the back of her left arm. A streak of sudden heat flashed along her arm and she jumped in astonishment with a small yelp. For Annie, who never missed a trick, this didn't go unnoticed. She looked at Mary curiously. 'What's up, lass? You got summat to say?'

'I... I... It's just... I don't know. Something seems to be happening to my hands. I haven't felt it before.'

Without speaking, Annie reached behind Mary's back, grasped her hands for a split second then dropped them instantly.

'They're red hot, girl! Don't touch me, just hold them above my arm and let's see what I can feel. Ahhh yes – the warmth is soaking into me arm. Give 'em 'ere, hold 'em over this littl'un's leg and let's see what 'appens.'

Seconds passed, then a sigh and a weary voice came from the fox – *Thank you, thank you* – and the animal, with relief, promptly went to sleep on the table. Mary gazed at the small creature, then at Annie wide-eyed – 'Did you see that? He went straight off to sleep! But he spoke first – did you hear it or was that my imagination?'

'No, love, I didn't – but if you did, that's wot matters, ain't it?'

Annie looked at Mary shrewdly.

'It's comin' time, Mary,' she said now firmly. 'I want you 'ere for an hour each day after school, reglar like if you can make it. There's a whole lot to teach you and time is a-goin' on. You up for that?'

'Oh yes, absolutely, Annie – you know how much I want to do what you do!'

'By the time we've finished, girl, you'll be doin' a darn sight more 'cause you've got more abilities and we 'ave to wake 'em up and make the very most o' them – soon as!' And the old woman patted Mary's shoulder decisively. 'Last week's lesson, now – what d'you remember about cleaning up them wounds? And I want all the names o' the 'erbs you need from the off!'

Half an hour later, Mary looked at her watch in consternation. Oh no! She was well and truly late for afternoon lessons. Still thinking of the fox, she sped off through the lanes.

Both teacher and subject were Mary's favourites. Mrs Hunt enjoyed her vivid imagination and the

English teacher did her best to make up for the lack of understanding that Mary met with from some of the other staff. Now she looked reprovingly at her watch as Mary came through the door but simply motioned her to be seated. Mary slid gratefully into her seat and did all she could to escape further attention while she made up lost ground.

Even though absorbed in the work, however, her thoughts insisted on straying to the small, lone fox recovering in Annie's care. Judith Hunt, watching her keenly, couldn't help noticing that, despite her enjoyment of the exercise, for Mary other matters were intruding.

'Everything okay, Mary?' she asked as she wandered around the room in her usual fashion during such an exercise. 'Anything you need help with?'

'Oh no, thank you, it's fine, Mrs Hunt,' Mary replied, recalled hurriedly to the passage in front of her. She must concentrate on the present; the little creature was in the best hands and her own part in all this would become clearer as time went on. If only things would happen faster though!

Lizzie Paige was at the school gates as Mary approached. Lizzie lived in her direction – it would be great if they could walk at least part of the way home together. She approached the other girl diffidently, waited for a reaction. Lizzie did not disappoint.

Though largely in silence, the walk seemed companionable. Before Lizzie turned off, she stopped and looked steadily at Mary. 'We could do this more often. We both live this way – shall we give it a go?'

Mary felt a small rush of she didn't know what. Was it pleasure? Happiness? 'Yeah, why not?' she said simply. And that afternoon, for once, she turned into the Darlings' drive with a small smile on her face. Her mother would be watching keenly from the living room window, as usual, and would notice the smile. Wouldn't she be curious!

The fresh scents and colours of spring continued to lighten the memory of winter's chill, although a nip in the air was still noticeable. Mary shivered as she traced a pattern with her finger in her breath on the bedroom window the next morning. Remembering colder days and nights made her think, sadly, of all the creatures that would *not* feel the coming warmth. Not for the first time, she began to think how she could help some of them to survive.

'Are you coming? Breakfast's ready,' came Mrs Darling's voice from the bottom of the stairs. 'Come on, now, I know you're at the window staring at some creature or other out in the garden but time's going on and you'll be late!'

Mary smiled to herself. Her mother knew her so well, sometimes!

'Coming,' she called as, grabbing her school bag, she ran from the room. Mrs Darling looked at her keenly.

'Anything special on today?'

Mary smiled, for a rare moment the smile reaching her eyes. She could see that her mother had sensed something, was waiting expectantly to hear about it, knew that she should mention her walk home with Lizzie Paige, and that this small sign of progress after so long would please her. She would wait, though; better that she had something more conclusive to report than a simple walk home.

'No, nothing in particular, just a pretty good day yesterday. I had English and Mrs Hunt told me more about Milton Upper. Seems an okay place once you get to know it.'

'Diana Lord is a year ahead of you and has always been happy there. Her mother says it's a good school and the teachers are fair. They encourage the pupils to make the most of themselves in any way they can. I'm sure you'll be a lot happier with time and some friends.'

🦋

There was now something to look forward to and Lizzie smiled across the rows of chairs as the classes filed into morning assembly. With ten weeks to go to the end of term, and for those moving on to university or elsewhere, the mood of assembly was thoughtful. Mr Staddon was taking the opportunity to issue a new piece of wisdom each morning, especially for the benefit of the school leavers, and today his theme was *Ambition*.

The school, in general, liked the Head and so all years listened respectfully as he talked about things like Strength of Character, the inevitable Hard Work,

Hopes and Dreams. He ended with The Power of Dreams and as Mary listened to this, her own heart responded. She could enter into this. Most of her life had been powered by dreams. She knew how they could transform the world and life in general; they were her chief escape from the daily business of living and her loneliness – her dreams, her love of wildlife and, now, the astonishing, developing gifts that would enable her to help all creatures. She felt eyes on her, looked across the hall and met Lizzie's. The two girls exchanged glances of what felt to Mary like mutual understanding.

The brief exchange did not go unnoticed. Watching from her place further along in Mary's row, Paula Bagley saw this development and grimaced, then just as quickly smirked. A quick glance at Lana showed her that the blonde girl had also noticed the glances between Lizzie and Mary – and not with pleasure. The three cronies and their latest recruit put their heads together during break, Paula taking the lead.

'I've had some ideas,' she confided to the others, 'if we're clever, we can nip this matiness in the bud and cause a load of hassle for the gippo.'

Lana surveyed her immaculately varnished nails, expressionless, as she waited to hear more. She listened as Paula outlined her plan, gradually paying more and more attention with increasing interest as the details unfolded. 'Hmm, this could be good,' she said reluctantly. 'If we're successful, it could end in a real disaster for Darling. That we,' and she looked at the three others, deliberately uniting them all, 'have to mix with her sort is, in itself, an insult. She deserves everything that's coming to her!'

Their latest recruit, a new girl on the block from a more expensive school whose parents had been forced to downsize on all fronts, sat silently, uncertain as yet whether she really belonged to this cohort.

'Well,' Lana went on grudgingly to Paula, as she flicked a stray hair from her pullover, 'I'm quite impressed. You've outdone yourself for once. We'll plan it over the next couple of weeks but if we succeed, it'll slap a dirty great blot on Darling's records and, with luck, be a big step towards shoving her back where she belongs – in the gutter!'

THREE

The next three days were peaceful. It was great to be left alone by the Fellowes bunch and Lizzie seemed her sort of person: straight, honest and funny. Maybe, just maybe, she had found herself a friend at last.

As Mary walked home with her that afternoon, both their minds were elsewhere. End-of-year exams might be in the offing but school holidays stretched ahead as well, with the prospect of exhilarating, golden days of freedom. Long walks and fruit picking; exploring the countryside; checking out the reported sightings of ospreys and the extremely rare visitor to these regions, the great grey shrike, usually in Autumn/Winter but occasionally spotted in early Summer, together with other birds at the old stone quarry; and cycling on the common. All this and freedom that she could share and enjoy with someone now, so much *not* tethered to lessons and homework – all so alluring.

'Going anywhere for the summer?' asked Lizzie.

Mary thought for a minute before answering. 'Don't think so. My father's just been given some important responsibility at work and doesn't feel he can take time off and Mum's busy with the Hospice fete. Anyway, they've had to spend a fair bit on my uniform and other bits and pieces for the move and it's all been quite expensive. You?'

'Just a week with the grandparents in Northumberland. They're getting old now and we need to make sure they're okay. Otherwise, no, we'll be here the rest of the time.'

Mary swallowed. Should she, shouldn't she? What did she have to lose? Only her pride – not worth much when it came to actually having a friend. She decided to risk a rebuff.

'Is there… Would there… Do you think…' she stammered, then stopped. Maybe it was too soon.

'Are you thinking we could meet up in whatever time's left?' asked Lizzie. 'Because if you are, yeah, great.'

Now Mary really had something she could talk about! Mrs Darling, in the act of putting a tray of baking in the oven, turned to catch the grin on her daughter's face as she entered the kitchen. Her excitement was unmistakable. Hanging up the oven gloves, Susan Darling enquired with what appeared to Mary a casual interest – 'Had a good day, then?' and, having heard it all, smiled broadly. She threw her arms around the girl and gave her a huge hug. 'Well, this deserves celebrating, doesn't it? Sit down and we'll treat ourselves to a glass of elderflower wine while you tell me all about it.'

The following day began badly. Mary, exhilarated by the possibility of her new friendship and affected, too, by thoughts of the fox at Annie's, had not been able to sleep. Her mind buzzing, she had tossed and turned restlessly. The morning saw her listless over her breakfast with the result that her mother was forced to remind her repeatedly of the time. Now, as she ran down the road, satchel flung carelessly over her back, her mind was on the day ahead and she didn't notice that the strap on her satchel was not pushed home into the buckle.

Oh hell! Jerked by her running, the strap had given way and now the contents of her satchel were flying out everywhere. Cars slowed and hooted as she ran into the road to retrieve them; a van crunched over a pack of pens before she could grab them; and, as she scrabbled frantically at the books and other bits and pieces, the full significance of her situation washed over her.

She was going to be really late. And it couldn't be worse: double maths first period with Lasher. Hell on earth! What a nightmare!

'You need some 'elp, love? Here's a pen, look, and there's your rubber over there…'

One or two motherly passers-by came to her aid but Mary was miserably aware that the first period would be well under way by the time she reached the school. Fastening the bag at last, she stood unhappily, wondering if she should bunk off. The temptation was immense, the prospect of facing the maths master almost too awful to contemplate. But no. Her fault – her problem. She'd just have to take the rap. Shoving her hands in her pockets with a huge sigh and sinking heart, she headed for the school gates.

As she had feared, the first period was well advanced and Lasher in full flow as she entered. There was a hush as her classmates looked up at the uncomfortable figure in the doorway.

Lasher was talking as he wrote at speed on the board. Alerted by the sudden hush, he turned to see what had caused the silence. The satisfaction on his face was immediately obvious and she could almost hear his purr of pleasure as he took in the situation. In a flash, her mind registered his thoughts – *Ah! The gipsy brat, eh? Late for my lesson, eh? Well, well...* And she shrank within herself. Oh no, it had happened again! The energy flow within her had started to swell and rise and, with it, came the other developing powers. It must happen with any strong feeling on her part, then. She'd have to look out for that, though what she could do to stop it in its tracks was anyone's guess. Feelings weren't easily controllable by the mind, in her experience, especially if they were strong.

'Come here, girl!' he beckoned. Mary advanced unhappily. Hell's teeth, the loathsome creep would milk this like mad now and she had no defence. And, as she came nearer, she felt the darkness emanating from him again. She stopped, unwilling to advance further.

'Come here, come here! I haven't got all week! Now – you obviously think you have better things to do with your time than attend my lesson, so entertain us, Mary Darling. Just what has been so much more important this morning than your presence in my maths lesson – hmm?'

The focus of all eyes, Mary was silent. What could she say? He had the whip hand. She had no reason that he would accept and she knew that he knew it. She squirmed with embarrassment, shifted from one foot to the other and, as she did so, the energy flow within her became even more forceful. She paled with horror. Oh God! What now? Each time it made its appearance, it went one step further. Last time she had nearly imploded. A shudder shot through her frame as she fought to control herself. What would happen this time? One minute became three as Lasher waited for her to respond. Finally he spoke.

'Well, girl, yet again speech seems to have deserted you and I'm wasting more of my valuable time as well as that of your colleagues who did – unlike you – have the courtesy to turn up when they should. It's time an example was made of this rudeness and one, Mary Darling, that you aren't likely to forget. YOU – COME – WITH – ME!'

And, grabbing her by the arm, he dragged her to the corner of the room, thrusting a large sheet of cardboard and a thick felt pen at her. Mary flinched as, with a belch of garlic breath, he bellowed in her face. 'Now write, girl, in large block capitals – I AM RUDE AND IGNORANT! And when you've done, you'll stand in this corner holding it in front of you for the rest of the lesson! It will remind us all of what we have to suffer constantly in your company! What's more, when I've finished here, you will take up a position with that board in the corridor outside the Headmaster's door for the rest of the morning!'

Breathing hard, the maths master swelled with satisfaction. A few of the class tittered. Several remained silent in sympathy. All of them recognised that Lasher's punishment was way out of line for their year group: it was reducing Mary to the level of a First Year. The Fellowes bunch sneered openly. Mary flushed scarlet. This was worse than anything she had imagined. To have to stand there for the rest of the lesson with this board was shame enough: to have to repeat it outside Mr Staddon's door was too much. She couldn't do it. Maybe she should make a run for it now rather than wait until the end of the lesson and, as she considered this option, she felt a rush of energy inside her as though the force beginning to take her over was in sympathy and preparing her for a rapid exit.

Triumph all over his face, Lasher turned back to the board and his writing. The snickers died away and, calm restored, the class returned to work. Mary, taking quick, shallow breaths and clenching her stomach muscles to control her agitation, stood with her head down, holding the board. Could she stand it for the rest of the lesson or should she leg it now? No. She wouldn't let this scumbag win, wouldn't give him even more satisfaction from seeing her run – she'd die first! From time to time, the Fellowes bunch looked up at her, pulled expressive faces at each other and sniggered. She stared back at them with as much indifference as she could muster. Occasionally, she met Lizzie's horrified and sympathetic gaze across the classroom. Most of the time, hot with mortification and mounting outrage at Lasher, she focused on the floor. The end of the lesson couldn't come fast enough for her, even though she knew that, when it did, her humiliation would simply begin again outside Mr Staddon's room. What a nightmare! Lasher was a monster. How would she ever live this down?

At that moment, the force within her, now throbbing and bubbling uncomfortably, chose to remind her even more forcibly of its existence. She had moved her gaze to the large wastepaper bin on the other side of the master's desk at the front, was imagining it bursting into flame with a loud blast, visualising the shock on those smug faces, when instantly, the bin did just that. It burst into flames, the paper and other detritus in it billowing smoke as it caught fire. She recoiled, then stared in horrified fascination as shrieks and screams broke out everywhere. The room was immediately full of bodies struggling to get out of the door as panic reigned.

As they pushed and heaved, the inevitable happened: some of her classmates became wedged in the doorway. God! How frightful! Was it really her doing this? She could only watch aghast, her feet rooted. Those jammed in the doorway were only able to struggle free when Lasher seized the classroom's fire extinguisher, directing it forcefully at the flames. With smoke billowing everywhere, he rushed between windows, opening them and bellowing at the class to help. In the midst of the panic, through the smoke, the figure of the Head appeared in the doorway. The two men conferred hastily whilst the class finished opening windows and setting upright the desks and chairs that had been overturned in the rush to get out of the room.

Slowly, a semblance of order was returning but the whispering, shock and general agitation continued until, a minute later, Lasher finished talking with the Head and returned to the front of the room.

'Right – now, which of you was responsible for starting that?' he barked. With everyone staring around at everyone else and no answer forthcoming, he strode back and forth around the room, glaring at each pupil in turn as if willing them to confess their part in the débâcle. Finally, he stopped and turned to fix Mary with an evil look. All fear had left her by now. All feelings of loneliness and of being thought weird had disappeared. At last, she just might have been given something valuable, a gift that could defeat Lasher – all of her enemies – in time and if so, when she was ready, this toerag would know about it, that was for sure! She stared back at him stonily.

Responsibility had to involve a *conscious* act, didn't it? She hadn't intended starting that fire – it had simply started of its own volition, hadn't it? Well, okay, she may have lent a hand along the way but she still had to establish that. She had to know, beyond doubt, that she had played a key part in that incident and if so, how, because – sure as night followed day – she wanted to be able to do it again! The seconds ticked by as they stared at each other in mutual contempt until the bell for the end of the lesson was heard. Lasher turned away from her with a scornful gesture.

'I will get to the bottom of this, you bunch of no-goods! This had to be started by someone and if anyone saw who it was, you had better come forward because you haven't heard the end of this. The whole class will be in detention after school every day this week until I get an answer!' and, ignoring the wave of protest that greeted that announcement, he motioned to Mary – 'You, girl, follow me!' – swept up his books and strode off through the door.

With a last resigned look at Lizzie over her shoulder, Mary followed him, battling her own mixed emotions: the shock and horror she had felt was now a compound of wry pride and fascination at the discovery of what she could apparently do with so little effort. Oh boy, if she could really do it, could actually set things on fire, this was going to be something big in her life. She must – absolutely must – grab the first chance to have another go at it! It would need practice too. She'd have to make sure a power of this sort would be well under her control. Oh boy, what a gift! At last the source within her had given her something worth having!

As the maths master left her, smiling broadly and openly at her humiliation, Mary viewed his departing back with loathing. If only a bolt of lightning would descend from above and strike him down! What a shame the source of all this energy that was growing inside her hadn't given her *that* ability. Wait a minute, though – if she really had this gift of being able to set something – or someone – on fire and she practised it enough, at some point in the future she could set *him* on fire, couldn't she? *That* would solve the whole problem. And no one would connect it with her. It could easily be seen as an act of God! Or the work of demons. Yes, demons – that'd be a good one.

Lost in her imaginings concerning the maths master's early demise, Mary suddenly became aware that the air around her was changing. Slowly, gradually, the colours were beginning to materialise. She had missed the signal. Oh gosh! The music next. That could mean another animal needing help and she was stuck here with this wretched board. Unable to stop herself, tears of humiliation and rage at herself, as well as at Lasher, trickled down her cheeks.

Not much in her short life had been able to reduce Mary to tears but now she had other more defenceless creatures to think about and the fact that she'd been placed in this position where she could do nothing to help them was too much. She choked back a sob and clenched her fists in frustration. How she hated humans! Somehow, they always managed to louse up life for the rest of the planet.

Just at that moment, Mrs Hunt appeared round the corner of the corridor. 'Mary, my dear, what on earth are you doing here?' she asked and, as Mary recounted her tale of woe, the English teacher gazed at the girl with compassion. The damp cheeks and wretchedness in every line of Mary's figure was unmistakable.

'Give me that board, Mary,' she said crisply, 'and go to the lesson that you should be attending. I will sort this out!' and, as Mary vanished round the corner, the sound of raised voices from the Head's office followed her down the corridor, through the open window as she made her way past it and through the grounds. How much, she wondered, would Mrs Hunt say to Mr Staddon and how much might that affect the scumbag who had been a major cause of her misery since her first day at Milton Upper!

FOUR

The colours, fading now, had done their work and, as before, the musical tones heralding the next stage had begun. Next would be the cry – she had to be out there ready to respond! Instinctively, she raced towards the trees at the side of the upper playing field. This was where she must station herself.

Not a moment too soon! Only seconds after she had settled herself quietly in place against one of the trunks, the cry sounded. This time she was ready. Silently, she waited for it to give her some idea of the location. A few minutes later, it was repeated. Still no clear position. Minutes passed before she began to pick up the faint voice.

Help! came the plea. *Help me, please!*

She concentrated, closed her eyes and focused her thoughts. She knew it would come to her in time. Perhaps it would get easier as she became better at it. *Where are you? Please tell me where I can find you.* She sent out the thoughts as forcefully as she could. Another wait. No reply. Frustration building, she tried again. This so-called gift of hers wasn't up to much if it was going to take this long to find a casualty. At this rate the poor thing would be dead before she got to it!

More minutes passed. She let the thought trickle more slowly from her mind. Immediately the reply came back. *The tall bushes behind the big oak.* Ah, so that was it – she mustn't force her end of the conversation, then it would flow. Wasting no more time, she ran to the tree, scrambled behind it and dived into the bushes. *Where? Where? Which bush? There are so many. And what are you? Are you in the bush or on the ground?*

My wing's hurt, I can't fly; I'm on the ground in the bottom of the bush.

The voice was weak. Right. A bird. Oh God – a bird! This would be even more difficult. Unless it was a parrot – and that wasn't very likely – there'd be no colours to guide her. Most birds did tend to blend into the background. Useful for camouflage, of course, but equally useless when they needed help. And they were fragile. It would be so easy to cause more damage. She sent out a quick plea. *Please, help me to find you or this could take forever.*

Minutes passed while she continued to search, down on her hands and knees under low, dense bushes, gently parting the feathery branches and carefully separating the heavier ones in order to make sure that the injured bird did not suffer further harm.

Am I getting nearer? Can you see me?

I think so but there are still branches in the way.

Uh-huh – the voice was beginning to sound slightly louder. She was obviously getting near. Suddenly it became clear.

I can see you through the branches in front of me.

Slowly, Mary parted the leaves in front of her and, yes, there it was! Cowering at ground level in the centre of the dense bush, a thrush was looking up at her in desperation, one wing drooping, clearly hurt.

How did you do this? Without thinking, the words came, unbidden, into her head. Response was swift. *A buzzard was chasing me and I flew into the window of that shed.* Ah, she'd been right: thinking the words spontaneously – just like an ordinary conversation in her mind – made all the difference. Struggling to send out the thoughts, trying to force it, somehow made the process much slower. How many times had she been told she lacked patience! Okay – lesson learned. The shed in question could only have been that of the school gardener.

How did you escape?

The buzzard went after another bird and I managed to drag myself into the bushes.

Oh gosh! Picking it up without causing further damage wouldn't be easy. No choice, though, she'd just have to do her best. She peeled off her school jumper.

I'll try not to hurt you. Please help me as much as you can.

At least there was one bonus – while she'd been searching, she'd felt her hands becoming warm, just as when she'd taken the fox to Annie, and it seemed to send it to sleep. Clearly this was a sign of something she might have to expect, though as yet she still didn't know what other good it might do.

'Mary! Mary!'

Oh damnation – Lizzie! What bad luck. It was too early in their fledgling relationship for Lizzie to be involved in this but what choice was there? She had no other excuse for scrambling around in the bushes. Without a decent reason, Lizzie would think her off her rocker. What a time for her to appear. Okay, well, too bad. She'd just have to get on with it and stop faffing about!

'Lizzie, I'm over here, in these bushes – *how weird can you seem? In the bushes!* Can you come and help?' Thank goodness for Lizzie's practical side. She wouldn't waste time asking questions – she'd just get on with it.

Seconds later, Lizzie appeared behind her. She took in the scene at a glance.

'What do you want me to do?'

Another minute or three passed before their combined efforts paid off and the thrush was cradled gently in Mary's pullover. It must have been feeling the warmth from her hands because it was looking distinctly sleepy. Lizzie looked at Mary questioningly.

'What happened? How did you end up here?'

'Mrs Hunt rescued me from outside Staddon's room.'

'Did he see you?'

'No – he was on the phone. I could hear him talking.'

'So why didn't you come back to the lesson?'

'I just had a feeling that something was wrong out here.'

'You just had a feeling?'

The silence between them grew. Mary flushed. Yes, it sounded lame even to her. But it was too early to try and explain to Lizzie what she was experiencing. They were only just on the edge of friendship. Oh hell!

'Anyway, what are *you* doing here?'

'I needed a book from my bag in the cloakroom so decided to come and look for you.'

Mary was touched. 'Thanks for that. Look, I know it looks odd but I'll explain all this later. Let's just get this bird to someone who can help, shall we?'

Hang on – no time like the present. This would be a good opportunity to let Lizzie meet Annie, wouldn't it?

'Hey, how about *you* come with me? It *is* almost lunchtime, after all.'

Long seconds passed as Lizzie stared at her expressionless, then nodded.

'I've got a dental appointment in town this afternoon anyway, so I may as well go straight there from wherever it is you're heading. Wait a sec while I just grab my bag.'

Carrying the small bird carefully, the girls made their way out of the school gates and headed down the road to the High Street. Each was silent, wrapped up in her own thoughts. Reading Lizzie's mind, Mary answered her – 'We're taking it to see a friend of mine. Her name's Annie and she heals anything and everything. All her remedies come from nature and she's brilliant. You'll see.'

'How d'you know her?'

'I found a cat torn up a bit – in a fight, I think – and was taking it home to see what I could do. Annie happened along, spotted us and took me to her cottage. She sorted out the cat in no time and it just kind of went on from there. Now, we're good friends. Up to now, she's been my only friend.'

The last bit was added hesitatingly. After all, she didn't want Lizzie to think she had "victim" stamped on her forehead and was desperate for a friend, even though inwardly she knew the latter was somewhat near to the truth.

The front door of the cottage was firmly shut and no amount of knocking brought anyone to open it. The girls stood undecided.

'How about the back?' suggested Lizzie. 'P'r'aps she's round the back?'

A small wooden side gate led to the back garden where immediately they saw that the upper half of the stable door to the kitchen was open. In the centre of the garden stood a large metal cage and there, to Mary's relief, was the fox – curled up, asleep. Just at that moment Annie appeared, clambering through the fence at the bottom end of the garden, her arms piled high with greenery.

'Mary, girl – I didn't expect to see you till later! And who's this you've brought?' She looked at Lizzie keenly as she approached. Then, without waiting for an answer, 'And what's that you've got there? Let me see, lass…' And, noting Mary's anxious glance in the direction of the cage, 'You can see that little feller when we've seen to this one, lass. Redcoat's all right; this one needs us now.'

Depositing her gatherings in the cottage, she took the small bird from Mary and laid it gently on a towel on the kitchen table.

'Well, little feller, let's see what you done 'ere… Ah, I see, it's the wing's the problem, ain't it?'

Mary looked down at the bird then, knowing that Lizzie was listening, said tentatively, 'I think it may have flown into a window.'

'Hmm, that'd make sense. Now, take note, girl, it's important to see how bad this is afore we can do right by this little chap. We need to know just what treatment to give him, right? So, look 'ere, lass, we 'ave to make a thorough examination. Don't rush it, take it easy, right?' Mary nodded. There was silence as Annie parted the feathers, examining the bird more carefully, making soft reassuring noises to it all the while.

'So,' she finished her examination, 'it's actually a small injury and if we take care and go easy, we can get away with binding it. Then, over the next few days, we'll give it a bit of 'ealing and see 'ow that 'elps.'

As the girls watched, Annie went to work carefully with tape, securing the wing against the small body in its natural position, murmuring gently to the small creature as she did so.

'Hold the good one up there, Mary, so's I can get the tape underneath. That's it, lass, 'e 'as to be able ter balance and the other wing'll 'elp him. There – done now – let's see 'ow 'e does wi' that.' Annie stroked the small creature gently. 'All done now, little fella – you'll be fine. We'll rest you up and keep you safe and warm and you'll soon be better.'

The three of them watched in silence for some minutes as the thrush struggled to remain upright.

'Will he be all right, Annie? How long will it take for the wing to mend?'

'Well, 'e might be a bit awkward for a bit but we'll see 'im right until 'e can manage 'isself. As to mending, lass, we'll just have to keep an eye on 'im. Each case is different and you can never say. Now a bit o' water in that small dish – not too much, else 'e'll drown 'isself – and there's a bag o' seed over by the kettle. Put some in that tray and we'll find 'im a temporary 'ome where 'e feels safe.'

With the thrush safely ensconced in one of the small cages that Annie kept for her avian casualties, a warm blanket placed over it, Mary sent out a silent message – *You're safe here. Annie'll take care of you and I'll be back tomorrow.*

Thank you!

The little creature, nestling in the corner of its cage, opened one eye and looked at her gratefully before settling down to sleep.

The immediate concerns dealt with, Annie looked from one girl to the other, and Mary, recognising the question, responded – 'Annie, this is Lizzie, she's…' she hesitated.

'A friend,' Lizzie completed it for her.

Annie looked from one to the other in silence.

'Well, 'ow about that then – took me ages to get a smile from you, me girl, now you're grinning yer 'ead off! Now then, shall we go out and look at the fox and then would you girls like a cup o' my lemongrass tea? Part o' your learnin', Mary girl, this 'ere tea'm good for loads o' things – 'ealthy skin, coughs and colds – I'll give you a list, people 'oo didn't oughta take it, too. You can't afford to make mistakes, chuck!'

Mary nodded, her nose prickling with pleasure. This was her world. This was what she wanted her life to be. She glanced across at Lizzie. Would she be able to understand that and really be the friend she wanted? If only...

FIVE

As she raced back to the school, Mary's thoughts and feelings were mixed. On the one hand, her intuition told her that a real friendship with Lizzie was on the cards; on the other, she had yet to explain the strange happenings and her talks with animals and she wasn't sure, by any means, how Lizzie would react. After all, there was no denying it did sound weird. And that was *without* everything else: the spooky energy thing; her growing ability to read people's minds; the gift she apparently had of starting fires; and, worse still, the fact that she possessed a disturbing urge – *and* possibly the power, with all these developing abilities – to destroy people as well as objects! That was awesome. She, herself, hardly understood what was happening here, never mind making someone else understand it.

Not only that, she wasn't used to sharing *anything* with anyone. This was a whole new ball game. Too many blows in life had given her a thick streak of cynicism. Was this potential friendship heading for more disappointment and, even if it were genuine, did one have to tell friends *everything*? What did friendship involve anyway? She knew what she might want it to be but she still had to find out whether that idea had any truth in it.

Lizzie, meanwhile, was also preoccupied. Open, energetic and generally involved in some practical activity, that evening she was thoughtful. Her parents, she knew, never worried too much about her because, faced with a problem, she would either sort it herself or talk it over with them. Her two brothers were equally outgoing and uncomplicated and so the Paige family home was generally one of ebullience and frank good humour.

This evening was different. Normally talkative, Lizzie was unusually quiet. Her mother, she knew, would notice this and she had every intention of talking to her about it all later. Her mum, being outside the situation, would know best how to handle it, whereas she, herself, was too close to it to find the right balance. Her intentions were thwarted however: Mrs Paige was diverted by a telephone call from her sister which went on for ages, certainly longer than usual. Well, too bad – it was a good time to clean out the rabbit's hutch while she figured this one out for herself!

There was something here she didn't understand. Things seemed to be going on that she'd never encountered. A mystery and no mistake. All she knew

– and she didn't know how she knew but somehow she was certain – was that whatever Mary was involved in, it could simply *not* be bad and her own support and friendship were needed. By the end of the evening, she'd made up her mind. She liked the unusual, shuttered girl she was getting to know. Mary had been alone for too long; it was no wonder she was a bit odd and found it difficult to get on with other girls. She, Lizzie, could sort this; she'd let this friendship develop – if that was where it was headed – and then everything would be clear in time. Meanwhile, she'd simply put all the weirdness on one side and just get on with life. Yes, that was the way!

Much to her relief, Mary had managed to get through that afternoon without incident. Good job, she thought wryly on her way back towards Annie's small cottage; she must be notorious throughout the school by now. If only Lasher would leave her alone for a while, things might have a chance to calm down. After all, it wasn't as if she set out deliberately to cause mayhem. The man was a moron; he seemed to come looking for trouble and generally in *her* direction.

Annie was waiting for her, sitting on the grass next to the fox's temporary quarters. 'There you are, Mary girl. Redcoat and I were wondering when you'd show up.'

She nodded towards the fox, standing now and looking eagerly in Mary's direction. Immediately the words flashed into Mary's head – *Been waiting for you, Mary. Think you'll be pleased at how I'm doing!* She shook her head, still bemused and half wondering if this strange, unexpected form of communication was her imagination.

'Come, lass, come and see Redcoat, he'm nearly ready for us to let 'im go. Made great progress and much faster than I thought. You tread carefully, now, young feller me lad, when we let you go. Don't want you back 'ere with any more o' them nasty snare cuts, you 'ear me?'

The fox gazed back at her, its head on one side, then sat back on its haunches with what appeared to be almost a smile as Mary approached. It held up its paw for inspection. Annie grinned.

'Looks as if 'e knows you, girl; you just said something to 'im? Just look at that big grin on the silly sap's face!'

Mary smiled as she neared the cage. 'Gosh, Annie, the wound's almost gone. Doesn't look as if he ever had anything wrong with it – you've worked miracles!'

'Nothing you won't manage once we get on with your learning, girl; there's no time to waste, that's for sure – you've a deal o' work ahead an' I 'ave to make sure you'm ready!' Annie smiled affectionately as she spoke but the smile belied the intent look she cast upon Mary.

'Don't you forget, Mary, I'm always on *your* side, never mind what the rest o' this flaming planet is up to, you and me'll make sure you get where you 'ave to get. It's a long road, girl, an' it ain't goin' ter be easy but this looks ter be one of the most exciting things facing you, lass, and I aim ter be there for the ride as long as I can. The time'll come, though, when you'll leave me way behind and that's all ter the good 'cos – make no mistake, girl – there's a lot at stake 'ere, massive stuff ter be done. You remember that. Annie's never wrong!'

And she nodded emphatically as she put a comforting arm around Mary.

'Now, say 'ello to Redcoat properly and then we mun leave him another night. We'll let him go tomorrow. You come 'ere after school and we'll take 'im out together. You want to sound 'im out 'bout that now afore we start our lesson?'

She watched Mary with interest.

Mary looked at the fox, now gazing back at her quizzically – *Did you hear that, Redcoat? D'you understand? Only one more night then you'll be back out into your old haunts. Annie says you'll be fine to leave us tomorrow. How about that, then?*

Something proud, something primeval in its eyes, the fox stared back – *I feel fine, Mary. You and Annie have done good things for me. Thank you.*

You must come back if you ever need us again, Redcoat, or if any of your friends need our help; you know that, don't you?

I know, Mary. I'll put the word out.

See you tomorrow, Redcoat, before we say goodbye!

It won't be goodbye, Mary – I'll be seeing you again.

As Mary and the old woman settled in the kitchen, Annie looked keenly at the girl. 'Now, Mary girl, there's something biting you and we got to clear it, ain't we? Can't start your lesson with you somewheres else now, lass, can we? So… What's troubling you? You just tell old Annie and we'll sort it. Come on, out with it, lass.'

Mary flushed. She might have known. Nothing much escaped Annie. She'd picked up on her anxiety. It was opening up time. Flaming Norah! This wasn't going to be easy. She wasn't used to talking about feelings or opening up on things that had happened to her. She hesitated then took a deep breath. Just get on with it. Annie was different: she could be trusted. She'd understand.

Falteringly, she began. Gradually, details of her early life in the Home came out then the foster homes before her adoption by the Darlings. She didn't fudge any issues or hide the difficulty she'd been for the Darlings at the start.

Her experiences at school were another thing. Determined not to make herself appear too much the victim, she had to make sure, nevertheless, that Annie realised how important this fledgling friendship with Lizzie was to her, how much it could mean and her worry that the other girl might think her too strange. Haltingly, she talked about loneliness and, listening closely, Annie heard and understood all that Mary didn't say.

She rose and gave the girl a hug. 'Now, my bird, 'ere's what's goin' ter 'appen. You'm going to bring that lass over 'ere and Annie'll 'ave a proper chat with 'er while you go off and collect some important 'erbs and plants ter treat these 'ere critters you keep bringin' in. All right, my bird?'

Mary was silent. She would have to trust Annie, she knew that.

'I know this feeling, girl, from the inside. I've always walked me own road, Mary, been a lone wolf, as they say. And, although I've been 'appy enough that way, it ain't right, I know, for everyone. Your life, my bird, is going ter pull in people on a grand scale and you'm going ter need a few solid friends, starting now. Lizzie seems a decent lass – you'll do well ter 'ave 'er on your side. And she'll be there, girl. You'll 'ave the friend you want – I promise you. Will you trust old Annie ter do it right, Mary?'

Mary raised her head, looked her in the eyes and said simply, 'Yes, Annie, I know you will.'

The old woman hugged her warmly. 'That's settled then. Drink up now and we'll make a start on this 'ere lesson o' yourn!'

Mary's heart was light. With almost a smile in her step, she whistled on her way home. For once, it was a whistle with hints of hope. She was always happiest in the spring; now there was a scent of optimism in the breeze, a tremble of promise in the air and a real sense of an impending fresh start.

For the first time, the force within her seemed to offer promise rather than threat; if she could work with it positively, it would help, not hinder, her. If she could only control it – and herself – it would be all for the good. That wasn't all. Strangely, for the first time, she was picking up a sense of urgency: a task lay ahead, a mammoth task, a mission of sorts. She was not mistaken, she was sure of it. The exact nature was still unclear but it would be of major importance and on a scale yet to be imagined! All at once, goose bumps were starting up on her arms as excitement mingled with fear and trepidation.

Would she be capable of handling it? Of course she would, there would be no choice; but she also sensed a mighty struggle ahead with massive opposition – more than she could even, at this stage, envisage. Battle or not, though, in the end she *would* emerge victorious!

If she'd been a fly on Mr Staddon's wall that afternoon, however, Mary's optimism might have undergone a few tremors. As he sat staring across his desk at a mathematics master dumb with rage, Keith Staddon was resolute.

'I trust we understand each other then, Gordon. It would be most disappointing if I were to discover at a later date that my express wishes had been disregarded. It would also be somewhat depressing, in the event of such a discovery, to have to extend the current exceedingly short list of suitable candidates for Deputy Head, to include more external applicants!'

Seething with frustration, the mathematics master strode from the Head's office ten minutes later, his brow knitted in silent fury. *So Staddon was a fan of the gipsy brat, was he? Thought he could protect her, did he?* Well he'd see about that!

SIX

Morning sunshine filtered weakly through a thin cloud as Lizzie set off for school next day earlier than usual. The Paiges believed in action over words and Lizzie was a Paige through and through. Opportunities for getting to know Mary properly included walking to and from school so she would meet her where their paths joined and that would give her a chance to start asking some key questions!

The figure in the distance coming towards her suddenly picked up speed as Mary spotted her. Both girls began to run at the same time and smiled broadly as they met. Both started to speak at once.

'I thought I'd meet you...'

'I hoped I'd see you...' They both laughed.

'Did you go back to see Annie after school?' asked Lizzie, tentatively.

'Yes, and we talked about the fox – she said we'd release him today.'

'Can I come with you?'

'If you want. Are you sure? You don't have to.'

'I know, but I'd like to – very much – if you don't mind.'

'Oh that's great, only…' There was so much that would need explaining and she didn't know how or where to start – and now Lizzie's expression was telling her she'd have to explain why she was hesitating. Oh damn!

'There are things you might not understand,' said Mary slowly, 'things I don't quite understand myself yet.' She paused. 'You might think me weird. And I don't want that.'

There! She'd said it. No going back now. This conversation would have to run its course. Lizzie would have to ask what she wanted to ask – and they'd both have to live with the outcome. That was all there was to it. Lizzie stopped walking, stared at her for a long moment then looked around. Without noticing, they had arrived at the small road leading to the railway bridge on the outskirts of the small town. A small bench a bit further on, under one of the few big trees in that area, was empty.

'Look – another twenty minutes and we'll be at school. It's still only eight thirty – we've got time to stop and talk for a bit here. We need to clear the air, don't we? And, to be honest, I *have* got some questions.'

It was a defining moment for both of them.

'Come on,' she urged, 'if we're going to have any sort of friendship, we need to start off the right way, don't we?' And she grabbed Mary's arm, pulling her towards the seat. 'So shoot – what's this all about?

Why would I think you odd? And what exactly is Annie teaching you?'

Mary bit her lip and took a deep breath. She had known this moment would come. Now it had. It wouldn't be easy: this sharing business was a bit too touchy-feely and her inner thoughts and feelings had always been carefully cloistered. People didn't normally understand her – and she didn't normally care. This time she did, though, and Lizzie was right – she had a right to know. If they were going to be friends – real friends – then Lizzie deserved to know at least some of it, what she felt able to tell her, without the really weird destructive bits for the time being. Right then! An inward sigh. She'd give it a go and see where it took her.

Minutes later, when she had finished, there was a long silence. Lizzie had listened with ever-widening eyes, her expression ranging from amazement to scepticism and then incredulity before, lastly, reluctant wonder. Mary had not exaggerated, she had simply related events as they had taken place. Her own astonishment and disbelief, her genuine lack of understanding and her obvious wonder had done the rest: Lizzie was finally convinced.

'But how can – how does – this happen?' she asked. 'I don't understand where it all comes from in the first place. I mean, how can you know what the creature is saying if it doesn't actually speak? And how come you hear and see all these signals? The cold and the whistling and the colours… and… and everything,' she ended lamely.

'I know, I know – and I don't know the answers either,' said Mary. 'I'm as surprised as you are. All I can say is that I seem to hear the words… in my head,' she finished, her voice tailing away, 'and I ask myself, too, if it's just my imagination.'

'And how do you reply? Is that in your head too?'

Mary flushed. 'Are you being sarcastic?'

Lizzie was immediately apologetic. 'No, no – I'm being serious. Do you just think the reply and the animal hears you?'

'I suppose so. I told you, there's a lot I don't understand still, so I can't be certain.'

'Does Annie know all this? What does she think?'

'I think she knows more than she lets on at present – we haven't really talked about it yet.'

Lizzie continued to look at her wonderingly. 'Is there anything else I need to know?'

'Well, I'm not mad – or a witch – if that's what's worrying you, and yes, I suppose there are other things we should probably talk about but not now. It's almost ten to nine and we're going to be late if we don't dash. I can't afford any more trouble, especially with Lasher. Can we leave it there for now? Haven't I said enough to show you that I'm not a weirdo? That you don't have to worry about anything? And,' she hesitated, 'can we still carry on as we are? I promise to tell you the rest when we get a proper chance.' How she hoped none of this would endanger this friendship she wanted so much!

Lizzie stared back in silence for a few moments, before she grinned, sprang to her feet and threw Mary a light shoulder punch. 'Guess it's okay. Guess I can put up with an oddball who hears things! Guess it's not catching! Come on – let's get going – we'll just make it if we run like mad!'

The two girls pelted the rest of the way, Mary's heart lighter for the conversation that had just allowed her to be open with someone for the first time; and Lizzie's spirits seemed as high as, well, as Lizzie's spirits were generally. What a relief! How she wished she could be as uncomplicated as Lizzie. How much easier life seemed to be for those who didn't over-think everything!

The girls were looking forward that afternoon to seeing Annie's work and the wildlife always around her. As soon as they arrived, Annie was direct. 'Now, Mary, I'd like you ter go an' get me some wild plants that I've written down 'ere. It'll test what you've learned so far. An hour or summat like should do it, lass, an' meanwhile, Lizzie 'ere can stay and 'elp with some cleaning an' preparing them cages. Away you go now an' we'll release old Redcoat when you get back!'

Once Mary was on her way, Annie turned to Lizzie. 'Now, young Lizzie, you and me 'ave important matters to discuss an' no time ter waste. That there lass'll be back soon an' I need ter tell you a few bits about 'er an' find out summat about you so's we pool our knowledge. You all right wi' that, girl?'

Seconds later, both seated at the broad, old kitchen table, she continued.

'You serious about this 'ere friendship with Mary, girl? 'Cos I ain't 'avin' you upsettin' 'er now. She's 'ad enough trouble in 'er life. What she needs now is a friend, not someone who's going ter cause 'er even more trouble!'

And, pausing no longer than the time needed for Lizzie to nod mutely, Annie swept on. Half an hour later, Lizzie had most of the picture. Annie had not pulled her punches. Mary's troubled background, her loneliness and the unhappiness at Milton Upper had been laid bare.

'She's 'ad ter be strong all 'er young life an' she'll 'ave ter be even stronger, if I know me onions. There'll be jealousy an' envy an' all sorts for Mary ter battle along the way, so if you really mean ter be 'er friend, you'd best be serious about it, Lizzie Paige, an' just as strong. 'Cos if you let Mary down when she needs you, girl, you'll 'ave me ter sort!'

A silence fell whilst Annie surveyed the girl keenly. Lizzie stared back unfazed. 'All right then, Annie – so tell me more. Exactly what is it that Mary has to do?'

'I don't know all of it yet meself, lass. All I do know – in me blood, bones and teeth – is that Mary's got important work ahead. This 'ere gift of 'ers is more than I can match. I can 'elp her some o' the way but there's a long old road ter travel yet. Mary's goin' ter need all the friends she can get. An' she's only got me presently. So you need ter be sure you ain't goin' to chicken out when it gets ter be tougher than you expect. And the big question, girl, is – *Are you up ter it?* 'Cos if you ain't, you best back off now! There ain't no p'rapses or maybes, girl, you'm either up for it or you ain't!'

Lizzie was silent for perhaps half a minute while Annie watched her keenly. Then, raising her head, her chin jutting firmly, she looked Annie in the eye. 'Mary's got some bad enemies at the school, Annie. She's told you some of it but I'm worried there's a lot more to come. Nothing she's done, just some people are prejudiced against those who are different, things they don't understand, see as a threat. And Mary *is* different, isn't she? Her skin has this brown wash to it like leather, her eyes are that funny sludgy colour and they change sometimes – get a kind of faraway look – and she's sort of… in a different place a lot of the time. I can't really explain it; they just say she's away with the fairies or she's a witch – or worse.'

'An' you, girl? 'ow do you explain it? 'ow do you manage ter get through to 'er? An' why don't any o' this bother you?'

'I don't really know, Annie. All I can tell you is – it just doesn't. Mary's okay as far as I'm concerned. My mum and dad brought us all up – my brothers and me – to give everyone a chance. Dad calls it "cutting people some slack" and we never judge anyone on how they look. So Mary's colouring doesn't bother me and if she doesn't want to talk to some of them, well, I can understand it. Some are real bozos but others are plain nasty and Mary's become their target. She needs someone on her side and, now I know her better, I like her. So I guess that someone has to be – is going to be – me,' she ended, with a firm nod.

Annie smiled her approval.

'You'm direct and down-to-earth, girl, and that's good enough for me. Mary *is* different – but then, she 'as ter be: 'uge tasks lie ahead of 'er with some 'eavy boulders in the way. 'Er life ain't destined ter be easy, girl, and now, 'earing this, I see the battle's already begun. You strike me as being a trusty lass and sturdy enough. Yes, you'm okay, girl. Mary's got you and me now. It's a start!' The old woman nodded to herself, satisfied.

'Well, I'd like to tell you a bit more about my side of this, Annie—' but Lizzie was interrupted by approaching steps as Mary appeared at the stable door, laden with plants and greenery.

'Think I've got it all, Annie – want to take a look?' As Annie took the load from her, Mary looked anxiously from her to Lizzie. 'Everything okay?'

'Everything's fine, Mary,' said Lizzie, 'just fine. Annie's been telling me all about the other creatures you two have saved. I'm impressed!'

And she went across to Mary and without a word, gave her a big hug. 'You two are going to put all the vets around here out of business if you're not careful!' She threw Annie a small nod of reassurance. The old woman nodded back in recognition.

'Come on then, you two, time ter give Redcoat some time afore we let him go. The lad's been waiting for this moment like crazy!'

The fox was, indeed, up and waiting. As they approached the cage, a voice reached Mary – *Been waiting for you, Mary. Going to let me out now?*

Yet again Mary was taken aback. Would she ever get used to this? Had she really heard the fox speaking? Was she certain she wasn't imagining things? Annie and Lizzie were both waiting, Annie's face showing she'd noticed the change in her expression. There was silence. How should she play this? Again Redcoat's voice reached her – *Mary? I am going today, aren't I? You did promise...*

She'd just have to run with it. The longer she dithered, the stranger it would seem. Her mind decided, she threw the small fox a mental response. *Yes, Redcoat. I did promise and you are going. Can we just stroke you and say goodbye before you go?*

Of course, Mary, open the door – I promise I won't disappear straight off!

'We can open the door, Annie, he won't shoot off,' she said confidently, 'he knows we want to say goodbye properly.'

And as the cage door was opened, Redcoat came out quietly and sat before them.

Goodbyes over, three pairs of eyes were misty as Redcoat streaked across the garden and vanished silently into the undergrowth.

Lizzie leant forward in wonder as she stroked the fox gently. She could hardly believe this was happening, that any of this was taking place. She was here with Mary and this old woman, witnessing some sort of communion between Mary and a wild fox and stroking it! Nobody would ever believe her. How could they? Her parents would never believe any of it – even if she could tell them, of course, which was definitely not on. Annie's words had been clear: Mary's gift, whatever it was, had to be protected. It was nowhere near time to go public on any of this. Lizzie had got the message. Oh yes. Loud and clear, thank you. And Lizzie knew how to keep her mouth shut.

SEVEN

Games afternoon. Great! It would fly! Freedom, wonderful freedom – to be herself! She could feel the joy bubbling through her already. For once, her wiry build would have real benefits, ideal for virtually any field event she chose – the only exceptions, up to now, being any that needed strength. Athletics – like gymnastics – appealed because it was something she could do alone. Relying completely on her own resources, she could soar and fly to her heart's content. Brilliant! Miss Batchelor seemed to understand her, too, let her do her own thing, and that was such a relief. No restrictions, no dictatorship. The games mistress would be observing her as usual but that was fine. She'd show her what she could do when she was ready!

Jill Batchelor looked up from her clipboard and eyed the girls. The big event was Sports Day in a month's time and another couple of entrants were still needed for the 400 metres. She was looking for those entrants today.

As the girls all trooped out of the changing rooms in their usual groups and cliques, she stared, felt like punching the air. Wonder of wonders! Mary Darling was not alone. She was actually talking to another girl! Who would have thought it – Mary Darling and Lizzie Paige chatting like old buddies!

No stranger to the class mafia, she also observed the covert glances and sour looks from the predictable quarter as the two chatted happily. The Fellowes girl and her clique were making no effort to conceal their vindictive expressions.

In fact, the entire class had noticed the budding friendship and more eyes than those of the games mistress were on the pair. They were all aware of the situation and especially familiar with what usually happened in games lessons. Mary was skilled in gymnastics and had also done well in field games, yet was always the last choice when it came to any team selections.

The Fellowes clique had considerable influence and the other girls feared the repercussions for themselves if they showed her even the smallest favour. Little could be done to change this since no one would "grass" on the class tyrants. More than one staff meeting, however, had heard Jill report how any selection process worked, and how Mary's face always remained expressionless as she stood waiting, with no hint of emotion at being passed over every time, until there was no option left for a team but to take her.

Yet, despite that isolation, Mary always played hard for the team that ended up with her, notching up an impressive number of runs or goals and showing no reaction to the lack of support from the rest of the team. Only once had Jill spotted a chink in the girl's armour, only once had she witnessed an unguarded, spontaneous response: when the Cobb girl, significantly heavier than Mary, had – deliberately, she was certain – stepped backwards in the batting line directly onto Mary's foot, crushing her toes and making it impossible for her even to hobble out to play her turn. On that one occasion, Mary's face had, instinctively, displayed unmistakable fury: Jill had seen her fists bunch involuntarily, despite her pain – and the Cobb girl had shrunk back instantly. The moment had passed without further action but the games mistress had seen enough then to tell her that Mary was no pushover.

Ah, so that was it. She had reported back at the staff meeting that evening. The rage, obviously simmering beneath the surface with Mary, was merely contained. How difficult it must be for her to control that anger and frustration – *not* to lash out at her tormentors. Almost impossible to shine in any sport when battling such isolation! It must be verging on the unbearable. The staff – with the one exception – had all concurred with undisguised admiration; Mary's position was well known – and documented.

Following that incident, they had all agreed it was time to harness that fury, channel that undeniable energy, and the school's Sports Day would offer the ideal opportunity. Untried as Mary was in track events as yet, it was time to find out how much power lay beneath the guarded surface.

Today, Jill intended to pit the girl against two of the seasoned players, her best runners and not unpleasant girls either. Lizzie Paige could complete the line-up – that would tell her what she needed to know.

The Fellowes clique had also chosen athletics. The 400 metres happened to be Lana Fellowes' own specialism and was she proud of it! Tall and sturdy enough to last out, she seemed to take pride in barging her way to first over the finishing line and was determined that no one was going to deprive her of her triumph.

Aware that overt competition at this stage between Lana and Mary would inevitably result in open friction, Jill had decided on separate trials for the two until Sports Day itself. She had no intention of creating more warfare for Mary before it was unavoidable.

Her whistle got grudging attention.

'Right, come on, everyone, let's have you lined up. Quick now – warm up as usual!'

The 200-metre dash was the first and the girls were tried out in groups of five. Mary came in fourth. Undistinguished there, then. Oh well, there were definitely others better in that event. The 400 metres followed and, predictably, Lana Fellowes won her trial in her usual bullish fashion. The tall girl smirked with satisfaction as she looked about her and, her two cronies having finished their own heats, the three sneaked off to a far-off corner of the playing field for a furtive smoke.

This did not go unnoticed by Jill. Good, couldn't be a better time! She was about to test Mary. Better they were out of the way than hanging about to cause trouble for the girl at such a critical stage. Lizzie was also running in this set and, as the two girls lined up with the others, they grinned broadly at each other.

'I'll let you win, shall I?'

'You reckon? I'll show *you* how to win, smart Alec!'

And they laughed good-humouredly. Jill smiled to herself as she watched.

'I just have a feeling,' she had said to her colleagues, 'there are unexpected reserves there and either the 200 or 400 will suit her. I know she can do this and it'll help her so much. It's time. She needs to shine in some area, and success in this could make such a difference, give her the confidence she needs and show the others she's a real player!'

Standing on the starting line, the nerves had struck. Everything seemed to be critical these days but, somehow, the next five minutes felt especially important. Running lightly on the spot, shaking her hands and circling her shoulders to loosen up, once again she felt the energy flow begin to kick in. And how! Her pulse quickening, heart pounding, a violent pulsing and throbbing was spreading rapidly through her body as everything in her began straining for the off. Come on, come on, why didn't Miss Batchelor get on and shoot the pistol? She couldn't last much longer. This force was becoming irresistible. And then it did go off and they were away! Clare Robbins, Caroline Merry, Jane Dart, Lizzie – and her.

Hey – what was this? Something new was happening. From the off, a burst of different power had started up in her legs. Not only was the energy mushrooming instead of simply rising through her body, her legs were taking on a new strength and stamina. A force was taking over completely, enabling her – unmistakably and without the normal breathing needed – to draw away from the others. She could sense the distance between her and the others increasing, just far enough to seem natural but *with no effort at all on her part*. Frigging hell! Still, no point in worrying about it now, no time; she must just go with it and think about what it meant later. There was no doubt though – another weapon had just been added to her armoury. How utterly weird!

Exactly one minute and fifteen seconds later, Jill had her answer – Mary Darling had swept the board! And, for a first attempt, the time wasn't bad either. The girl could only get better with practice! Well, well, well… First time and already home and dry in first place – with both Clare and Lizzie a full two point eight seconds behind her! She had her last two entrants for the 400 metres.

66

Falling in behind the rest of the girls as they trooped back up the sports field, Lana Fellowes and her cohorts could hardly believe what they were hearing. Snatches of various exchanges were enough for them to deduce that, in their absence, Mary Darling had – somehow – managed the impossible. In horror, they exchanged disbelieving glances. How had this happened?

'Quick – find out more!' snarled Lana.

'Here – say that again!' yelled Julia Cobb, grabbing at one of the group immediately in front. 'What was that about Darling?'

'Get lost, Cobb – shove off!' Julia Cobb had, without thinking, chosen entirely the wrong informant.

'Leave it, Jules – we'll get the rest later!'

The rest, from a more compliant source, would do nothing to pacify the enraged trio.

Mary, meanwhile, alone in the changing room waiting for Lizzie, was experiencing a rerun of an earlier mysterious experience and, as before, she was baffled. Like the previous fragments of an exchange between Staddon and Lasher that she'd picked up unexpectedly on the airwaves, she now seemed to be tuning in to bits of another remote conversation! From the Fellowes bunch this time, the random bursts of talk were ripe with swear words. Loathing, spite, envy – corrosive, all of it – was coming through with force. She had tuned in to violent rage.

Where was this coming from? Why was she hearing it? It *had* to be a step forward from her earlier experience. So did that mean that she'd be able, in time, to hear complete conversations taking place miles away? Wow – that could be wild! She might find she could listen in to all sorts of risky stuff anytime, anywhere! Better not think of that now. She'd handle it when it came up – *if* it came up.

This vile stuff was the business at present. Why was she hearing this? Where were the Fellowes bunch and what or who had rattled their cages this time? The trio were completely fired up. The object of their rage was certainly in for a hard time! She'd better keep her ears open if she could, try and keep track of this…

EIGHT

Halfway through the week, there was some excitement as Mrs Hunt announced that Lana Fellowes' parents had offered to donate the end-of-year class prize and their offer had been accepted: a cheque for £50.00 would be awarded to the student with the best all-round performance.

Only a few exchanged wry smiles at this obvious attempt to curry favour in all quarters as Lana smirked self-importantly while flashing her own parental "sweetener", an obviously expensive wristwatch. Her two closest cronies, basking in the reflected glory, were also clearly enjoying the attention.

For some reason, Mary felt a deep sense of unease. Was this linked to the ugly fragments of their conversation that she had, somehow, picked up on the airwaves the day of her 400-metre success? How could it be? And yet, the unease within her refused to budge. She'd just have to keep an eye open. Maybe she'd better warn Lizzie.

'You going to the fair this year?' asked Lizzie.

'Are you?'

'Absolutely! We always go. Want to come with us?'

'What – your whole family?'

'Yeah – tradition. Like the Milton Carnival. So?'

The girls were heading home through Radison Park and the unexpected suggestion was a shock. Oh heck! What to say? How to play for time? Was this how friends behaved? Coming out with sudden invitations to do things with no warning? She needed time to think.

'Well, I don't know them.'

'So? It's about time you did. Come to tea on Sunday.'

'What? Just like that? You haven't even asked them if it's okay—'

'Yes I have. I just didn't tell you that first.'

There was silence. Mary was struggling. Such a riot of foreign feelings all at once – the unexpected invitation, its suddenness and spontaneity, the friendliness and warmth. All of it astonishing! But what if Lizzie's family didn't like her? What if they thought her strange? She'd never been asked to tea before. What would happen? How did you behave? What if she couldn't think of anything to say? She wasn't used to conversation, especially at first meetings. She'd have to think about this, come up with some excuse. But Lizzie was ready for her.

'Sunday's the ideal day for us and my folks won't take no for an answer, so I'm coming home with you. Then we can ask your mum, so's I can go back and tell mine it's on!'

Before Mary could reply to this trump card, the sound of barking – loud, agitated barking – broke into their conversation.

'Over there,' said Mary pointing at a cluster of trees in the direction of the lake. 'Come on!' and she galloped off with Lizzie in pursuit.

On the other side of the copse, the reason was obvious. A bunch of youths – ages around twelve to fifteen – were ranged around the edge of the small lake, yelling and hurling stones at a black and white dog swimming round and round, looking desperately for a place to land and escape the persecution. The torment had clearly been going on for some time as the girls could see that the animal was becoming exhausted and the barking was a cry of desperation.

Without even a second's pause for thought, Mary pelted towards the group. As she ran, the same flow of increasing power that had enabled her to win her 400-metre trial began rising forcibly, adding both speed and strength to her slight form so that the fury with which she hurled herself at the apparent ringleader – a burly youth of, perhaps, fifteen – was a complete astonishment to both of them. Shoving him with all her might into the lake, she turned glaring, fists clenched and teeth bared, on the others. Taken unawares by the ferocity of this attack, the ringleader gave a shocked yell, which was followed by a similar bellow from his sidekick as, a few feet away, he was treated to the same fate by Lizzie.

'Brill!' she said, punching the air and scowling with satisfaction.

The younger four, meanwhile, taken aback by this attack and deprived so unexpectedly of their leader and his sidekick, simply turned and fled, ignoring the struggles of the beefy lout who, it seemed, couldn't swim and was already shouting for help.

Pausing only to check that his mate was on the way, the girls raced for the other side of the lake where the exhausted dog was now heading. As Mary ran, she directed her thoughts repeatedly at the frightened animal – *Don't worry, please don't worry. We're here to help you. No one will hurt you now. You're safe, I promise. We'll take care of you.*

Lizzie, eyes on the dog, noted a small change in its pace. The frantic swimming was slowing as the panic and desperation that had been so evident gradually diminished. Arriving at the bank where it was heading, she watched as Mary moved forward step by step, leaning forward gently to greet the animal as it approached the bank.

Lizzie was no fool. Clearly a form of communion was taking place here. She watched in silence as Mary took hold of the dog – a male collie, she noticed – with immense care and gentleness, allowing it to take its time, easing it to the bank between both of them. As it lay on its side, eyes wide with fear and panting with exhaustion, Mary stroked it patiently.

Easy now, easy. You're with friends; we'll protect you. No more need to be frightened. I don't know how that foul business started but it'll never happen to you again. I promise. Just try and relax. We won't leave you.

Waiting until the animal calmed down, its breathing slowing by degrees to a comfortable pace, its flanks rising and falling at a more normal rate, Mary asked: *What are you called?*

And the reply came: *Lots of names by lots of people – some of them not good. Call me whatever you want and I'll answer.*

Lizzie, watching, saw tears gather in Mary's eyes, her teeth bite on her lower lip.

'What's happened? Why are you upset?'

'This poor dog's had a difficult life, Lizzie. Many owners, I think, but not much love, it seems. I was trying to find out his name and he says he's been called so many and lots of them not good. It's upsetting because I've been there too – more than once. We've got things in common, I think.'

Lizzie was silent for a few seconds, her face troubled, as she looked from the dog to Mary.

'Annie did mention a bit about that and I'm really sorry—' and she broke off, swallowing. 'Now's not the time to dwell on this – action is what we need. Shall we take him to Annie? The sooner we do something positive for him, the better, don't you reckon?'

It worked. Mary nodded quickly.

'Yes, you're right. He needs some special care and Annie's the best person for that. I'll just let him know he's going somewhere very safe and caring and then he'll come with us easily.'

'Won't your mum worry where you are?'

'She knows I go to Annie's sometimes after school to learn about herbs and plants so she usually allows me an hour plus travelling time. If I'm any longer, then yes, she'd worry but you're right, it's already later than usual – I ought to call at home first. That okay with you?'

'It'll give us that chance to ask her if you can come to tea on Sunday,' said Lizzie firmly, 'and my mum doesn't worry unless I'm a couple of hours late – she knows me well!'

Mary closed her eyes and focused on the dog. Two minutes later, he rose to his feet and followed the girls unsteadily as they made their way towards Mary's home.

Mrs Darling was taking off her coat as Mary opened the back door. Her eyes opened wide as she took in first the wet dog and then Lizzie. She smiled a welcome. 'Well, you must be Lizzie,' she said, and looking at the collie, 'and this is?'

'Mum, we can't stop, we've just rescued this poor dog from some vile yobs and we have to get him to Annie because he needs special care but I knew you'd worry if I was any later—'

'And anyway, Mrs Darling,' broke in Lizzie, 'I wanted to ask you – can Mary come to tea with me and my family, on Sunday?'

The words came out in a rush and Mrs Darling smiled as she looked from one girl to the other.

'Well now, girls, let's not rush this. Mary, you and Lizzie can spare a few minutes to sit down and tell me properly what has happened and *I* will then run you all to Annie's place but first things first. While I make some tea, you take this towel and dry this poor animal who seems to be shivering fit to burst.' And she was right. The poor dog did now appear to be suffering from the aftermath of its ordeal. Shaking from head to foot, it looked a pitiful spectacle and in need of both warmth and nourishment.

'Then you can give him some of this corned beef and some biscuits since I have no dog food and was certainly not expecting a visitor.'

While Mary dried the collie, she reassured it gently. *Don't worry, we'll look after you, no one'll ever hurt you again and, what's more, if I have my way, once we've sorted things, you'll come back here to live with me… if you'd like that, of course.*

Susan Darling and Lizzie watched as, by degrees, the poor animal slowly relaxed. With the dog drier, fed and watered and explanations over, Mrs Darling stood up decisively.

'Coats on, girls, let's get your animal friend out to the car. I'll wait while you get things sorted out with Annie before we run Lizzie home. Mary, I want both of you in the back, with the dog on a towel across your laps. Happy though I am for you, and more than willing to help, I refuse to have my car filled with damp dog hair!'

Mary had never been so happy. They'd helped this super dog to escape from the clutches of a load of yobs; her mother had met Lizzie and clearly approved; Lizzie equally obviously liked Mrs Darling; and now they were all on their way to Annie's with the dog who would find there the care and affection he so badly needed. Hey – perhaps now was the time to ask her mother if she could keep him! Steady on, her instinct was saying, don't rush your fences, take it easy, one step at a time.

The dog would be fine with Annie until her mother said yes. And she would!

Lizzie and Mrs Darling chatted away happily while Mary focused on the dog: *You're going to a special friend of mine for a while where you'll be happy and very safe. After that, I'm going to try and keep you – if that's okay with you?*

As one ear twitched slightly, she knew that the dog had heard. She could wait for an answer.

NINE

'So, what now?' The girls were on their way to Annie's cottage the next morning.

'I'm going to keep him,' declared Mary firmly.

Lizzie eyed her curiously. 'Have your mum and dad agreed?'

'Not yet but they will!'

Annie, however, was adamant. 'We 'ave ter report this poor animal to the police,' she announced firmly when they arrived and, as Mary protested, 'It's no use, lass, this ain't a bird or fox or somethin' else wild. Someone might 'ave reported him lost and then there'd be trouble if 'e were spotted. And then you couldn't keep 'im, anyway.' And, in answer to Mary's snort of disbelief, she added, 'I know, I know, but we 'ave ter do things proper like, girlie. Now, 'e's 'ad a comfortable night and a good meal, so come on, it's down to the police station and we'll take it from there!'

With a heavy heart, Mary took hold of the lead that Annie had found for the collie and told him the situation.

We have to take you to the police station for now and I'm hoping they'll let you stay with Annie until we know that no one's coming for you, but we have to go and see what they say.

The dog was silent. Tail drooping, its body language spoke volumes as the small, dejected cavalcade made its way to the local police station. Here, the desk sergeant was sympathetic as he viewed the downcast girls, the subdued dog and the weather-beaten old woman.

'I'm sorry, ladies, but this is a matter for the dog warden. I can tell you now that the dog will have to go into kennels while the warden tries to find out if he has an owner. Then, if he isn't claimed in the next seven days, the kennels will have a decision to make. They can either keep him – somewhat unlikely, I'm afraid – or they can try to rehome him, which may be where you come in, or they might decide to put him down.'

'Oh no!' said Mary. 'That can't happen; it mustn't happen. I won't let it!'

The sergeant eyed Mary with curiosity as well as interest. Unusual to encounter such intensity in one so young and evidently not short of determination either, this lass!

'Does he have a name, do you know?'

'No, but I know what I want to call him,' said Mary eagerly.

'I'm afraid that'll have to wait, young woman,' said the desk sergeant, 'until he's yours – *if* and when that happens. In the meanwhile, it's the dog warden we need, so if you wait here with the dog, I'll see if I can get him over now.'

The girls and Annie waited sadly. Their mood was clearly communicating itself to the dog who lay with his head on his paws disconsolately.

The dog warden, when he arrived, was also sympathetic but firm. 'He'll have to go to *Rosemore*,' he said. 'You can visit him there, even take him out, I expect, if you ask them properly. Then, after seven days, if no one claims him and *if* your parents agree, he's yours!'

I'll be back, I promise, said Mary to the unhappy animal. *This is* not *the last you'll see of me,* and she stroked his head and back gently as he was taken away by a young policewoman.

A downcast little trio returned to Annie's cottage.

'Now, come along, girl, this won't do!' Annie was firm in spite of any doubts she may have been feeling. 'You being miserable ain't going to 'elp that there dog. We'm going ter sit down and 'atch a plan of action. And if you want 'im, I know you'll get 'im. Think positive, lass, 'cos miracles can 'appen even if we don't expect 'em!'

'Oh, d'you really think so?' Mary was only too ready to believe in miracles if it meant that the collie could be hers.

'But even if an owner doesn't come forward, you haven't asked your parents yet,' said Lizzie, direct as ever, 'and they may not be so keen, Mary.' And, as Mary pulled a face, she added, 'I'm not being negative but I know mine wouldn't be. We've had loads of family discussions about this and the same questions always come up. Who'll take it out each day when

I'm at school? Who'll make sure it's trained and fed? Where will it sleep? And you can't leave a dog for hours on end. What if your mum wants to go out for the day? You can't just leave it in the garden with all the risks that would involve. They're bound to bring up all these points – and they should. You have to think through all the practical aspects. Too many people don't think about the dog enough before they take it on.'

Mary, of course, had not thought this through. Her heart was completely in charge at the moment. 'Yes, well, I thought you'd be on my side,' she said unhappily.

'I am, you know I am, but someone has to think of the arguments you're going to face and prepare you. I know you want this dog. I know what it would mean to you, really I do, but you have to think of your parents' side too. It's their house, Mary, and their rules. I'm sure they'd want you to be happy but they'll be thinking of all the practical aspects, whereas you're only thinking with your heart at present. Look – why don't we think up answers to all the practical arguments they'll bring up, then you'll be ready for them! Come on, I *am* on your side.'

Annie looked from one to the other and, seeing the sad expression on Mary's face, joined in quickly, 'We'll go back on Monday and see where they've taken 'im and you can visit while 'e's there, at least.'

'I'll come with you if you want,' said Lizzie, 'and, as that bloke said, they'll probably let us take him out!'

Sunday was always a relaxed day in the Darling

household. Susan Darling was generally either up to her elbows in compost or planning her seasonal garden layout. Tom Darling usually seized the only opportunity he had in the week to read the Sunday paper in leisurely fashion over a peaceful coffee in his study. Mary would either accompany her mother into the garden, where she would spend her time in close scrutiny of flowers and any form of wildlife that moved, or she would lie on her bed, gazing abstractedly into the air, occasionally turning the pages of her latest book.

Her parents had become used to their daughter's solitary ways, so it was no big deal that this particular Sunday found Mary in a reflective mood. It was clear, however, as she lay on her stomach in the grass, that there was an extra dimension to her quietness this Sunday and her mother couldn't help but notice.

'Is something bothering you, Mary?' she asked gently, pausing in her weeding. 'Would you like to discuss it?'

There was a silence as Mary hesitated. Then, 'Can I have a dog?' she asked abruptly.

Susan Darling laid down her trowel and looked at her. 'Is this to do with the dog you and Lizzie rescued?' she asked carefully. Mary was silent.

'I see it is,' continued her mother. 'I think perhaps we had better sit down and discuss this properly, hadn't we?'

'She really wants this dog,' she reported to Tom Darling later that evening when Mary had gone to bed. 'I honestly believe she won't give up on it and, you know, I actually feel it might be a very sound idea.'

'But what about the practicalities, Susan? Even if this particular dog is released and Mary can have it, have you both considered who will look after the animal? We've never had a dog – what do *you* know about keeping one? Where will it sleep? Is it house trained? What about its meals? Who will take it out each day? It'll need exercise and Mary will be at school. What about when *you* want to go out? It can't be left in the house for hours on end. If it's left in the garden the risks are legendary and, anyway, it's cruel to leave a dog on its own for that long, regardless of where you leave it.' Tom Darling was a pragmatic man. 'I'm not at all sure either of you know what you could be taking on. And from what you've told me, this poor animal needs some stability now. You can't just turn it in, you know, if you decide further on down the line that you don't want the responsibility!'

Susan Darling was nettled. 'I know that, Tom, I'm not a complete idiot! Mary and I have discussed all this and I'm still convinced that it'll do wonders for her. She has the beginning of a really decent friendship with this girl, Lizzie, she seems to be coming out of her shell at last, and a pet of her own would help even more to dispel the loneliness and insecurity that's still lingering there – you know it would!'

Tom Darling surveyed his wife. It was not often

that Susan dug her heels in over something. The fact that she was hanging in there, that she had not been deterred by any of his arguments, meant that she was serious about this. It looked as if he would have to give it serious thought – and fast. If this dog was likely to become available in the next couple of weeks, they could not afford to dither.

He nodded slowly. 'Okay. The most I will say, at this point, is that I will give it thought. You can tell Mary that she would do well to give serious consideration to the issues I have raised tonight! I will expect well-considered and informed answers when we discuss this again and, if she wants to convince me that this dog is necessary to her, I will need to be certain beyond doubt that she has sound replies for all these aspects of its care!'

Armed with this knowledge, that her mother lost no time in passing on the next morning, Mary set off for school beaming. At the junction of their paths, she waited for Lizzie with a broad grin.

'Hey – you'll never guess!'

'No need – it's written all over your face! Go on then – how did you do it?'

'Well, it's not going to be easy – there are loads of conditions – but I'm sure I can fix it. I just have to make sure everything's taken care of – and Mum's going to help! Coming to *Rosemore* after school?'

'Of course!'

And so the school day began well for both girls. As time went on, though, Lizzie became uneasy. Very uneasy. Pleased as she was at Mary's news, she could see that her friend was so preoccupied with her father's conditions that she was oblivious to most of what was going on around her. The behaviour of the Fellowes clique, the complicit grins, whispers and notes passing back and forth – clearly an irritant to the rest of the class – appeared to have escaped her friend totally. Mary was smiling dreamily into the distance, seemingly unaware of any of it.

It did not, however, escape Lizzie who realised very swiftly that something was afoot. She consoled herself with the thought that there was little time left before the summer holidays for them to cause much grief and, anyway, Mary was not alone anymore. She, Lizzie, was around to look out for her now. Had she understood the nature of the plan the trio had hatched, though, her unease might have been greater and her confidence far less.

TEN

On the outskirts of the town, *Rosemore* Kennels took in paying guests as well as the less fortunate, and were well known for their rapid turnover of the latter. Large, immaculate and well-run, they had an impeccable reputation. Having run all the way, the girls were at its gates within ten minutes. Panting hard, they approached the reception desk. The woman behind the desk listened patiently to their gabbled account of the previous day's events.

'So, can we see him, please?'

She looked at them for a few seconds in silence before pulling a large ledger towards her. Turning the pages rapidly, she came finally to an entry made the previous day, then reached behind her to a large board on which hung a number of keys. Selecting a bunch, she struck a bell on the desk to summon a colleague. Having explained the situation to her colleague and left her in charge, the woman gestured to the girls to follow her.

Mary and Lizzie were impressed by the security. Doors that had to be opened with keys gave way to rows and rows of wire pens until, in the rear of the last pen in the final occupied row, they spotted a forlorn black and white figure. It was the collie they had rescued the previous day. At the sight of Mary, he leapt up and ran towards the front of the pen. Mary's heart went out to him as he pawed eagerly at the wire.

Have you come for me? Oh please, have you come to take me away?

Once again, Mary was thrown temporarily by the communication. Again, she wondered if her imagination was working overtime, then decided to ignore that possibility and simply get on with it. She allowed her own thoughts to respond naturally.

I'm sorry – not yet. We are going to take you for a walk, though, if that's okay?

Oh yes, yes please – just get me out of here. I hate being caged in.

I know that feeling, thought Mary, *flaming Norah, do I know that one!*

'We can take him out, can't we?' she asked the woman. 'Oh please let us take him out!'

The woman, who had started to shake her head, looked from the girls to the dog, saw the longing on Mary's face and the transformation of the dog. She thought for a moment then relented. 'As long as you keep him on the lead and promise to have him back in half an hour – and I want both your names and addresses first.'

'Yes, oh yes, anything, just please let us take him out!'

The fields adjacent to the kennels were ideal walking territory. Birdsong filtered through the branches of the trees as they strolled around while the collie sniffed interestedly at various grassy tussocks, clumps of wild primroses and the trunks of more than one tree.

'What'll you call him if you can have him?'

'I thought Laker might be sort of right, seeing as we rescued him from the lake. What d'you think?'

'Have you thought of asking him what *he* thinks?' replied Lizzie.

The old distrustful Mary surfaced for a second. Was this a wind-up? She wouldn't discuss any of it with Lizzie if there *was* a chance that she was making fun of her. Seconds passed while she digested this possibility. She looked at Lizzie, uncertainly. 'Are you serious – or is this meant to be a joke?'

For a brief moment Lizzie was stung. 'Of course I'm serious! Who do you think I am, Mary Darling? Would I be here with you, backing you up, trying to understand and be your friend if I weren't serious? You've got a perishing nerve!'

The two girls stared hard at each other over the collie's head for a moment before Mary relaxed, softened and grinned apologetically. 'Sorry, I'm sorry – old habits and all that. I've never had a real friend so I'm not used to it. Can we start again? Please?'

'Hey, I'm an airhead too,' said Lizzie immediately. 'I should have known you might think I was taking the Michael, as my dad says. I'll remember that. Look, I don't know how this business works but it's obvious you can get through to creatures somehow, so I was being serious. Why don't you ask him what he thinks – about going home to live with you *and* about the name?'

'Erm, okay then, here goes…'

I've made up my mind that I want you and I'm going to do everything I can to make it happen so, if that's on, d'you want to come home with me, be my friend? You'll never have to worry about being left on your own ever again, I promise!

In response, the collie jumped up, planted its paws on Mary's shoulders and licked her face.

'I think that means "yes" to the first question,' she told Lizzie with a smile.

And how d'you feel about the name Laker? Because if I can have you, that's what I'd like to call you.

No problem – can I call you Mary?

'Is that a grin?' asked Lizzie disbelievingly, as the dog lifted its head and opened its mouth wide to display a broad set of white, gleaming teeth, understandably not in mint condition but looking exactly as if he was, indeed, grinning.

'I think so,' said Mary, 'so I guess it's another yes.'

'Hey, that's great! Can you teach me to do this, d'you think?'

'I don't actually know what I'm doing myself yet. All I know is that, somehow, if I think it, it seems to get through but I'd rather you kept all this to yourself – or I think others might think me weird, don't you?'

'Oh yeah, sure to. It's not exactly common, everyday behaviour, is it? Don't worry – your secret's safe with me!'

And the two girls grinned as they walked on.

For Mary, the episode marked an important turning point. Here was an acceptance she'd never experienced before. Lizzie was becoming her friend, someone she could trust. There wouldn't be too many like this in her life. It felt so good! The only small blot on her landscape, though, was that same deepening sense of something in the wind, something *not* good! She'd been so immersed in the joy of having her first dog that she'd been paying scant attention to the warning signs that normally informed her of impending trouble. Now one of those warnings was insisting on being heard. How long had it been trying to get through? She tried to think back, to remember when she'd first had the feeling. It was after the games lesson, wasn't it? After she'd heard those ugly exchanges. She'd meant to warn Lizzie at the time and realised that she had forgotten to do that as well. Was it too late? Flaming hell! Oh well, no choice but to go with the flow and see what happened.

Every day that week the collie was treated to a walk, twice with Mary on her own, on the others with both girls. This dog would *never* feel abandoned again! The day was approaching when Mary could claim him for her own and she was determined to confirm this without any further delay. At the end of the collie's week at *Rosemore*, she decided to share her news with the ladies who ran the kennels, by now firm friends with the girl who so clearly loved the black and white collie.

The manageress, aware of Mary's hopes, had decided to do everything she could to help. Touched by the happiness on her face as she sat on the floor, hugging and stroking the collie, she smiled delightedly at Mary's ecstasy and kept silent about the fact that she'd already turned away potential adopters.

'We *will* need to do an inspection visit first, I'm afraid,' she said, 'as we have to be sure that all our dogs are going to good, suitable homes where they will be loved and cared for in the right way. I know *you* love him but we have to meet your parents and be certain they're happy about this, too. After that, you can all come and collect him but make sure your parents know that there will be documents to sign and a fee to pay.'

That night, Mary approached Tom Darling. Her adoptive father was not yet as close to her as his wife. A kind man, he was, however, still something of a stranger and, despite having braced herself, she was filled with considerable trepidation as she entered his study. Her usual appeals went out to whoever might be listening. *Oh please, please, let him say yes. I want Laker so much. I must have him!*

'Can I talk to you?' she asked tentatively and, when he nodded, continued, 'Mum's told me your conditions if I want to keep Laker, bring him home to stay with us, I mean, and I've thought about all of them and… and…' She paused, uncertain quite how to continue. 'And I know I can do it all and Mum says she'll help me and it won't be any bother to you, really it won't. Oh please, can I keep him?'

The last bit came out in a rush as, unaware of it, she shifted from foot to foot, trembled slightly and twisted her hands together pleadingly. She'd never wanted anything so much in her life. He had to say yes, surely he would, surely…

The silence between them lengthened as Tom Darling surveyed his daughter. Then – 'What do we have to do next?' he asked gently.

ELEVEN

Something was afoot. As Mary entered the classroom, the air was stiff with tension. Pausing in the doorway, her eyes met Lizzie's and the unmistakably apprehensive signals that Lizzie was sending out told her that something was very wrong. The hairs on the back of her neck began to prickle in response and her gaze went immediately to the Fellowes clique. Huddled together in the corner, they were waiting for something. As Mary entered, they stopped whispering, straightened up and moved to their desks, smirking.

The fortnight had passed in something of a blur for Mary: the inspection visit, Laker's joy when collected from the kennels, and then his first week with the Darlings had taken up most of the time left after school and, Mary's homework completed, most nights had seen her fall into bed and asleep almost in the same moment.

It had been decided, for the time being, that Laker would sleep in the utility room, an idea firmly squashed when Mrs Darling, going to wake Mary on only his second morning with them, discovered him sleeping soundly on the floor beside Mary's bed. As she entered the room, he leapt up, barking furiously.

Awake in a flash, Mary leapt out of bed and grabbed hold of him. 'Sshh, quiet, Laker, quiet! Sorry, Mum, he's only—'

'I know, don't worry, love, he's only defending you. Do you think you might let him know, please, that I'm not an intruder and he doesn't need to protect you from me in future? I don't think your dad would take kindly on his days off to the noise I've just been treated to! Oh, and if this is going to be a permanent arrangement, no need to worry Dad with it but, er, d'you think it might be an idea to bring Laker's bed upstairs?'

The two conspirators grinned at each other before Mary flung herself across the room and clasped her mother in a spontaneous hug.

Lizzie, too, had been fully occupied during the two weeks, helping her mother to prepare for one of the charity fairs that Ellen Paige had long supported. As a result, the girls had seen little of each other for the fortnight.

The following week arrived with a flourish. The morning sun, beaming through Mary's bedroom window, dappled the carpet as she dressed cheerfully, recalling Laker's excitement that weekend. The two of them had bounded round the large fields near *Rosemore,* Laker relishing all the spring scents while gambolling through the grass and chasing birds with obvious recognition of the fact that he had no intention of actually catching them. On the Sunday – even better – the whole family had enjoyed a visit to the grounds of a National Trust property not far from Milton Cross. Laker, compelled to remain on his lead for some of the time, was then permitted to run free in a designated area with other dogs, running and chasing them joyously, until going-home time.

It was a milestone for Mary: content for the first time in her life, she was no longer alone. The Darlings, watching her running up and down with Laker, agreed that a turning point in *all* their lives had been negotiated safely and that the right decision concerning Laker had been made. For the first time since Mary had come to them, the closed, uptight face appeared open and relaxed. And so the week, for her, began positively.

The first clear indication of something amiss came as a troubled-looking Lana Fellowes left her desk after registration and approached Mrs Hunt with a serious expression. Morning lessons were delayed by a quarter of an hour as the two of them left the room. As they did so, Mary turned to Lizzie, her face worried.

'There's something bad going to happen – I can feel it.'

Lizzie stared at her.

'I felt something was up, so you're obviously feeling it too. But what exactly d'you mean? How bad? Where? When?'

'Sometimes I get this feeling – it's a really weird sensation – it just tells me that something's about to happen and it isn't good. And sometimes I can see, too, what people are thinking or doing behind the scenes and that usually isn't good either; it's quite scary. I'm feeling that now. I've had it for quite a while and I meant to tell you about it, then I got distracted by all the stuff with Laker.'

Lizzie's face was serious. 'Have you been right before – when you've had these feelings?'

'Yes.'

'And this one now: is it something to do with you, d'you think?'

'Erm, don't know, wait a minute… Yes… Yes, I think so,' said Mary slowly. 'I don't know why but I'm afraid, Lizzie. My stomach's tying itself in knots. I'm picking up trouble. I can't get a fix on it yet but I'm picking it up. Oh, Lizzie, I wish I wasn't but I am, and I don't think I can do anything to avoid it, either. It's started already.' She swallowed hard.

'It's Fellowes, isn't it?'

'Feels like it.'

'I just knew she and those cronies of hers were up to something, I knew it! They've been smirking away for the last few days and it had to be for a flaming reason!'

Just at that moment Mrs Hunt came back into the room, followed by a satisfied-looking Lana Fellowes. Head lowered, she made for her desk, throwing her cronies a small triumphant glance from beneath her lashes, not missed by a now anxious Lizzie.

'Right, everyone, class reader out and turn to Chapter 6,' said Mrs Hunt crisply. 'Lindsay, I'd like you to read, please.'

Although the lesson proceeded, all interest for Lizzie and Mary was swamped by the increasing tension. Sitting across the gangway from each other, they spent it alternately trying to work and exchanging uneasy glances. Mary's shoulders were set firmly. This was no small matter. The butterflies in her stomach were increasing by the minute, not helped by a vision of something like a small cupboard that had flashed through her mind just as Mrs Hunt had asked her a question which she hadn't heard because she was so distracted. Her silence had not done much to improve matters, while the mental image that had come and gone lightning fast – like some sort of advertising her father had mentioned once, she could never remember the name – had left her bewildered.

There it was again, the same image! The quickest flash – then gone! Not long enough for her to spot any telling details, just a very small cupboard that looked familiar but vanished so fast that she couldn't be sure. What could that mean? Screwing up her eyes and clenching her fists in an effort to hold the image, she was unaware that her desperation was speaking volumes to Lizzie sitting only feet away.

As the double period ended, faces were clouded and the usual rush for the door subdued. The following lesson, physics, was normally popular but today was different. Everyone knew something was wrong and was awaiting the next development. Mary and Lizzie remained at their desks until they were alone, the Fellowes bunch clearly gloating as they sauntered out behind the others.

'Look, all you have to go on at the moment is a feeling,' said Lizzie. 'I know you have experience of usually being right but there's always a first time for the opposite, isn't there? My family believes in thinking positively. My mother says negative thinking encourages the worst to happen; something about the Law of Attraction. You attract what you keep thinking about, whatever it is that's scaring you. And, anyway, you're not alone anymore. I'm here now and I absolutely refuse to let that filthy bunch win!'

Mary looked at her gratefully. Everything Lizzie was saying was right, but these feelings that came upon her had done so more than she had let on – and had always been right. She was afraid now and, her instinct was telling her, not without foundation. Sometimes people attracted vileness just by breathing; they didn't actually have to *do* anything wrong or unpleasant in order to end up a target for someone's viciousness. It had happened several times before, in the Home *and* in her foster care and, each time, it had been ugly.

Fellowes and her cronies hated her because she was different, not because of anything she'd ever done but exactly the reverse: because of things she had *not* done, could *not* do, was not *capable* of doing – maybe because she was disadvantaged by her background but certainly because she was contemptuous of theirs.

Worse, she couldn't – wouldn't want to – alter this, and Fellowes and her cronies knew it. They simply didn't understand her and she certainly couldn't understand them. As a result, she must suffer their hatred and although she had no idea what was coming her way, it would be malignant – without doubt – and there was little she could do to protect herself. What a bummer!

With little appetite for food, the girls wandered round the sports field at lunchtime, making sporadic attempts at conversation but only too aware of an imminent threat.

The afternoon register taken, Mrs Hunt was in the process of gathering up her books for her next lesson at the far end of the school. For Mary and Lizzie, it would be maths: in Mary's current frame of mind, torture itself – she was certainly in no mood right now to bear the brunt of Lasher's bad temper. Perhaps bunking off was still an option. Should she grab it while she could? Too late! The door had opened to admit the Head.

With a troubled expression, he headed for Mrs Hunt, an envelope in his hands. As he handed it to her, the teacher looked at him questioningly. He looked round at the class. 'Stay where you are, everyone!'

Then, turning back to Mrs Hunt, he beckoned to her to follow him. Outside the door, he could be seen gesticulating in the direction of the corridor, shaking his head, waving his hands and shrugging his shoulders. Mrs Hunt seemed to be also shaking her head in denial.

After a few minutes, Mr Staddon opened the door. 'Right, Mr Lashley will be here shortly!' he announced crisply. 'Mary Darling and Lana Fellowes, follow us, please!' and, as a babble broke out and Lizzie stared in shock, he and Mrs Hunt walked off down the corridor, a satisfied-looking Lana Fellowes behind them, Mary trailing wretchedly in her wake.

TWELVE

'You what? Are you serious?' gasped a horrified Lizzie as she faced Mary in the corridor at the end of the afternoon. She took in Mary's ashen face. 'Bloody hell! You are, aren't you?'

Lizzie was swearing! That meant she was really mad.

'So, Fellowes lost that famous new watch of hers that she only wears to show off her parents' dosh and you're supposed to have swiped it?'

Mary nodded, her shoulders slumped in despair.

'What? And they don't believe you? They really think it's *you*? They must be bonkers! Don't they know you wouldn't steal a crumb even if you were starving?' She shook her head, bemused. 'Anyway, that watch is so glitzy, it's vulgar. Only Fellowes and her sort would want to flash it around. They need their heads examined! That *bloody* cow…' Her voice tailed off as words failed her. 'And they found it in *your* locker?'

'Yes – and I've had this vision flashing through my mind the last couple of days and didn't realise what it was.'

'Vision? What vision? You didn't tell me.'

'Because I honestly didn't realise what it was. It just looked like a small cupboard and it didn't last – just a flash and it was gone.'

'And you didn't think to question it? Tell me about it? Honestly, you must be crazy to let something like that just go through your head without talking about it! I might have had some ideas that would have helped – if I'd only known! I just don't understand you – what good does it do if you just hug it to yourself? That's plain barmy!'

'Okay, okay. I get the message. There's no need to go on. Anyway, it's too late now – the damage is done.'

'But, in any case, you haven't been able to get into that locker for at least two weeks! I thought you said the key had gone missing!'

'Yes, it had,' said Mary, miserably. 'It disappeared from my desk two weeks ago and I was going to report it and try and get another but I didn't get round to it. Don't you remember I had to use my spare kit the last two games lessons?'

'Yeah, right, you did. So, how did they get in, then?'

'Staddon used the master.'

'What made him do that?'

'Well, they said they had to start somewhere when Fellowes reported the watch missing and they didn't want to give us any warning, so they searched the lockers first.'

'And it was in yours! Well, how bloody convenient!' Lizzie really was worked up – that was the third "bloody" in less than three minutes. 'And they think you hid it there? When you haven't been able to get into your locker for the past week?'

'Fellowes said I could have hidden the key and just pretended I couldn't find it.'

'Yeah, well, she would, wouldn't she? Brazen cow's been planning this all along! Bet she or one of her mates took it from your desk in the first place!'

Mary was silent, for once her usual spirit lacking. The worst thing, the thing she couldn't forget, was the expression on Mrs Hunt's face. Not that she'd said anything – just her look was enough. It was almost too much to bear. Mary had been struck dumb by it. The thought that Mrs Hunt could think her a thief was so painful that she could hardly find the words to deny the charge. She had done, of course, but to little avail, it seemed, since the evidence against her shouted so loudly. Now she faced Lizzie, her shoulders bowed, miserable beyond compare. What could she do to save herself? Where were all the powers that had seemed to be growing inside her and what good were they to her now?

Lizzie stared at her, appalled. This wasn't the girl she had come to know. After all her battles in life, to let this arrogant bully who'd persecuted and tormented her from the moment she'd arrived, to let her and her hell-hag suckers win over her like this – well, it was just *not* an option, as her father would say. It couldn't happen. It wouldn't happen! She would have to do something to help Mary. Just what, she had no idea – yet – but she'd think of something. She would, she most certainly would – and she clenched her fists passionately.

On the journey home, neither girl was in any state for idle chatter. Lizzie, generally the more talkative of the two, was deep in thought.

'Look, don't wait for me tomorrow morning,' she said as they reached their junction, 'I may be late – there are a few things I promised to do for Mum before I leave. See you there.'

Susan Darling, feeding roses in the front garden, caught sight of Mary's face before she reached the gate and although Mary made an effort to adjust her expression, her mother's face told her that she was too late. As she lifted the latch, Laker, who had been waiting for her sprawled peacefully on the path in the sun, hurled himself at her so that she was able to bury her head in his coat for a minute before turning to face her mother now looking at her questioningly.

'What on earth has happened? You looked as if someone had died as you walked along that path! I saw you! Are you all right? What *is* the matter?'

Mary struggled with herself, holding her breath in an effort not to break down. This was dreadful. All her life up to now, she'd been used to keeping things to herself and it hadn't been difficult because no one had been able to penetrate her protective outer shell. Now, though, she had two friends who'd done just that: Annie and Lizzie were already both much closer to her than anyone else had managed. Not only that, Susan Darling had given her all the support she'd needed to bring Laker home, and controlling her feelings and expression now was much harder than before. Her sense of injustice was acute, the pain at being accused of theft almost unbearable. Her eyes stinging, distress written all over her, she looked at her mother. What could she say? What would they think of her? They wouldn't want a thief in the family, would they? Laker chose that moment to jump up and lick her face. That did it. Mortified, Mary burst into tears.

Mrs Darling was horrified – but no more than Mary was. This was practically unknown. Defiant yes, sulky yes, silent – oh certainly! Yes, definitely guilty on all those charges. But emotional? In tears? Completely without precedent! She'd always been determined to remain remote, unreachable, and had maintained this from the beginning of her time with the Darlings. No one was going to breach the wall she'd erected so carefully around herself. Never! And yet, that was exactly what was happening now! She seemed, overnight, to have become a different person. This was so, so hard to handle.

Spontaneously, her mother reached out and put her arms around Mary. 'Come here, my darling, come here,' she said, and clasped Mary in a fiercely protective hug. The two of them stood like that for several minutes while Mary sobbed and sobbed, deep, heart-rending sobs that made her whole body shake. Laker, recognising hurt and unable to reach any other part of her, rubbed himself against her legs frantically all the while. Eventually, the sobs subsided and Susan Darling, now seriously alarmed, took Mary by the hand and led her indoors. Sitting her daughter down at the kitchen table, she poured mugs of hot, sweet tea.

'Now, what's this all about?' she said firmly, fixing her eyes on Mary's tear-stained face. 'I want to know everything and don't even think of keeping any of it back – we've had enough of that in this house to last a lifetime!'

An hour later, with the entire sad tale in her possession, Susan Darling was filled with mounting rage. From all that she had heard and – more telling, perhaps – all that she recognised had *not* been said, Mary had had a traumatic time at that school and she and Tom had been unaware of it until recently when one or two unguarded remarks, let slip at a coffee morning with some of the mothers, had alerted her to the notion that all might not be sunshine for her daughter. She had not, however, suspected the extent of Mary's difficulties. Now she had a clearer idea and Susan Darling was furious – with both those at the heart of the problem and even more with herself for not investigating further before this point of no return. She could see exactly where all this was heading: the plan seemed to her to be fairly transparent with Mary cast in the role of arch criminal. Well, she would see about that!

Impulsively she got up and pulled Mary to her feet, enveloping her in another hug.

'We will sort this out, my love, don't you worry. This will be dealt with – and soon. Now, you go and change out of your uniform, take Laker out for his evening constitutional, get some fresh air and leave the rest to me!'

Mary went upstairs, marvelling at how much – unusually for her – she had divulged to her mother and, surprisingly, how different she felt having done so.

As she left the room, Susan Darling picked up the phone. The conversation she had with the person at the other end might have filled Mary with trepidation had she heard it, but Susan Darling was in no mood for diplomacy. 'So, we will see you tomorrow morning then,' she finished, 'when I trust this matter will be completely resolved!'

A second phone call, this time incoming, after Mary had departed with Laker, simply strengthened her convictions.

'So, I'm assuming, Tom, that you will want to accompany me on this occasion?' she asked her husband later when Mary had gone to bed. 'I think we're at a major crossroads here with Mary: she's just beginning to open up and give us her trust, and I feel we should show her that it's justified. This situation is actually quite serious. This bully of a girl is obviously on track to portray our daughter as a thief and Mary is powerless to prevent it. We need to show her that she's not alone, that we believe in her, that we're right behind her and – most importantly – that truth and justice are stronger than lies and deceit. We also need to present a united front to the staff at that school! One of them at least, I believe, needs to know that Mary is *not* a homeless tramp, and just because her background is not known, it does *not* constitute grounds for treating her like a hooligan gipsy with delinquent tendencies. He seems to be as big a bully as the Fellowes clique – if not worse.'

'Strange that it's the Fellowes girl,' said Tom Darling. 'Graeme Fellowes seems a decent enough chap, for all he's Head of Finance at *Maynard's*. Our paths have crossed a couple of times in the last year and I didn't get the impression that he's over conscious of his position. Odd that it's his daughter behind all this. I do agree with you, though. It's taken us seven years, going on eight, now, to make Mary part of our family and feel that she's loved and valued; we can't let a nasty, arrogant little snob make her feel worthless and ruin all we've managed to achieve. Our daughter may still have one or two problems but they don't include being a thief and we must make sure the whole staff and the entire school know it!'

THIRTEEN

With the exception of the Fellowes clique who sat nudging each other, triumph written all over them, the class was subdued the following morning. With tension still prevailing, Mrs Hunt's expression was serious. When she picked up her bag and rose to leave and a relief teacher entered, it was clear that something was happening somewhere. As Lizzie rose and followed her out of the room, curiosity turned to astonishment. Whispers began everywhere and the relief teacher was compelled to restore silence.

Mary was as astonished as everyone else. What on earth was happening? Why was Mrs Hunt not taking the lesson as usual? And where was Lizzie going? Eyes fixed firmly on her reader, she struggled for outward composure. Heart thudding uncomfortably, she shivered. Clearly her developing powers were not allowing her to use them in her own interests yet. Would they ever?

A low buzz reached her ears from the Fellowes clique. They, too, were clearly curious. If only she could erase, dissolve – whatever the word was – make them evaporate. Never had she detested anyone so passionately; even the old bags in the Home hadn't been so vile. The trouble with people like Fellowes and her hangers-on was their belief that money made them superior to other people, made them special – yeah, special flaming scumbags! Arrogant, nasty lowlife!

Until now, she'd been able to distance herself from them; her protective wall had shielded her and she'd seen them as mere irritants. Now they had become more than just bullies who tormented her. Their hatred practically sizzled in the air and she could actually feel the danger she was in.

The same feelings of fear that she'd experienced in the Home when she was younger – only worse – had resurfaced. For a rare moment in her life, she felt totally vulnerable, at the mercy of thugs, and the thought of being powerless to combat their sickening lies made the bile rise in her throat. Her rage and frustration, contained for so long, was threatening to choke her.

Wait a minute – she was forgetting something, wasn't she? What about her gift? If she could heal, then she could also destroy, couldn't she? *Couldn't she?* And evil was there to be destroyed, wasn't it? Yes, it was. Maybe she should stop controlling these urges; maybe she should let them take over, instead, do whatever it was they could do. And maybe it should have been done a long time ago.

Just as these thoughts were taking over, the classroom started to disappear behind a mist forming before her eyes, a mist that was slowly changing colour, becoming crimson, clouding her vision and gradually obscuring it completely. With fear flooding her veins as this mysterious blindness took over, what seemed like a voice – though barely recognisable as one – began to penetrate the red mist. Her heart hammering, gradually she began to realise that in a strange sort of way, a message was being delivered to her and, as she strained to understand it, the meaning became clear: the powers being gifted to her must be used only for salvation and regeneration of life – *not* destruction. Destruction of objects, obstructions, non-human threats of any sort, yes – in due course. But even when that became possible, destruction of life? Certainly not. Probably never.

Furthermore, if she disobeyed this injunction, her other powers would be lost to her for good. No second chances. Jeez – the big one and no mistake. The odd voice continued. She would be permitted some leeway: if ever on the verge of disobedience, the same crimson mist would appear to warn her before she proceeded. It would be unmistakable – and she would then proceed at her peril.

And if her own life were threatened by humans? The voice was insistent: *You may, in time, use your powers to assist your escape – but not to destroy life, even that of your enemies. The job you are here to do will have to be completed without any killing by you, and you will have to stop others from committing their atrocities without using your gifts to destroy them.* Perhaps she would be allowed to disable enemies? Hmm, presumably that would be open to discussion in the future. For now, she must *not* act without permission. Currently, anyway, the boundaries were unmistakable.

The message delivered, the mist began losing its colour, the crimson diminishing slowly. Then, gradually, the vapour began melting away and the classroom was reappearing before her eyes. No time seemed to have passed and everyone around her was still as they had been before this strange episode; only she had taken yet another step forward in this mystifying saga, without knowing why and what she was here to do!

Swallowing hard as tears gathered behind her eyes, she returned to her present plight. What must her parents be thinking? How could she have exposed them to such shame? And her greatest fear of all resurfaced: after this, the Darlings would surely not want to keep her. Just as things had been getting so much better all round and she had begun to feel that, at last, maybe she belonged somewhere. Oh no, no, it was too much; she couldn't bear it.

And then, as if she didn't have enough to think about, that wretched cupboard image was here again, flashing through her mind like lightning, but – wait a second – this time there was something that hadn't been there before. What was that she'd glimpsed? She struggled to capture the memory that had vanished just as fast as the image had flashed upon her. A glint of something had caught the edge of her mind – something silver, she was certain of it! What could that have been? Why hadn't it been there before? Why now?

It was hopeless. She couldn't think clearly, her head was thumping, the ache intensifying, her brain flooded with too many anxieties. So many questions needing answers. No one she could ask. Her head drooped in despair.

Her mother had been extra comforting that morning, but her whispered words of comfort had done little to dispel the fears that had assumed immense proportions by the time Mary had reached the classroom. And now here she was, facing those fears alone – with no Lizzie either! Where on earth had her friend gone? For the umpteenth time, she shook her head in disbelief. How could this be happening? What had she done to incur such hostility, such viciousness? She could hear the Fellowes bunch giggling openly now and, with the blood starting to pound in her ears, nausea swept over her. Feeling faint, she grasped the edge of the desk hard for support.

Minutes passed as she stared hard at it, forced herself to focus on the grain, to think of things that managed, generally, to soothe her, things in Nature. And, for several blessed moments, her usual solution seemed to work as her spirit left the classroom and she was away amidst trees and hedgerows, flying through the air with birds and butterflies, running with wildlife, happy and carefree. If only this could continue forever…

Then, in the next moment, she came back to her current surroundings with a start, as the door opened and Mrs Hunt entered. A hush fell as the teacher looked the length of the room. What now? Had Mrs

Hunt come for her? She hardly dared breathe, felt the blood rush to her head, a buzz in her ears. It seemed as if everything was happening in slow motion then, as – no! Good God! It was Lana Fellowes and her bully buddies who were being summoned!

A babble broke out as the door closed behind the group and it was minutes before the relief teacher could restore calm. Mary, meanwhile, was in a state of complete turmoil. What on earth was going on now? First Lizzie, now the Fellowes bunch. Would it be her next?

With another twenty minutes before break, concentration on any work was proving impossible for everyone and there was a low hiss of whispers as opinions flew back and forth with increasing intensity.

The bell for morning break signalled the usual rush for the door but Mary remained where she was, staring ahead rigidly. She might as well stay put. There was no one for her to talk to and, with no idea what to think or do, she could really only await the next development. She didn't have long to wait. Just before the end of break, the door opened again, this time to reveal a triumphant-looking Lizzie accompanied – stranger and stranger – by a smiling Mrs Darling!

Rooted to the ground, her feet incapable of movement, Mary sat and simply stared at them both. It was left to Lizzie to run forward, haul her to her feet and grab her in a gigantic hug. This was followed closely by Susan Darling who did likewise.

'It's all okay, Mary,' shouted Lizzie, 'you're in the clear! It was Cox who planted Fellowes' watch in your locker – we found one of those silver buttons of hers at the back. It must have come off her cuff when she was planting the watch and she didn't realise it, but it was unmistakable! You know what a fussy cow she is over her buttons – well, this time they were her downfall because no one else has anything like them. I suddenly thought, last night, that whoever planted it might just have left something incriminating behind. It was an incredibly long shot and I didn't have much hope at all, but I couldn't think of anything else so I came in early and got Staddon to open up your locker. I hope you don't mind. And her bad luck, huh – there it was, caught under that funny lip of metal that sticks up at the side!' All this was delivered in almost the same breath, Lizzie crowing with triumph.

Mary was stupefied. All this time Lizzie had been on her side, working to establish her innocence – and she had been thinking herself alone! Apart from that, it seemed a highly unlikely coincidence that Lizzie had thought something incriminating might be there and it was! Eyes brimming, she could hardly swallow or speak for gratitude and relief; all this emotional stuff was so foreign. So this was friendship! No one had ever spoken up for her like this in her whole life! And what about her mother? What was *she* doing here? She looked from one to the other, struggling to find words to express her feelings, but although her mouth opened, her tongue seemed glued to her palate and nothing came out.

'It's all right, Mary, I know what you're trying to say,' said Lizzie sympathetically. 'Don't worry, you'll get there later; just relax, it's over. And the Fellowes bunch won't know what's hit them by the time Staddon finishes with them,' she added.

'But, Mum, how come you're here?' Mary managed at last.

'We arranged yesterday evening – Dad's in the car, by the way – to come in and see Mr Staddon, ourselves, to sort out the obvious injustice. There was no way that our daughter, whom we know well enough by now, could possibly have committed this crime and we were determined to uncover the truth somehow. Thankfully, we had help. Lizzie's mum rang me last night to discuss what had happened and then Lizzie told me her plan which we felt was a reasonable move. As it turned out, her idea was right, thank God, but even if it hadn't been, we would have got to the bottom of it, somehow. Anyway, after finding the button, we were able to work out what had happened and when Lana Fellowes and the others were confronted with the evidence, they confessed immediately. It was a clear plot to blacken you, Mary. You've made some bitter enemies, love, through no fault of your own, and Mr Staddon realises this. He'll be asking all their parents to come and see him immediately and I imagine those girls will spend some time at home while he decides what's going to happen long-term!'

'Either way, Mary, you're free of the snakes!' Lizzie was exultant.

Overcome with all sorts of feelings, Mary looked from one to the other. Profound relief at being exonerated was spreading from her head to her feet and mingling with a joy beyond belief. The tension draining away was almost palpable. She could hardly take it all in! What a super friend Lizzie was turning out to be! And what great parents she had! How rich she was! Humbled, she looked from Lizzie to her mother, moved beyond words that they should have so much belief in her. The changes in her emotions felt staggering. Most impressive for her was the discovery that there *was* justice in this world after all!

'Right, girls, that'll do for now. Come on,' said her mother firmly. 'You both have permission to take the rest of the week off and you're going home. We'll stop on the way for some lunch and you can relax! It's all over!'

In the Head's office, there was anything but jubilation. Lana Fellowes and her cohorts stood, red-faced and humiliated, before his desk. Fellowes, however, was unable to hide a mutinous expression that said it all: she'd get the gipsy one day, if it was the last thing she did, and pay her back good and proper for this indignity. Oh boy, would she!

The Head had not minced his words. 'I shall be contacting your parents immediately,' he finished. 'What you have plotted against this poor, defenceless classmate has shown me that you are potentially quite dangerous and I will need to give serious thought to your immediate as well as long-term futures. In the meanwhile, you are all suspended. Collect your belongings and leave the school now!'

On the Friday of that week, three sets of parents gathered in the Head's meeting room. All expressions were serious. Mr Staddon had had time to consider the options and by the time the meeting ended, it was generally acknowledged that he had been more than fair.

'I shall, therefore, leave it with you,' he concluded, 'to take the necessary action in relation to your daughters as well as Mary Darling. If they are to return next term, their conduct will have to be second to none. They will be in separate classes and under constant scrutiny. They have caused a great deal of anxiety and unhappiness to this unfortunate young girl since she arrived. Through no fault of her own, she has endured a degree and calibre of hostility that, in all my years as a teacher, it has never been my misfortune to encounter – until now. I have decided, therefore, that some public recognition of this, as well as appropriate compensation, is owed and your judgement might take into account the fact that Mary's behaviour in response to your daughters' nastiness has, I understand, always been exemplary.'

The Head stood up – a clear signal that the meeting was at an end – and the parents, faces troubled, led the way out of his office followed by their daughters.

FOURTEEN

'So you liked them?' Lizzie was disbelieving. Mary nodded. She'd expected this. 'Fellowes' parents and you *still* liked them?' Another nod.

'They apologised,' said Mary, 'handsomely, Dad thinks. They made no excuses for Lana, they actually seemed furious with her, *and* they were really decent about it all. Said they intended accompanying her to the school and making her apologise publicly. I said that was awful but they insisted it was part of their plan, whatever that means.'

'Well, I think they're right. She's a nasty, cruel bully who thinks far too much of herself. She and her bunch have terrorised others for too long. It's time she suffered some public humiliation. They *all* need bringing down. I hope your parents agreed – it's only right she should grovel – they *all* should! Teach them a lesson they won't forget!'

'Well yes, Mum and Dad did agree it was the right thing to do in the circumstances. I'll be really embarrassed but the parents are all insisting.'

'Absolutely! You deserve it! So what then? Are they coming back to finish the term?'

'Staddon's still thinking about it but he did ask me how I'd feel having them around.'

'*And?*'

There was silence as Mary studied her feet.

'You are such a pushover!'

'Well, they *are* going to be split up into different classes and he said they'd be under close scrutiny and their parents have guaranteed they'll be keeping tabs on them.'

'Huh – and you swallowed that? Well, I think you're bonkers. Did you get it in writing?'

'Actually, yes, and they made Lana write an apology too. Oh, and one other thing…'

'Yeah?'

'The parents all agreed with Staddon that the apology was needed in a more tangible form – something practical, not just words – so they've clubbed together to buy me *and* you new bikes! My parents and yours came up with that idea.' A noisy few minutes followed.

The staff were vocal in their responses to the episode. With ninety-nine per cent in Mary's favour, the loner in the opposite camp stayed significantly silent. Notably, too, the same individual was absent from the first assembly of the week when a public apology for anti-social behaviour and unequivocal personal oppression was tendered by an extremely red-faced, inwardly resentful trio of bullies – their latest recruit being released from any involvement – to their equally embarrassed former victim.

Graeme and Liz Fellowes, ashamed of their daughter's behaviour and determined that she should learn the error of her ways, had been implacable. Haggle, argue, coax, plead and sob as Lana might, they had remained unmoved.

'I will drag you there if necessary,' her father had declared the night before. 'I am ashamed enough of you, Lana. I am warning you now, do not – I repeat NOT – give me an excuse; if you do, you will see exactly how despicable I find your conduct! In fact, I'm currently wondering just how you can be my daughter!' And he fixed her with a glare of such ferocity that she fell silent immediately.

'And now, let us hope that we may move on to more worthy pursuits!' The Head's tone was conclusive. 'Sports Day will shortly be upon us and from all I have heard, we have some promising young sportswomen in our midst, so I trust we may put all this firmly behind us and aspire to higher levels of achievement!'

Another week followed without the Fellowes clan, a week in which the atmosphere lightened for everyone; a week in which Mary's classmates, relieved of her enemies' influence, began to include her in conversations and break-time activities; a week in which she, too, began to relax, open up to the general banter and even laugh at humour she was learning to understand. It was also a week in which Lizzie took it upon herself to begin coaching Mary for their big race on Sports Day later that month.

'But you're supposed to be racing *against* me,' Mary protested. 'You're not supposed to be helping *me* to win!'

'Hey, it's got to be a fair race, though,' said Lizzie. 'I don't want to win against someone who isn't much good!' A remark that earned her a good-natured thump on her shoulder.

Walking into the staffroom, Jill Batchelor punched the air. 'You wouldn't believe how much that girl's improved! She's almost a different person!'

Judith Hunt, one of the only three teachers to hear this and understand immediately who was being praised, smiled approvingly, while the second of the three was immersed in marking. The remaining staff member was careful to control his expression – the interviews for Deputy Head were only a week away.

Mary, meanwhile, oblivious to any of this, was revelling in a new-found contentment. Life felt so good, she could hardly believe it. She had a great family, a wonderful dog and two super friends at last who seemed to care for her as much as she cared for them. Her classmates weren't bad either, now she'd come to know them a bit, and they'd become more human towards her. And then there was her wildlife interest and Annie's lessons in healing that she was absorbing with increasing delight. Everything seemed, almost overnight, to have been reversed. It was rather like coming out of a wilderness into endless greenness and fertility.

The last month had seen a dip in the colour activity, and silence from her other developing powers, but then there had been so much else to handle that she felt quite grateful for a breathing space. She wasn't sure she could have handled it all. In any case, something was telling her the breather was only temporary.

Sports Day came with acres of unblemished blue from which the sun radiated simple good cheer. Mary woke with an inner grin. For now, at least, there was everything to hope for and nothing to fear. Her mind on the race to come, she sprang out of bed – and straight on to Laker's outstretched back! At least, she would have done if, even as she leapt, she hadn't spotted that her landing could injure him considerably. Twisting sideways to avoid him, she hit the floor awkwardly, her ankle giving way beneath her as she fell.

The damage was immediately evident: a vicious stab of pain, as she tried to stand, told her that. She tried again and fell back on the floor. Oh no! It was the 400 metres this afternoon. How could she run like this? Laker, too, was concerned as he stood over her, licking her face gently while she struggled to heave herself to her feet. Finally hobbling towards the stairs, she winced, tears threatening. Her mother's expression as she stood at the bottom reflected her own.

'What on earth have you done? I heard the thump – did you fall? How bad is it? Come into the kitchen and sit down – let's have a look at you.'

An hour later, ice-packs on the offending ankle,

Mary sat sipping hot, sweet tea. 'It's better already,' she declared. 'I'll be fine to run, I'm sure!'

'Well, you can just think again, then,' her mother replied. 'That ankle is definitely swollen. It's a bad sprain if nothing else and you'll only make it worse by trying to be brave. No running for you today, miss!'

'I might as well have saved my breath,' her mother said as they set out for the school two hours later. Sprayed and strapped up, her newly-washed and pressed sports gear giving no hint of the incident, Mary was dressed for action.

'Now remember, Mum, you mustn't say a word, not one word, about this – promise me! Promise me!'

Her resigned mother sighed. 'Only if *you* promise *me*, miss, that the slightest hint of pain and you will stop immediately! You just promise me that. If you don't I will risk your wrath, my girl, and tell everyone!'

Lizzie was waiting and as Mary stepped out of the car, a slightly questioning look crossed her face. 'You okay? You're later than I expected!'

'Yeah, I'm fine, just had a couple of things to do that I'd forgotten.'

'Right, well, we've got an hour before the race, so shall we go and get a drink?'

Mrs Darling had spotted people she knew and so they took their drinks over, Mary doing her best to stroll casually so as not to attract attention or place an undue burden on the wretched ankle. Of all the days for this to happen, it would be today, wouldn't it! Oh well, it was done and that was that. The only thing to do was get on with life! Her ankle didn't seem too bad at the moment; with luck, it would hold up at least for the race. Keeping her weight on the other foot whenever possible, she took care not to turn too hastily. Not long to go now, then it would all be over.

'You all right, Mary?'

Oh hell! Miss Batchelor had been watching her – she'd spotted something! An unexpected light flashed in her head rather like sheet lightning before, unexpectedly, she was in her games teacher's mind. Gosh, this power had taken a marked leap! Until now, her ability to read minds had not only been haphazard but given to timing out, too, just when she needed it to continue; now it seemed to have started up for a definite purpose. If she could direct it at will, that would be very useful in the future. She must work on that. For now, though, it was more important to suss out the present situation. Miss Batchelor had clearly spotted something wasn't quite right. The question in her teacher's head confirmed it. *Was Mary not standing quite as she should?* Damn! If she didn't convince her, Miss Batchelor would stop her from running.

'Fine, Miss Batchelor, absolutely fine!'

Hmm, did that sound a bit too defensive? Yes – the teacher's mind was still questioning. There was something she couldn't quite put her finger on.

'Are you sure? There's nothing I should know?'

'No, really, everything's great. Look, it's almost

time, isn't it? Sorry, I really must get ready, concentrate.'

Lizzie chose that moment to point out that Lana Fellowes had arrived and was preparing to line up so the moment passed but, as Jill Batchelor turned away, her expression remained uncertain, and Mary could still read her mind. It was unconvinced. Well, no more time for that now – she had a race to run.

The others were warming up on the spot. She and Lizzie joined them. She must be careful to seem as if she was joining in but watch her ankle while doing so. Now was not the time to tax it; that moment would come at the critical point in the race. Warming up had finished. The starting pistol was being raised.

Miss Batchelor was counting, 'Five, four, three, two, one!'

They all tensed, bent to the line, poised. The starting pistol sounded. They were away! Hmm, the ankle was letting her know it was there. If it stayed at this level, she'd be okay, would at least finish the race even if she couldn't win. 'Uhh... Uhh...' She could see Lizzie on her left out of the corner of her eye; she seemed to be doing slightly better than before, actually running almost level. It was this wretched ankle, wasn't it? This was proving difficult, worse than she had expected. The pain was rising now, beginning to stab at her. At this rate, she wouldn't be able to keep up her pace for long. And then, without warning, the same power that had helped her to win her trial heat flashed in and began working for her; she was accelerating – faster, faster and yet faster! Oh wow! Lizzie and someone else had fallen behind her and no one was out there in front. Her surroundings were shooting by in a blur. Not far to go now. All she could see was that finishing post. One last sprint should do it.

'Uhhh… Uhhh… Uhhh…' Breathing hard, gasping now, 50 metres, 40, 30… The final stretch was in sight… upon them…

And all at once, a burst of extra speed came from nowhere and she streaked for the finishing line to touch it split seconds ahead of her rivals – before collapsing in a heap on the ground, clutching her ankle.

FIFTEEN

Lying on her back in the grass, eyes closed with Laker at her side, Mary was smiling to herself. Hard to believe yesterday really happened. What a fabulous day!

'Good evening, parents, pupils and friends, and welcome to the eighth prize-giving of Milton Cross Upper School!'

On the last day of the school year, the hall was packed – on the stage, Keith Staddon and two of his most senior members of staff; at the front of the hall, seats arranged for the music pupils who would end the evening with a short recital.

The atmosphere was buoyant with expectancy and smiles were widespread as the awards commenced. When the class English award was announced, the applause was enthusiastic and as Mary went up to receive it, the only face not cheerful was predictable. It was the first time she had received any such recognition and she couldn't stop grinning. Hey, it couldn't get much better than this! What a super surprise! How lucky she was to have such an inspirational teacher in Mrs Hunt who, beaming with pleasure, handed her the handsomely bound edition of *Shakespeare's Plays*. The Darlings, too, were smiling broadly. Lizzie, standing, clapped until her hands stung, her grin from ear to ear expressing her feelings more clearly than words, a response amply echoed by Mary when Lizzie was later awarded the end-of-year class prize – ironically, the money donated by Lana Fellowes' parents, for high achievement in all subjects!

The other significant development that day was also satisfying. Filtering through to the pupils, almost at the last minute, had come the news that the new Deputy Head would be a newcomer – from a school in Yorkshire.

'Whacking! Absolutely bloody great,' declared an unrepentant Lizzie. 'So he didn't manage to pull the wool over their eyes, after all. Didn't think the governors had it in them; stupid old buffers hardly know the time of day!' She punched the air triumphantly. 'Bet that stuffed him!'

Mary grinned. Lizzie's language was becoming increasingly colourful these days and the more passionate she became over something, the more emphatically she would repeat what she knew her parents would disapprove of if they could hear it!

Both girls might have been slightly less jubilant had they seen Lashley's vindictive reaction to both the decision and the awards. 'I'll show them all,' he snarled. 'Think they can keep me down, do they? Well, we'll see about that! And you, gippo, you enjoy your fleeting pleasure while you have it – it won't last!'

And they would have been somewhat perturbed, too, had they seen the new "friends" that Lana Fellowes was cultivating – unknown to her parents.

The holiday weeks passed like a dream for Mary. Happiness she'd never experienced before! In the warmth of the growing friendship with Lizzie, the twenty-four hour companionship from Laker and the increasing closeness of her family, she was beginning to bloom. She and Lizzie walked, cycled, swam in the local pool and spent lazy hours on the common or in one of their gardens with Laker sprawled between them, just lying on their backs chatting, getting to know each other and watching the clouds scudding overhead.

Those same hours also gave Lizzie the chance to see Mary's communication gift at work, and Mary the opportunity to practise it on the astonished creatures that happened upon the girls lying in the grass. Squirrels flashing along branches; rabbits and field mice scuttling around them; water voles emerging cautiously from their burrows in the riverbank beyond Annie's cottage before dipping and slipping playfully into the water; fox cubs scampering around the base of a beech tree; and, on one memorable occasion, a family of deer. All responded to Mary once they had overcome their initial astonishment. It was magical.

When the two families met for lunch and hit it off immediately, Mary's happiness knew no bounds. Moonlight flooding through her open curtains, she hugged Laker. The dog – now curled up on her bed when no one was looking – licked her face fondly. "Close" was an understatement for their relationship: Laker was everything to her and she talked to him constantly, knowing that he understood all of it.

The last week of the holidays began with sunshine and looked set to continue that way.

'You haven't had any more contact with animals in trouble, have you?' said Lizzie as she and Mary strolled along towards Milton Cross town. 'D'you think that's all stopped?'

'I was wondering that, too,' replied Mary. 'I certainly hope not but it's true there hasn't been any need in the last few weeks. Mind you, I don't think I could have handled it with everything else going on. So glad that's all behind us.'

'Yeah, me too; wouldn't like all that again, I can tell you! So, the animal thing, then. What are you going to do? Just hang around and wait, I suppose, until something happens?'

'Yeah, not a lot I can do really. Still carrying on lessons with Annie, though, and I'm learning so much. Her knowledge is stupendous! She says I'll leave her behind at some point but that seems a long way off. Sometimes I struggle to keep up; there's so much to remember about all the herbs and wild plants and that's only one of the areas I'll have to master. There are others, too. She says they'll come naturally when the time is right. Don't know quite what that means – but she says when it happens, it'll be obvious.'

Lizzie looked at Mary curiously.

'Well, I'm obviously still in the dark about a lot of this but, hey, I'll just watch and learn as I go and accept what I don't know until I do!'

'Me too, you know. I still don't understand it all but Annie says I have an important part to play so I'll just wait 'til it becomes clear.'

As the girls took their usual route into town, discussing the new term and what it might mean, they were oblivious to the few cars that passed them, as well as the usual country sounds, which was why it took some time for them to register the thin wailing that reached their ears as they approached the railway station on the outskirts of Milton Cross.

It was Mary who stopped in mid-stride, hand on Lizzie's arm and finger to her lips.

'Sshh, listen – I can hear something.'

'What? Where?'

'Sshh. I don't know yet, just listen. It's coming from over there – near that fence. Come on, let's take a look.'

And as they raced over to the steel fence bordering the railway, they could hear distinct wails of anguish.

'It's a cat,' said Lizzie. 'Sounds very distressed. But where is it?'

'Let's fan out over this area,' said Mary, 'and search. You take that half and I'll take this. Fast as we can – sounds like it's in real trouble.'

Combing the area quickly but thoroughly – the

yowling sounding more and more desperate all the while – gradually they reached the part furthest from the steps to the railway bridge where a drain, half overgrown, was visible. It was from this that the sound was coming!

'Oh no, I don't believe it! The poor creature's down this drain! We have to get this cover off somehow.'

'Looks like it's already been up once, recently too, but we'll still need a metal lever, something solid,' said ever-practical Lizzie. 'You stay there, talk to it or something, while I run to the railway office – they're bound to have something we can use!' And she raced off.

Mary, meanwhile, was in turmoil. What if the animal couldn't hear her down there? What if it were in danger? How far down the drain was it? What if they couldn't reach it? Had Lizzie thought of all that? She was interrupted in all her wonderings by a voice inside her practically shouting – *OH, JUST GET ON WITH IT, GIRL, FOR HEAVEN'S SAKE!*

Hurriedly, she squared her shoulders, took a deep breath and began to send out her thoughts to the creature. *Hello, we're friends, please calm down. Don't move, just talk to me. We're going to help you, get you out of this awful place. Are you a cat? What happened? How did you get in there?*

The yowling stopped and there was silence for several seconds. Then a thin, piteous voice answered her – *Yes, I am a cat and I was eating some food that a kind little girl put out for me outside her garden when this dreadful person, a man I think and very rough, came up behind me and shoved me into this dirty old sack. Then he tied it up and bashed it several times against something very hard which knocked me out, I think. He must have stuffed me down here after that. It's very dark and I'm really frightened. Something's broken, I think, I can't move one of my legs, my head is very painful and something wet has run into one of my eyes. I'm stuck here in this awful place and I can hear water rushing down below. Please can you get me out soon?*

Mary sat back on her heels. Oh, the poor thing. Annie's term for the dirtbag who'd done this came into her head – "bustard" was right, too good in fact!

I'm just waiting for my friend to return with some equipment so that we can do just that, so stay still and don't worry – it won't be long now.

At that moment, Lizzie came rushing down the steps leading a harassed-looking railway official – who turned out to be the station master – panting and laden with metal rods and ropes.

'I know the drains round here,' he said; 'there's a bend in the pipe in that one about two feet below the ground, so the animal's probably landed in that bend. Safe for a bit but we have to get it out fast because if it's moving around trying to escape, it could easily slip further down and then we're in trouble!'

Don't move, said Mary mentally to the cat. *Stay completely still. We're going to get you out but we have to do it while you're in that bend. If you slip further down, we'll lose you!*

'Here, hold that end and don't let go, while I tie the other end to this rod,' and the railway official produced a rod with a large hook on the end. Levering off the drain cover with an effort, he pointed a large torch down it and, in the light of the beam, all three of them could see a small dirty sack tied with cable, lying in the bend as the station master had predicted.

Minutes later, the filthy bundle lay on the ground near the top of the cover, the movements inside it telling them that their efforts had not been in vain. The cat was alive. As Mary drew it gently from the sack, she had to swallow several times in an effort to control her feelings. Howling in pain, the small ginger cat was a pathetic sight and had clearly been the object of cruelty. Bashed against something hard? And the rest! The small, bedraggled creature's head was bleeding on one side, a front leg was bent at an awkward angle and its jaw was clearly broken. Not only that, the cat's back looked suspiciously out of line with the rest of its body! In spite of her efforts, it was getting hard to stem the tears. This poor, poor creature had done nothing to deserve this dreadful treatment. Why were some people such monsters?

'Can't stop any longer, girls,' said the station master gathering up the ropes and rods; 'must get back to my work. Must say, it doesn't look much like saving, poor creature. Best put down now, if you ask me!' And, without further ado, he turned and hurried off.

'Oh no!' said Mary vehemently. '*That* is definitely not going to happen!' And, before Lizzie's pitying gaze, she took off her cardigan and, covering the cat with it, gathered it up with extreme gentleness.

'What are you going to do?' asked Lizzie. 'It's

obviously in heaps of pain and might not be curable. Shouldn't we just take it to the nearest vet's and leave it to their judgement?'

'No, they won't take the time. I'm taking it to Annie and we'll work out together what's best for it. You don't have to come, honestly; it'll probably take quite some time and my sports gear can wait as far as I'm concerned. But you go ahead and get yours – I really don't mind.'

'You have to be stark raving bonkers – don't you know by now that where you go with any animals, that's where I'm going too? Come on, stop jabbering and let's just get this poor creature to Annie before it dies on us!'

SIXTEEN

The journey to Annie's took longer than usual as the girls walked slowly, carrying the small animal with the utmost gentleness. Deep in thought, Mary was struggling with herself. How could anyone inflict such pain on a helpless creature? It was worse than gross. The fellow was a monster and needed to pay for his cruelty. Animals were so vulnerable. She'd have to give this serious thought later – the priority now was treatment for this poor cat. If the fury bubbling away deep inside her were allowed to surface, she'd become violent. The urge to destroy the vile cause of this poor cat's pain was huge, but she'd been warned what would happen if she gave in to such vengeful impulses and the work ahead of her was too important.

If only Annie could tell her the little cat could be healed. Her insides were churning at the thought of the alternative. They must save it, they must! Meanwhile, *she* must stop raging, control herself, be calm, positive and reassure the cat as much as she could.

Don't worry, she said to it, *it'll be all right. We're taking you to someone brilliant who will put your poor body back together.*

The cat said nothing in reply, only whimpered from time to time. As Mary continued to reflect on the situation, she became aware of a curious sensation crawling along her arms. Seconds later, her hands began to tingle. What now? It felt as if insects were darting about under her skin. 'Hhhuhh!' That was a particularly sharp prickle.

'What's going on?' said Lizzie. 'Why did you gasp?'

Groan. She'd have to explain. She couldn't hide things from Lizzie now; that wouldn't do their growing friendship any good.

'Something's happening to my arms and hands. They've been getting really warm the last few minutes and now my hands are verging on hot. Feel...' She held out a hand to Lizzie who touched and dropped it in the same motion, with a sharp intake of breath.

'This poor cat should be hating it,' she continued, 'but look here – all this heat and it's gone to sleep! I don't know what's happening but whatever it is, the cat's loving it!'

They stopped and stared at the creature. It certainly did seem completely happy. The whimpering had stopped, its eyes were closed and it was sleeping peacefully.

'Well, we can't just stop here. As long as the cat's okay with the heat and it isn't too much for *you* to bear, we're only about ten minutes away, let's just push on to Annie's. Then maybe we can sort out what's going on.'

Annie, up to her arms in one of her herbal concoctions, took in the situation instantly. Signalling Mary to lay the cat on the vast kitchen table, she waited while the girls recounted what had happened.

'… so we think its back is damaged, its jaw is sticking out at an odd angle so it must be broken and its head is bleeding, Annie. Please, please say you can save it,' said Mary.

'Yes, the railway man thought we should just have it put down,' said Lizzie, 'but we were determined to give it every chance.'

'Well now, let's have a look at the little fellow and see what can be done.' As Annie spoke, she lifted away the cardigan with care from the small creature. There was silence as the three of them stared down at the cat. It was a silence that continued for some time as the cat opened its eyes, stretched and looked around it.

'You said the jaw was sticking out at an odd angle, didn't you?'

'Yes, it was. It definitely was, wasn't it, Lizzie?'

'Absolutely!'

'And its head was bleeding?' Silence. 'And its back seemed injured, too?' More silence.

Annie looked from the cat to the girls while Lizzie's astonishment finally found expression in a squeak of disbelief. 'There's nothing wrong with it!'

'Did *you* carry it all the way, Mary?' Mary nodded. 'And did you feel anything as you carried it, lass?' Another nod. 'Tell me everything, girl.'

And as Mary told of the warmth spreading down her arms into her hands and increasing in intensity, Annie's expression became thoughtful.

'We'll just feed the little soul and then talk some more, okay?'

Minutes later, with the cat fed and ensconced in a warm bed, the three of them sat down to talk and, by the end of that conversation, the enormity of Mary's latest gift had finally sunk in.

'You'll need ter practise it, lass, again and again. You know that, don't you? This 'ere gift o' yourn needs working – you can't just let it sit there. 'Cos the more you use it, the stronger it'll become.'

'I know, Annie, I'm not taking it for granted, I feel quite humble. In fact, I'm wondering why it's been given to me when I have such violent feelings towards so many people, especially those who treat animals with such cruelty. When I think about the moron who hurt this little cat, I want to set him on fire! The worst thing is, I know I can do it! But I also know I mustn't give in to this because I've already been warned that, if I do, I'll lose this gift and it's so important to me to save animals that I can't risk that.'

She looked from one to the other. Annie and Lizzie were silent.

'Can you really set people on fire?' asked Lizzie, looking disturbed.

'Well, I've only done it with paper so far but I'm pretty sure I could, yes. But you needn't worry, I'm not allowed to use it to damage anyone. The Voice inside me has said so. If I do, I'll lose all my gifts. I guess I've got it for a reason, though. It'll probably come in useful at some point, you never know.'

'Well, you can't let anyone else know this – or about the healing – not yet, can she, Annie?'

'You ain't wrong there, girl. It be much too early for people out there ter know 'bout this, Mary. You'm going to have ter keep this 'ere 'ealing under wraps a fair old while. And the other mebbe forever. And you…' looking at Lizzie, 'you, girl, 'ave to 'elp with that. There be too many 'oo'd be out ter use 'er for their own reasons – and not good ones neither! No, we need ter keep this to ourselves, lassies, while Mary gets strong enough ter 'andle what's coming ahead. You clear on that, girl?'

For Mary, there wasn't the slightest shred of doubt. The healing was the big one, wasn't it? This one power put all the others in the shade. Sure, the others were there for a reason, they would help her when needed, she was certain, but this one took priority over all else because at last she knew why she was on this planet!

Healing and saving wildlife was her reason for being; she was quite clear on that score. Oh boy, she'd guard this with her life and, meanwhile, take every opportunity to practise it!

SEVENTEEN

The first day of the new school year, buzzing with activity on all fronts, seemed to flash by in minutes and, as they walked home slowly, both girls' minds were preoccupied.

'So that's that,' said Lizzie, 'first day over. What d'you reckon?'

'Great! Some of it – like the homework for our new sets – seems fair, though I wasn't expecting so much of it. Thought we might get off lightly this first week but they've loaded us straight away.'

'Fellowes was boot-faced – not a happy bunny at all, was she?'

'Hacked off by her class, I should think – just as her parents will be!'

'Yeah, *and* without her happy clappers! Staddon's split them up just as he said – smart move, that! Did you see all their expressions when their names weren't called for our class and we got up to leave the hall? Really teed off! At least we don't have to suffer them anymore!'

And so they continued on their way home.

Susan Darling and Laker were waiting as Mary came up the path towards the kitchen door.

'Good day? Ah, I see I didn't need to ask. Sit down, have a cup of tea and tell me all!'

'So she seems to be in the top set for most subjects,' she told Tom Darling later. 'The only one that's let her down is maths.'

'Hmm, predictable, really, given the history with that Lashley chap. Good thing, though – at least she's out of his reach. And it's no problem. We can always get her extra coaching if need be.'

'You never know, things may improve with a new teacher.'

'Hmm, wouldn't count on it. Unfortunately, past experience tends to leave its mark – my hatred of art stems from the art master who told me in front of everyone that, since all my work looked as if paint had just been flung at the canvas, it baffled him that I should want to continue with it!' They both laughed.

The number of exam subjects staggered both girls at first. Gradually, however, they settled down, with plenty to discuss on their way to and from school.

Once they had left the town centre, their journey took them past a small lake that was home to a couple of swans and a variety of small fish. Mary had taken to bringing a slice or two of bread in order to feed the swans on their way home and the birds were fast becoming accustomed to the afternoon ritual, making their elegant way towards the bank as the girls approached. It was with surprise then, a week later, that they saw only one swan hovering at their approach before it turned and set off across the water.

'Where's the other one?'

In response to Mary's anxious question, Lizzie pointed to the far side where the swan was heading. There, partially obscured by a fallen tree trunk covered with vegetation, a white form could be seen half leaning on the trunk and struggling occasionally, it seemed, to escape from something holding it back. Without hesitation, the girls pelted along the bank towards the other side of the small lake. Halfway round, the way was blocked by dense vegetation.

'We can't get through,' panted Lizzie as she struggled with particularly troublesome brambles, 'we need machetes for this lot!'

'Can't waste time like this,' gasped Mary, battling thorns. 'I'll follow its mate and swim over there! See if you can wade out a bit ready to help as I get it over here – just hope we're not too late; the poor thing looks worn out. Don't know what's got it but it really looks as if it's on its last legs!'

Tearing off her shoes, socks and skirt, she leapt into the water and felt an immediate surge of power inside her lending speed to her strokes. As she neared the swan, she saw that she wasn't a moment too soon:

the poor creature had evidently been struggling for some time and was nearing the end of its reserves. One wing hung at an awkward angle half over its body, half in the air; the other was caught up with its feet in a mass of twine.

Hell's teeth – it was fishing line! Mary's heart sank. There was no hope of disentangling this beautiful creature from all that on her own without causing further injury! Lizzie would have to get over here and help. Together, they might have half a chance of getting the swan back to land; but then they'd still have to free it, somehow, from that mass of line before they could assess the damage. Not only that, they certainly would not – could not – do any of it without the bird's help. Strewth!

She hadn't got round to talking to the swans yet. Now, she had no choice: she'd have to make a start and reassure this wild creature that they were here to help and weren't going to harm it. Yikes! What if she'd lost the power? She hadn't done any talking with wildlife for some days now and, in the past, *they* had always called on her first! Like the healing, of course, she should have been practising it, shouldn't she! What if this one couldn't hear her? What if it didn't believe her and struggled? What if, what if… Oh hell! If she kept thinking of the what ifs, she'd never get started. Better just grit her teeth and get going.

Her mind made up, her feet touched the bottom – just as Lizzie's head appeared at her shoulder. 'I thought you could use some help,' she said simply, 'and this,' holding up her penknife with all its attachments.

Mary could have shouted for joy. Trust Lizzie to have her trusty camping knife with her. Thank God for her friend's practical streak!

The next moment, words sprang unbidden into her mind – *We're here to help you. Don't be afraid – just trust us and all will be well. It won't be easy but if you could possibly help us, it'll make everything much easier.* Almost as soon as the thoughts left her, the swan raised its head exhaustedly and looked her full in the eyes for a few moments. A faint, tired voice spoke in her head – *I've been struggling for ages. I haven't much left in me but I'll try. Tell me what to do.*

Just try and relax into our arms so's we can at least cut this line free, then we can carry you to land to try and remove the rest of it. You really mustn't struggle anymore as your wing may be broken.

'Okay, Lizzie, we need to cut the line that's holding it down first, then lift the swan between us.' Lizzie gave her a *What if?* look.

'Don't worry, it knows what to do. I'll give it some support while you get started.'

'D'you have any idea how heavy these birds are?'

'It's okay. I think I'm getting help on the strength front.'

And her strength did seem to be increasing by the second. Not only could she support the bird without effort but the swan seemed to be as light as air!

Within seconds, Lizzie had located the line in the water beneath the swan. Some minutes passed, however, before she managed to locate the source of the trouble. 'Got it!' she finally gasped in triumph, before sawing away determinedly with her penknife. The task wasn't easy as the line had wound itself around and between the clumped reeds which had then become entangled in the knot that had ensnared the swan. Breathing hard, Lizzie managed to keep going, however, until finally she straightened with a victorious grin. 'Done!' she announced.

With Mary on one side and Lizzie on the other, the girls manoeuvred themselves into a position from which they could clasp hands beneath the bird, then braced themselves before moving slowly and deliberately towards the bank. The bird was certainly no lightweight and with Mary having to move backwards against the water, the task might have presented more of a challenge than she had expected if it had not been for the continuing surge of strength within her that allowed her to take more than her share of the weight. Carefully they inched towards firm ground, the bird looking gratefully at them both as it arched its graceful neck, Mary reassuring it as they went.

When they finally arrived at the bank and could lower it, all three of them collapsed. Lizzie was no fool. 'Did you get some help on the strength front?' she asked. 'That was no lightweight bird and, sure as hell, I wasn't holding up much of her.'

Mary nodded. 'Good job, wasn't it? Don't reckon we could have done without it! You okay to go on?'

'Sure. Had we better try and remove the rest of this line?' said Lizzie.

Undecided, they looked at the swan, now lying awkwardly on the bank, resting its head, its eyes shut.

'I really don't know. Can we do it, do you think, without causing any further injury?'

'What about trying out your gift? We know you can heal – the cat showed us that – and I know you haven't done anything like that since but why not see if it'll get this twine off? Surely that ranks as healing?'

Mary stared down at the mass of twine and reeds constraining the bird. Could she do it? Maybe. Then again, maybe not. Oh, come on – what harm could it do to give it a go? Quite a bit if she didn't do it right!

'Mmm, okay, if you think so, but what if I make a pig's ear of it?'

'Oh rot! It's our best chance. After all, it's the line that's causing the discomfort and, once we remove it, the swan'll probably be fine. Look, how about a joint effort? You first and then I can pitch in with Excalibur here if need be! I'm willing to have a go if you'll help me. This blade is quite sharp and I'm sure we could make short work of the rest as long as we go carefully! Come on,' as Mary still hesitated, 'have some faith! I'm certain you can do it but even if you only manage half the job, it'll be a help.' She grinned. 'Think of our music lesson on *Swan Lake* and tell Odette here what you're going to do…'

Mary took a deep breath, squared her shoulders and passed her hands gently over the bird's body. Nothing happened. Oh no! It wasn't going to work! She knew it. She repeated the action. Still nothing. Looking up at Lizzie, she shook her head despairingly.

'Keep going,' said Lizzie, 'don't give up so easily, you've only just started – believe in yourself!'

Mary bit her lip in disappointment, then felt a lightning jolt as if someone had taken her by the shoulders and given her a robust shake. It felt like a rebuke. Pull yourself together, girl, it said, get serious! And the next minute a sharp surge of energy shot along her arms into her hands and the twine immediately beneath them fell away. Lizzie chortled. She'd been right – Mary could do it!

After that, the rest was plain sailing and the swan looked on in gratitude as the remaining lengths of twine lay around them. As they drew the last piece from its wing, the bird was free at last! Lizzie whooped with excitement.

'What about the wing?' she asked as they regarded it still standing up at an awkward angle. 'Can you ask it to try and move so we can see what happens?'

A sudden commotion attracted their attention – the casualty's mate had decided to lend some assistance! Their swan had seen its arrival and was trying to struggle forward but the girls could see instantly that the wing was damaged.

It's no good, please stop! Mary spoke to it hurriedly. *We think your wing is hurt.*

'It'll need specialist help,' she said to Lizzie.

'Hang about,' said Lizzie, 'aren't you forgetting something?' And she tapped Mary's hands then pointed at the swan.

Another half hour passed as Mary fixed her gaze on the injured wing with her hands close to, but not touching, it. Curious again, Lizzie held her own hand near Mary's but could feel nothing. She looked on fascinated, nevertheless, as, by degrees, the two parts of the wing straightened and came together. As the wing returned to its normal position, the creature bent its head gracefully and touched Mary's hands with its beak.

'It's thanking you,' said Lizzie in awe.

'But I'm not there yet, Lizzie, that was quite slow. It'll get faster with practice, I know it, and I want to keep it quiet for as long as possible because people would only want to make money out of it and that's not my way.'

Lizzie nodded. 'Okay, let's just call at the police station and report the twine. We can ask the police to contact the local sanctuary. They may be able to let people know how dangerous fishing twine is for wildlife.'

'You must be very proud of your daughter, Mrs Darling. No doubt about it – the girls did one tremendous job! It's a good job there were no other injuries but freeing the swan from that twine was certainly no easy task!' The policeman who had driven the girls home was emphatic. He had said the same to Lizzie's family, all of whom had been home by the time Lizzie arrived in the police car, causing much trepidation before the reason for her lateness emerged.

'It doesn't exactly surprise me,' replied Susan Darling, her anxiety at Mary's lateness now completely assuaged. 'So where is the swan now?'

'Some colleagues have taken it and its mate to the sanctuary at Becton Bridge. Bronwen Morley, who runs it, is wonderful with swans and will make sure it's okay before returning them both to Stellan Pool. She'll also get this some airtime as soon as she can and will let Mary know, as she'd welcome some help with the publicity side. I've given her your number; I hope that's all right. Anyway, without the girls' help, Mrs Darling, the poor creature would have had no chance whatsoever, so maybe you'll be wanting to let her off homework tonight?' And he grinned broadly as he left.

Susan Darling surveyed her daughter with a fond smile. 'It seems quite clear to me that any wildlife can stop worrying when you're around, my darling. Perhaps we should prepare for a future vet in this family. Your dad'll be pleased if so, that's for sure. Right now, up to the bathroom and a hot bath straight away – you're a real sight to behold – and those wet, muddy clothes in the linen basket *now please!*'

Mary grinned. The genuine pride and pleasure behind her mother's briskness was obvious. How super that, for once, it was because of *her*.

EIGHTEEN

'Don't forget – nothing about the swan. I really don't want the others to know anything we do unless it's absolutely essential!'

'Okay,' said Lizzie, with a curious stare. What a strange girl! Most people would have been pleased for others to know they had saved a swan! Still, that was Mary. So much about her was still an enigma. So much Lizzie still didn't understand. They were certainly on the way to being firm friends but their personalities were so different that, even though Mary was a bit more open now than she'd been to begin with, there was still a sort of shut-off quality about her at times. Sometimes her silences made it difficult to know what to think.

Still, at least she could make Mary laugh and she did laugh more these days. Of course, not having Lasher on her back had made a big difference and the Fellowes lot being out of the frame too was undoubtedly an immense relief. In fact, slowly, slowly, her friend was becoming quite popular, in part thanks to her own efforts – although Mary didn't know it.

Lizzie had made it her business to present her friend in an attractive light whenever the opportunity arose and, since Mary not only excelled at team activities but was also supportive when others had weaknesses, this wasn't too difficult. Since she had started to relax and smile more, talking and responding to jokes more easily as long as Lizzie was around, she was becoming used to mixing with everyone.

'You're extra quiet,' Lizzie said as they walked home a few days after the incident with the swan. 'Anything up?'

'Mmm,' replied Mary, after a few minutes' silence during which Lizzie mentally tapped her foot. Pressing her friend for a reply was useless – Mary would simply clam up. 'The local paper's been in touch about the swan business. They want to do an article on us.'

'Really?' It was all Lizzie could do to prevent her voice coming out as an excited squeak! She continued as casually as she could. 'Well, that's great – isn't it?'

Another silence followed. Ah! She might have known. Mary wasn't keen.

'So? What did you say?'

'Mum took the call. They want us to call them back.'

'Right. And?'

'Well, I just don't know – do *you* want our names and pictures splashed all over the Milton Chronicle for everyone to see?'

Aha, so that was it! Mary was publicity shy. Understandable, of course, but she seemed to be forgetting the priority here.

'Well, wouldn't it help to stop anglers leaving their lines in Stellan Pool and the river too? Come to think of it, in all rivers! Don't you think all swans might be safer if we made everyone aware of the dangers of just bombing off and leaving line behind them? Maybe they just don't realise what harm it can do. It would reach a lot of people, too!'

There was a silence while Mary digested this and Lizzie saw that she'd hit exactly the right note. Mary wasn't at all concerned about *their* part in the rescue – but she was very anxious that the swans should be safe and a report in the local paper would undoubtedly give a valuable airing to the subject. Lizzie, herself, wasn't trying to court publicity but, hey, it was rather exciting, wasn't it? It would be the first time anything like that had happened to either of them, so Mary should be jumping up and down with excitement, shouldn't she? After all, they had done something quite important. Shouldn't the world know about it?

'Okay then, but I'm not having *my* picture in the paper – you can, though, if you want.'

'Nah – won't bother if you don't!'

❧

In the event, both girls' photographs appeared in the local paper and the interview was fun, too – more like an informal chat – so that, after the initial hesitation, both girls relaxed and answered the young reporter's questions readily.

'Could you say how important it is for anglers to make sure they don't leave any fishing line behind them, even if it seems to be caught on some rock or something?' asked Mary.

'Yeah, this swan was lucky we were there,' added Lizzie, nodding emphatically. 'If we hadn't been, it could have died!'

Mandy, the reporter, nodded in agreement. 'Of course I will; that's one of the major points with this story, isn't it? We have to try and stop this sort of thing happening again. Tell me, it must have been terribly difficult to get the swan free of the line if you had to carry it back to land in order to cut all the line away. Swans are heavy and can be awkward, particularly if they're frightened. How exactly did you manage that?'

Mary threw Lizzie a warning look. Lizzie, no fool, realised what that look meant. 'Oh, I had my penknife on me,' she replied casually. 'It's very sharp, so it wasn't hard to cut the line free of the boulder that was trapping it. Then we just towed the swan through the water to the nearest part of the bank. It was quite easy really: it was so tired, it had no struggle left in it. And I think it knew we were trying to help!'

'Yes, then Lizzie cut the rest of the line away in short bits,' said Mary. 'It was her idea, too, to report it to the police who contacted *Becton Bridge Sanctuary* where it's being cared for with its mate until it's well enough to be returned to the pool. In fact, Lizzie did most of the rescue,' she added generously. The girl regarded her keenly for a few seconds then snapped her pad shut and stood up.

'Well, thank you both for all that,' she said. 'I'll get along to the sanctuary now to see how much progress it's made and perhaps we can get a photograph of you both with the swans when they're returned to the pool?'

'A successful hour, then?' said Susan Darling as she ushered Mandy out.

'Oh absolutely, but I'll be following this up when the swans are returned to the pool,' replied the reporter. 'The girls did a grand job and we must show the successful outcome. It's an inspiring little tale and I intend to keep in touch.'

She was thoughtful as she drove away.

'There's something here I haven't been told,' she said later to her editor. 'I can't quite put my finger on it yet. But I will – eventually. You can depend on it. And I'm going to keep an eye on those two – I've a feeling there'll be more to come from that direction, somehow!'

Mary was running. She was late, very late, and her mother, with plans for the day, would definitely be annoyed. To make matters worse, she and Laker were both soaked to the skin. Oh boy, was she going to be for it! But the heavens had opened without warning and she couldn't just leave that poor, miserable horse on his own in that quagmire of a field, could she? She pushed open the kitchen door and stood just inside, streams of water cascading to the floor around them.

Her mother's reaction was immediate. She flew at them in horror. 'Quick, quick – the utility room! Get those wet things off and let's get you both dry!' Half an hour later, with Mary in a warm, dry tracksuit and Laker towelled off, the three of them sat in the kitchen, Mary and Susan sipping mugs of hot tea and Laker sprawled near the Aga contentedly.

'Where have you been? You said it would only be a short walk this morning because of the weather – you've been over two hours, Mary! No wonder you were saturated!'

'Don't tell me,' she said, before Mary could answer, 'you came across some animal in trouble, didn't you?'

The response was an instant torrent of words. 'Oh, Mum, you should have seen it. This poor horse was stuck all by himself in a small corner of a really boggy field. There was no grass, no shelter and the small bit he had to himself was fenced off so he had hardly any space! Oh, Mum, he can't stay there; you'd have been so sad if you had seen him. His head was down, he's so thin and yet he had no coat. He was standing so still all on his own and he was soaking wet and lonely. It was really dreadful, so cruel. I had to do something so I went to see the owner at the farm and you won't believe what a complete moron he was! Didn't want to know, didn't care, told me to mind my own business and then just shut the door in my face! Oh, Mum, I have to do something for that poor, poor horse, really I do!'

Somehow she couldn't stop the words pouring out of her. Oh, surely her mother would help her to do something!

Susan Darling sighed, then, as if recognising the inevitable, she rose and went over to the kitchen dresser, picked up her telephone book and thumbed quickly through the pages to the number of the local horse sanctuary.

'Here you are,' she said, handing the small book to Mary. 'Call your friends at the sanctuary and report it now. See if they can start taking some action today and,' looking wryly at her watch, 'if you need to meet them somewhere to show them where the horse is I'll take you in the car, okay?'

'Oh, Mum, you're a star!' said Mary and she grabbed her mother in a delighted hug. The response from the sanctuary was sympathetic but cautious. Yes, one of their inspectors did happen to be in that day and yes, he would come out but only if it could be proved that this situation was ongoing. How often had Mary seen the horse at the location that was the basis of the complaint? Was it a regular occurrence? How did she know that on other occasions, the horse was not elsewhere, with company and also access to plenty of good grass or hay? Could this be just a one-off incident? Would it be possible for her to monitor the situation for a couple of weeks and report back to them?

Oh, for goodness' sake! No wonder so many animals had to continue in cruel situations for such a long time before anything was done. Could nothing take place in this world without having to cut through an entire library of red tape? How could she possibly explain that she had heard from the horse, *itself*, that its unhappy plight was a continuing situation? That the owner had no interest in its comfort and that it had been condemned to this location for some months? If she even hinted at communicating with the animal, they would think her a head case!

'Well, darling, you've done all you can for the moment,' her mother said carefully. 'You'll just have to monitor the situation as the man suggested.'

'But two weeks is too long!' burst out Mary passionately. 'That poor horse is suffering *now*. Why should it have to wait two weeks – maybe even longer – before it can be rescued? It's so, so unjust. I hate this world! I hate people! They're so cruel! Animals can't defend themselves. Why should they be treated like this?'

Susan Darling was silent. Seconds passed as she studied Mary's wretched expression. 'You're right, of course,' she said slowly. 'But sadly, my darling, you will come across incidents like this very often. They are part of the fabric of life, Mary. Unfortunately, the world out there is a hard and, at times, cruel one and you will come across lots of people who will disappoint and enrage you by their attitude towards animals and their treatment of them. None of it will be easy to accept and, although we will do our best, naturally, to prepare you as much as we can for the harsh realities, there are many that you will have to experience for yourself. But, Mary, remember that there are also some good people out there, people who care as much as you do about injustice and cruelty and who battle passionately against both. I'm sure you'll find them as you go about your life because like-minded people generally gravitate together, and a great deal can be achieved through the force of numbers, you'll see.' And she hugged her daughter comfortingly.

'Do you think a newspaper report on Mischief's situation would help? Should I contact that reporter? I'm sure she'd help us,' Mary said suddenly.

'I think, at this stage, you might do more harm than good,' her mother said carefully. 'Diplomacy will get you better results, at this stage, than outright confrontation. The man sounds as if he could be difficult and I would let things rest. The time will come when you may find the Press a useful aid but, at present, this poor horse could suffer more at the hands of that farmer if you try and involve the newspaper. Do what your inspector asks – monitor the situation, gather your evidence and take it from there.'

Mary carried her sense of outrage with her for the period that had been stipulated by the sanctuary's inspector. Monitoring he had asked for so monitoring he would jolly well get – but, along the way, she would also take comfort, reassurance and some healing to the poor creature at the receiving end of the farmer's callousness and so every day she visited the horse with carrots and love. Mischief, whose seemingly inappropriate name she'd established, soon looked forward to the girls' visits – for she had, naturally, recruited Lizzie as an aide and companion in this campaign – and when they went to the swampy corner of the lonely field where the horse stood patiently on his own, his ears flicked back and forth in appreciation as he nuzzled their hands gently. They took photographs and made notes on what they found, reassuring him all the while that before long his ordeal would be ended; and, on several of these occasions, Mary administered some healing for the sores on Mischief's back.

I can't remove them totally, I'm afraid, she told him, *because it will help your case, I think, to leave some evidence of the neglect you've suffered, for the inspector to see. That's why I took a photograph of them at the beginning and then we can argue that they've healed a bit during the two weeks because we've been treating them with herbal cream. But I've removed the worst soreness, I hope.*

The horse lowered his head and exhaled a deep fluttering breath through his nostrils twice before replying – *Thank you. Even this has made me feel better.*

At the end of ten days, the inspector made his visit and viewed the evidence that she and Lizzie had gathered, before calling on the owner where it was swiftly established that the man had no intention of taking any remedial action towards a situation which he refused even to acknowledge was unacceptable. And so, to Mary's delight, the long-suffering Mischief was removed, soon after that visit, to the sanctuary. Their friendly inspector, as he had become by then, was reassuring. Mischief would remain there, he promised, until a good, caring home for him could be found and, in the meanwhile, they could visit as often as they liked.

As the girls prepared to depart, following their first visit to his new pasture in a large, verdant field with four companions, Mary looked into his eyes and read the gratitude clearly visible in their depths, even without his fervently expressed thanks. Her own eyes brimming with feeling, she reassured him that all would be well now. She would continue to visit him here as well as in any future new home. And to herself, she vowed that, in the meanwhile, she would do everything in her power to find him an owner who would make him happy.

You know that I would have you, myself, if I could, she told him as he cavorted happily – through relief and contentment now behaving more in keeping with his name – *but I'm sorry, we don't own even a small field, let alone a superb one like this, and I think my parents would draw the line at sharing our living room with a horse, however wonderful I think you are!* He snickered and nuzzled her hand as she turned to go.

'What happened there?' asked Lizzie, still curious about the communication that seemed to go on when Mary was involved with any animals.

'Oh, nothing much,' responded Mary casually. 'Just reassuring him that I felt sure he'd soon have an owner of his own.' And, for the time being, Lizzie had to be content with that.

NINETEEN

Milton Cross had two proud families the following Thursday and, when the girls entered their classroom on Friday morning, the instant silence that fell preceded a burst of applause. Pink-faced, they made their way to their seats.

'Kept that quiet, didn't you!' and 'Good job we can read!' were followed by other similar comments and Mary, touched, went red with embarrassment. Lizzie, equally pleased, simply grinned. At break, as the other girls came up and congratulated them, the Fellowes set noticeably lurked in the background, their expressions betraying their jealousy for all to see.

'Oh, typical,' snorted Lizzie, 'we all know they're jealous as hell. But then saving a swan wouldn't even occur to them – they'd probably just have kicked off home and left the poor creature to die!'

It went on to be a satisfying though hardworking week. By Thursday morning, the class was ready for physical exercise. An hour of PE would be followed by field games.

'I am just sooo glad to get out in the fresh air!' said Lizzie, heaving a sigh of relief. 'I've had enough chalk and talk this week to last me a month!'

Mary, knowing her friend's preference for open air and physical activity, smiled sympathetically. It had been an intense week workwise, without a doubt.

'Right, girls, let's have some action! Come along, get moving; we want those limbs warmed up before we start on the jumps!' Miss Batchelor had arrived, unnoticed. The girls warmed up as usual before taking on the equipment set out around the gym. Mary enjoyed this more than anything else, her build and agility allowing her to take the pieces in her stride seemingly effortlessly. Lizzie, more sturdily-built, had to expend slightly more effort but still had no difficulty.

Today, however, her mind on other matters, Lizzie was not concentrating as she normally did – a lapse that would be her downfall. Mary, watching her in the run-up to the vaulting box, was surprised at her relatively loose approach and short take-off. This wasn't like Lizzie: she was tackling it rather clumsily, nothing like her usual smooth, fluid style. No, not like Lizzie at all.

The next round seemed more like Lizzie's normal approach. Perhaps it would continue like that now. She must remind Lizzie to concentrate. Fat lot of good all their ideas would be about volunteering over half-term at the swan sanctuary if she broke an arm or leg now! Hmm, that next run-up wasn't too bad but still not her usual form. What on earth could she be thinking about that was so important? She really would have to talk to her about it.

Oh no! She should have done it immediately! Lizzie's next take-off – for the horse, this time – was, once again, unusually short and the outcome a disaster! Everything seemed to happen in double-quick time. Lizzie hit the horse short, the horse collapsed under her as she fell to the ground, hands outstretched to break her fall, and the next minute there was a yell of pain as she hit the floor.

'My wrist, it's my wrist,' she groaned, clutching her right wrist, as Mary reached her. 'I hope it's not broken!'

Seconds later, Miss Batchelor was there and lost no time in confirming her fears. 'We'll have to get you to Casualty,' she announced firmly. 'Is there someone at home? Can we get hold of your mother?'

Fortunately, it was a day when Ellen Paige had no commitments, so within minutes she was at the school; the fact that Lizzie, normally dismissive of any physical injuries, was sitting in the school's medical room white-faced and trembling slightly, convinced her that this was more than the usual tumble from a tree or bike.

The simple fracture irritated as well as annoyed Lizzie who was mortified, too – after her initial upset – by her own carelessness. Mary, visiting her the following day, was deeply sympathetic. Of all the people to be incapacitated, it would have to be Lizzie. She was hating it already and the knowledge that she had been the cause of her own misfortune made it even worse. Mary, already missing her friend's presence, hesitated but decided to ask the question anyway.

'When do you think you'll be able to come back?'

'Oh, I'll be in on Monday,' replied Lizzie immediately.

'Oh, you think so, do you?' replied her mother coming into the room and overhearing this. 'Not if I have anything to do with it, Elizabeth Paige! Not unless you want the other wrist to suffer a similar fate!'

Lizzie groaned and rolled her eyes. Mary grinned. 'No problem,' she said. 'You can borrow my notes and I'll deliver them after school each day – if that's okay, Mrs Paige?' she added hastily, seeing Ellen's expression.

'Well, she can't write, Mary, she's not ambidextrous,' said Ellen Paige, 'and she *will* rest that wrist, otherwise she will be out of circulation even longer!'

'Oh, Mum—' began Lizzie indignantly.

'Oh Mum nothing! You will do as I say, young woman, at least for the next week, if not the following one as well. That wrist may be in plaster but a week – or even two – of complete rest won't do you any harm. Be warned, Lizzie – six weeks will become six months if you try to get going before you're ready!'

So it was that Mary had a week at school without her friend for the first time since their friendship had begun. It was a key fact which both girls would recall later on, with more than a little regret. Mary had been so absorbed during that week with notes for Lizzie, lessons with Annie and healing practice on the wildlife that Annie came up with, that she had failed to pay much heed to the fragments of conversation reaching her telepathically at the time. *Yes, around four... Plain white, no advertising... May have to wait...* The voices of Lana Fellowes and her cronies had been unmistakable but there had also been a male voice, something that Mary, puzzled, had simply shrugged off at the time but would recall in the days that followed, with regret that she had not listened in more attentively.

That Sunday, the Darlings took both girls out to tea in nearby Brancaster, a small market town not far from Becton Bridge, the home of the swan sanctuary where their casualty was recovering. Mary, ensconced in the back of the car with her friend, was as happy as Lizzie. It was great; she'd actually missed having a friend to share her thoughts and ideas which was definitely a first for her. Without thinking, she placed her hand on Lizzie's arm only to pull back, alarmed, when Lizzie quickly withdrew hers, staring at Mary suspiciously.

'What's the matter? What did I do?' whispered Mary.

'I don't know,' hissed Lizzie, 'but it was the strangest sensation. Didn't you feel it?'

'No, what d'you mean? What sensation?'

'I don't know – a sort of electrical current, a throbbing, all the way along my arm. Are you sure you didn't feel anything?'

Mary shook her head, bemused. 'Did it hurt? Was it uncomfortable?'

'No – just weird.'

The afternoon was an unqualified success. The sanctuary owner, Bronwen Morley, a wonderfully compassionate woman, clearly loved her work. She took them round, explaining how she and her small, dedicated staff of volunteers cared for the rescued birds – a mixture of adult swans and cygnets of all ages – and spent time preparing them for their return to the wild, where that was possible. If not feasible, the survivors would either remain in the sanctuary for the rest of their lives or be transferred to a lake owned by one of the patrons.

When they reached the small pre-release lake where about twenty swans at different stages of growth awaited release, the girls were overcome. Unaware until now that such places even existed, they were silent with wonder, though not for long. Very soon, one swan separated from the others and came swimming over. "Their" swan had recognised them!

I am so glad to see you. Thank you for all you did to save me!

Mary could hear the words forming in her mind and although still slightly unprepared, she allowed her thoughts to answer – *I'm so pleased to see you fit and well. We're doing our best to make sure that something like that doesn't happen again.*

Are we going back soon? We're happy here but we're missing our own pool.

Mary was touched. 'Will you be returning them to Stellan Pool soon?' she asked Bronwen Morley.

'We're actually intending to do just that tomorrow. What made you ask?'

'Oh, nothing; only they've been here some time and I wondered if they'd be missing their patch at Stellan Pool.'

Bronwen smiled. 'Of course; well, they won't have much longer to wait.'

Lizzie, suspecting what was taking place, did her best to divert attention from Mary. She turned to Tom and Susan Darling, who had been watching and listening quietly in the background, and drew them into conversation with Bronwen, leaving Mary free to talk some more with the swan.

You'll be going back tomorrow and we'll come and see you both regularly once you're there. Again, the words seemed to flow effortlessly from Mary's mind. Bronwen, who had been watching even while talking to the Darlings, had noticed the changing expressions on Mary's face.

'What's happening?' she asked Lizzie. 'The swan has clearly recognised your friend but it seems a bit more involved than that.'

'Oh, Mary just has that effect on wildlife,' replied Lizzie airily. 'Maybe she was a swan, herself, in another life!'

The journey home was a thoughtful one for them all. Tom Darling had been considering the sanctuary from a different angle.

'Right, you all,' he said now, 'clearly, Bronwen is doing a tremendous job and could do with more support. Swans are a protected species and belong to the Queen, technically, but that doesn't prevent some of the atrocities they suffer. They need all the help they can get. The Building Society can afford some sponsorship here *and* pull in some public support in the process! I've collected the necessary details from Bronwen so I'm going to push this through – everyone agreed?'

He need hardly have asked.

Sitting in the back of the car, only Lizzie could see the frown of concentration on Mary's face as the conversation about the sanctuary continued. Something was clearly going on. Tapping Mary on the shoulder and pointing to her head with a significant twist of her fingers, she raised her eyebrows quizzically. In answer, Mary nodded and put a finger to her lips before circling her finger in a forward movement which she and Lizzie had agreed would be their private sign for the first opportunity on their own. Lizzie nodded. This was clearly important and not for public knowledge. She could wait.

TWENTY

Annie handed her a cup of nettle tea and raised an eyebrow quizzically. 'So… 'as there been any change in Lizzie's wrist since you touched her arm?'

'Lizzie hasn't said so but then it might be hard for her to know because her wrist is in plaster. Why? Do you think there might have been? Touching her might have done some good? Should I try it again?'

'Now, don't go gettin' wound up, girl. Could be… I just wondered. Prob'ly runnin' afore we walk. We need ter get on with these 'ere lessons o' yourn – lost a bit o' time in the last few weeks, now, 'aven't we?'

She bent to pick a bunch of mint from her bucket and looked up from under her dense eyebrows. 'You still feeling the same about learning plant and 'erbal cures or 'as everything else taken top place now?'

Mary's response was instant. 'Oh no, Annie, no! I'm still completely, totally committed! Animals are far more important to me than people and I need to know *everything* I can use to help them!' She clenched her fists with passion as she spoke and, though Annie smiled, her next words indicated her concern.

'Well, there are some whopping boulders on the road ahead, lass, but you'll 'ave 'elp along the way. Some mighty important work's up there waiting for you – and long after I've moved on – but you won't be alone, girl. You'll 'ave powerful allies – equally powerful enemies, too, an' no mistake. But you'll come out on top, Mary, just you remember that. And always, *always* keep believin' in yourself, girl!'

'Never thought I'd say this – I am sooo glad to be back. Has the week dragged! Sitting around on your butt all day is so incredibly boring, you can't imagine! Still – need to catch up with everything now and especially the dodgy signals coming this way from Fellowes and her cronies.'

'Dodgy signals?'

'You don't mean to say you haven't noticed!'

'Well, I have been somewhat busy – your notes, the lessons with Annie and the wildlife cases she kept producing for me to practise healing. I haven't exactly been sitting around twiddling my fingers, you know. Anyway, what d'you mean – dodgy?'

'Something rotten's coming from that direction, that's what I mean – and I'm going to make it my business to find out what it is! Oh yes – and what were you frowning about in the car? Your hand signal said you'd tell me today.'

'Yes. I couldn't talk about it in front of you-know-who – that would really have put the cat among the pigeons. It's something you need to know that I haven't told you yet.'

There was no going back now – she'd have to tell her. She just hoped Lizzie wouldn't think her weird.

'Well, go on then – anytime this year'll do.'

'Well, I seem to be picking up bits of conversations between other people going on somewhere.'

Lizzie stared.

Heck, she knew it! Lizzie did think her weird.

'R-i-g-h-t. What exactly d'you mean – picking up? Where? In your head?'

'Well, yes, but they're not from me. You needn't think I've been making them up.'

'Okay, okay, no need to get hyper – I was just trying to understand.'

'Well, I've heard others in the past – when I was in the Home – and they turned out to be right, so I know it wasn't my imagination. These were definitely from the Fellowes set; only snatches here and there, though, so I took no notice – because I couldn't really tell what it was about.'

'What – nothing at all? No names or anything?'

'That's what I wanted to tell you. When we were in the car, I was picking up some more and then I did hear my name mentioned. And there was a man's voice, too.'

Lizzie looked at her friend in astonishment. 'And you didn't think any of this could be important?'

'Well, it's been going on for so long – odd bits here and there – that I just didn't realise.'

'How long has it been going on?'

'It first started in the Home and it's been there on and off ever since.'

'No – I mean the Fellowes bits?'

Mary thought for a moment. 'I guess they started up just after the newspaper report on the swan.'

'Oh – ace! This could be jolly useful and something I'd have thought I should know about as your friend who's supposed to be giving you back-up whenever it's needed – and you decide not to mention it! You're absolutely way out, you are! Are you crazy or what?'

This was going every bit as badly as she'd expected. Lizzie wasn't at all happy. Oh help – how could she make it sound better?

'Look – I didn't think I had anything concrete to go on, just a few snatches of conversation, that's all. Honestly, I just wanted to have more to tell you before I mentioned it. Anyway, I thought you'd think it – me – weird – that I could hear bits of conversations going on somewhere else.'

'Different, certainly,' said Lizzie dryly. 'Okay, no point in banging on about it. We just have to find out what we can *now*. I'm going to do some sleuthing, see what I can pick up. And if you "hear" any more "snatches" of conversation, perhaps you might think it important enough to tell me?'

'You being sarcy?'

'Just saying…'

And, with a faint sigh of exasperation, Lizzie went off in the direction of the sports field where groups of their classmates, standing around waiting for the doors to be opened, greeted her like a long-lost heroine.

Morning break, though, found her with a very serious expression on her face as she joined Mary in the corner of the quad.

'Fellowes either has a new crush or there's a bloke in her circle for some other reason,' she said in an undertone. 'She's been seen with a blonde guy in a silver sports car. He's been picking her up after school the last few days.'

'Well, that doesn't mean it's something to worry about,' said Mary. 'She's had a boyfriend of sorts for a good few months, even if she does seem to change them faster than her nail varnish. Don't suppose her parents like it one bit since it'll be bound to take time that they'd want her to spend on school work, but then she doesn't seem to let that worry her.'

'Hmm, I'm going to take a look, myself, tonight. You said you heard your name mentioned and I'm not getting good vibes about this. We'll see…'

At that moment, over Lizzie's shoulder, Mary caught sight of Lana Fellowes and her cronies staring across at them from the opposite side of the quad. The malevolent expressions on the faces of all three were unmistakable and, as she stared back, her own face expressionless, a drift of thought floated across to her – *It'll destroy her…*

She gasped, breathless for a second.

'What's happened? What have you heard? Come on – tell me!'

Lizzie grabbed her arm with her good hand as Mary

swallowed hard before relaying what she'd picked up. Lizzie's face paled. 'I just knew they were up to something! Didn't I tell you? This sounds serious. We must do more digging, find out what they're planning. Can you look into their minds somehow?'

'I've tried several times since this first started but no. That part of the gift hasn't been given to me – not yet. Maybe never. The bits of talk just seem to float into my mind by chance. I won't give up trying, though, and you never know, it may just start up for me like the other gifts. For the time being, I can only hear what comes across to me.'

'Well, anything you pick up from now on, you *must* tell me. Something's coming off and I've got a hunch it's big trouble. I'm really worried. We *must* keep our eyes and ears open. Can't afford to miss any clues!'

The man she saw meeting Lana Fellowes that evening simply added to Lizzie's fears.

'Don't think her parents would approve at all,' she reported to Mary. 'Flash car, older than Fellowes, early twenties, I'd say, and a bit rough – a shady look about him. Wonder what she wants with him. There's something crooked going on there, I just know it!'

Lizzie's fractured wrist was the least of her concerns in the week that followed. She watched the Fellowes set with a growing sense of impending doom and her anxiety for Mary increased by the day. Something was definitely in the wind. Despite her determined sleuthing, however, no one could – or would – talk and so she could find no concrete evidence that would incriminate Lana Fellowes and her followers; all Lizzie knew in her blood and being was that something bad – something verging on evil – was being planned and that "something" was aimed at her friend. Even worse, it was advancing steadily and she was unable to prevent it.

For the umpteenth time, she badgered Mary about her power to look into the minds of her enemies. 'Are you trying hard enough? It's a gift like the healing – maybe you need to practise it some more. There must be *something* you can do. Surely you can't mean to just sit there and let whatever ghastly thing is going to descend on you happen? Can't you ask for some help, some idea of what to do?'

Mary, herself, was wracked with uncertainty. The times she had asked herself this very question! But who to ask and how? Perhaps she should try the Voice that spoke to her from time to time. But how could she be sure it would hear her? She could feel the threat as strongly as Lizzie – even more so, given her heightened sensitivity and growing supernatural gifts – but, worse, Lizzie's desperate question had coincided with a slowly increasing awareness of something else that was filling her with dread. A sense of inevitability. What was going to happen would happen. And then, unexpectedly, the Voice spoke. *This is all for a reason, Mary. You must go through a baptism of fire in order to take a giant step forward.*

For a split second, she felt much older than Lizzie

– decades older than the fifteen years they would both reach in the next fortnight.

So what could she say to her friend? Knowing what she'd been told – that this would happen, come what may – how could she explain it to Lizzie, especially since Lizzie's knowledge of her powers was still so limited? The healing, a hint of the pyrokinesis and now the fragments of conversation that were causing all this hassle were the only gifts that Lizzie knew about. She'd been hoping to run the others past her friend gradually, in a way that Lizzie would find easy to accept. The pyrokinesis would be the toughest one to handle; she'd mentioned it fleetingly and seen the trepidation on Lizzie's face but she'd have to tackle that more fully when the time was right. Meanwhile, the current dilemma still needed resolving.

'Let's talk it over with Annie this evening,' she said. 'She's bound to come up with something.'

Oddly, however, the old woman was philosophical. 'Everything 'appens for a reason,' she said at the end of their tale. 'You'm 'ere with a mission, girl, and that ain't goin' ter change, whatever the Devil's 'andmaids do. Stay focused, lass, keep your eyes on the goal and whatever else comes up along the way. You'll be 'elped ter sort it. There's essential work for you ahead, Mary, and that ain't goin' away. You just stay focused!'

And beyond those enigmatic words, Annie would not be drawn. Instead, she led the girls into her garden, opened a hutch and took out the limp, sad little body of a rabbit.

'Now, Mary, I want you ter get some more 'ealing

practice in on this little critter what's been run over and just left by some two-legged vermin! You sit an' focus on this, girl, 'cos the more practice you get on that score, the better it'll be for you.'

Even Lizzie's anxiety was allayed temporarily by this task and she settled down with Annie a few feet away to watch what would happen.

The rabbit was a pathetic sight and, to an onlooker, it might have seemed a hopeless task that confronted Mary. Bones had, undoubtedly, been crushed and, although the small creature had been heavily dosed with pain relief by Annie, there was little doubt that the injuries were serious: vital organs had been damaged and were causing its suffering. She had to get started immediately.

Don't try and talk to it; get on with the healing, came the order from within her, and she extended her hands over the small animal, together with all the energy in her being, until she could feel the familiar sensation of heat.

Slowly, her awareness of Lizzie, Annie and the surroundings receded until she was alone in her circle with the rabbit and the extreme warmth that enveloped them both. It became increasingly hotter until she felt almost breathless. How long she sat like that was not clear. Concentrating completely on the rabbit, all she could register was the heat, at its strongest in her hands and chest, and flowing from her in waves to envelop the rabbit.

Finally, she began to experience cramp in her legs just before she became aware of Annie's and

Lizzie's elation, their voices congratulating her and Lizzie thumping her on the back. She came to with a jolt to see the rabbit bouncing around them, to all appearances restored to complete health!

TWENTY-ONE

The euphoria of the rabbit healing still clinging to them, the girls started home. As she said goodbye to Lizzie and continued on her way, Mary was still cherishing the memory of that final moment with the rabbit bounding around her, returned to health.

Misty-eyed with happiness, she turned the corner into her road. Spotting her mother in the front garden, she called and waved. What followed seemed almost unrelated, distanced – as if it were action in slow motion, in a film unwinding before her eyes.

An engine revving behind her became a roar as a white van from nowhere accelerated to race past her. At the same time, her front gate, slightly ajar, flew fully open as Laker, hearing her voice, charged through it. With a joyful yelp, he shot straight across the road towards her – and under the wheels of the same van which appeared to swerve deliberately in order to ensure that it hit him!

For what felt like an age but was probably only a heartbeat, Mary stood immobilised. In shock.

Everything had moved at half speed but with increased force: the sound of the impact as the van hit Laker throwing him into the air before he fell; his high-pitched scream that made her blood curdle; the sight of his bloodied body lying there; her mother running across the road. As the van accelerated even more and sped off into the distance, Mary, blood pounding in her temples, her heart racing, pelted towards her dog.

Her mother and she both arrived at Laker's body at the same time. Barely conscious, he seemed to be making tiny, futile efforts to move.

Holding back tears, she flung herself down and laid her head against his chest, listening anxiously for a heartbeat. It was only just discernible against the hoarse sound of his efforts to breathe. Blood trickling from his nose, his eyes half closed, one of his front legs was sticking out at an awkward angle and various cuts on his side oozed blood. She was beside herself. Her beloved dog, her pet, her life, was lying half-dead on the road. She could hardly breathe as terror overwhelmed her. *Oh God, don't let him die, please, please, God, I'll do anything you want, I promise – anything – just don't let me lose my dog. He's my life. I love him so much, God, don't take him from me. He's the only thing I've ever loved, please, please…* and, lying down next to him on the road, her usual control gone, she howled and sobbed her heart out.

'Call 999!' she shrieked at her mother. 'Call the police, call someone – don't just stand there!'

Susan Darling, herself distraught, ran back into the house.

By now, a small clutch of their neighbours had gathered hesitantly in a group a few feet away. All of them knew what Laker meant to Mary; not one of them could think of anything to say or do that might help her in this horrifying situation. They stood gazing at her in silent sympathy. Seconds later, Susan Darling's car backed out of the drive and, as she drew up near them and jumped out with a blanket, the neighbours stepped back.

'We have to take him to the vet, darling,' she said hurriedly. 'Now. Help me lift him, come on – fast!' One of the neighbours stepped forward to help and the three of them eased Laker – now clearly semi-conscious and in considerable distress from his efforts to breathe – from the road on to the blanket, placing him gently on the back seat where Susan had already tucked another. Mary, refusing to be separated from her dog, climbed in beside him, tears still streaming down her face.

TWENTY-TWO

At the surgery, preparations for their arrival had been made and a nurse was waiting. Laker was carried carefully into a prep room where their vet was ready with oxygen. As Stephanie George began her examination, Mary and Susan were ushered gently into another room and offered some tea. Her heart in her mouth, Mary refused at first – who cared a fig about tea when Laker could be dying? But the receptionist and her mother insisted and, minutes later, they were sipping the hot, sweet beverage – unexpectedly welcome, it transpired, for both of them.

Half an hour later, their vet appeared, looking grave. 'There is some way to go, I'm afraid,' she said. 'I suspect internal bleeding and there are other areas we need to examine. There's no point in your staying as it could all take some time and he will also need scans and other examinations. We need you to sign admission forms and then I suggest you go home and wait for me to call you.' She looked from Susan Darling to Mary sympathetically. 'I know it's not my dog lying in there and so it's easy for me to say, but please try not to worry too much – at least he's still alive. We've given him some pain relief and eased his breathing – and, Mary, while there's life, there's hope, you know…' Her voice tailed off as she studied the girl's tight, tear-stained face and she patted Mary's shoulder gently.

Susan Darling bit her lip, put her arms round her daughter's shoulders and squeezed her comfortingly. Mary, however, numb with pain, was barely aware of her surroundings. Her beloved dog, her friend, her companion, the only thing that had ever given meaning to her life, was lying close to death. What was left for her if Laker died?

The Darling household was a sorrowful place that evening. Susan was still horrified at what had happened. 'If only I'd checked that gate,' she kept repeating. 'If only I'd realised it was ajar and he could get it open! This is all my fault!' She was right, of course, but Tom remained silent, only reminding her later that everyone made mistakes, no one was perfect.

'I'm so, so sorry, Mary love.' Susan, wracked with guilt, tears filling her eyes, too, sat down on the bed and put her arms round her daughter; but Mary was beyond reach. Her chest tight with pain, she couldn't reply for sobbing. She stayed in her room, emerging only when the telephone rang with news from the vet.

'They've done all they can for him tonight, love. He's on a drip in intensive care and hugely doped. They have to do further X-rays and more tests before they can be sure, so they'll call tomorrow to let us know the position.'

It was a bad night for everyone. Mary's anguish was audible and Susan, who couldn't sleep for remorse anyway, was even more upset by the sound of her daughter's distress. She paced back and forth in the kitchen, made endless cups of tea which then went cold as, again and again, she revisited the events of the previous day. After futile attempts to sleep, himself, Tom eventually gave up the struggle and joined her.

Bleary-eyed, they surveyed each other gloomily in a brief silence from Mary's room. 'I can't begin to imagine what will happen if he doesn't pull through,' muttered Susan. 'She'll be inconsolable. We'll be right back to square one. That dog was everything to her.'

'*Is*, Sue, *is* – you're using the past tense already. We must stay positive,' replied Tom. 'There is still hope.'

Both of them, however, had in mind the phone call from their vet the previous evening. Compassionate and experienced as she was, she had been more explicit than either Tom or Susan had revealed to Mary.

'It's not looking too good, I'm afraid,' she had said, 'but it would be wrong for me to give you a verdict at this stage as we still haven't assessed all the injuries fully. We suspect more internal damage than we thought originally, and we have to look into it thoroughly before I can let you know the result. In the meanwhile, we've made him as comfortable as we can but it could be touch and go. The next twenty-four hours will be crucial. I'll ring you tomorrow as soon as I have a more accurate picture.'

'Well, I'll take the day off in case I can take some of the load off you,' said Tom and squeezed his wife's hand.

The morning brought no relief apart from a visit at lunchtime by Lizzie whom Susan Darling had telephoned to explain why Mary would not be at school.

'She's in her room, Lizzie, and isn't really interested in seeing anyone, I'm afraid,' said Susan.

'She'll see me, Mrs D, and it doesn't matter if she doesn't talk. I can at least sit with her and keep her company,' said Lizzie, struggling to keep her own composure. 'I've got a load of messages for her and I've told them I won't be back to school this afternoon, so I'm going up. Don't you worry about me!'

Half an hour later, there was a murmur of voices from Mary's room and, right at that moment, the telephone rang. Both Tom and Susan stared at it, neither willing to be the first to answer. Eventually, Tom picked up the receiver.

Steph George was direct. As they had feared, the prognosis was not promising.

'The injuries are severe,' she said, 'and I'm sorry to say this: Laker is a very sick dog. There is bleeding into his abdomen and his lungs are leaking too. This is creating a dangerous build-up of air around them that is causing them to collapse. Several ribs are fractured, as well as the front leg that you saw sticking out awkwardly. Ideally, we need to insert a tube into his chest and remove the excess air so that he can breathe normally again, but to give him the anaesthetic for this is too dangerous as he might not make it because of the internal bleeding.'

'Can't you control the bleeding somehow?' asked Tom.

'All we can do is apply a pressure bandage to, at least, try and slow it down. It's too dangerous to open him up at the moment although we may have no option if it continues. Even if Laker were to survive the anaesthetic, though, it would still be touch and go as there might be further complications.'

'Such as?'

'Well, the bleeding may continue, the bruising to the lungs may worsen and, of course, the fractures could require surgery at a later date. I hate to say this but, even if a chest tube is positioned, there's always a danger that his blood pressure might plummet, resulting in possible cardiac arrest and that could be the deciding factor. Naturally, we would take immediate action to resuscitate him but there would be no guarantees of recovery. If this were to happen, we would need something in the nature of a small miracle to bring him back.'

'What about surgery to stop the bleeding?'

'It would be much better if the bleeding were to stop naturally as surgery could be really risky. And, again, it's tricky for all sorts of reasons – which I would, frankly, rather not contemplate at present.'

'What should we tell Mary?'

'Just tell me the truth!' cut in a quiet voice from the doorway. Mary, her face drained of colour and the skin drawn tightly over her bones, stood looking at them steadily. 'Surely Laker deserves that at least.'

'Put her on the phone, Mr Darling,' replied Stephanie. 'I heard that and she's right. I'll be as kind as I can.'

Wordlessly, Tom Darling handed the phone to his daughter. Minutes passed as Stephanie talked to Mary.

'Yes, yes, I understand,' they heard eventually. 'When do you think you'll know? I see… So I must just wait to hear from you. As soon as you know for sure? Thank you.'

Her face was impassive as she put the phone down and turned to face them. 'I know the situation. She explained everything. I'm going for a walk now.' And, as Susan moved forward, she raised a hand. 'No thank you, Mum. Lizzie's gone home. I have to be alone for a while. I need to go out and just walk. I'll be back later.'

As Susan looked at him questioningly, Tom shook his head silently and mouthed 'Leave her.' When their daughter had gone, they sat at the kitchen table with a stiff drink and just talked – about Mary, about Laker, about themselves, the changes in their daughter and in their family, the difficulties they might face if the worst happened. And, finally – and reluctantly – about what they could do if their worst fears were realised. At the end, with nothing left to say, they simply sat.

Mary returned in the late afternoon, spent and drained of all emotion. She stood in the doorway dumbly. As Susan moved forward and held her in a hug, she buried her head in her mother's shoulder. Tom, who had been working in the garage, came into the kitchen at that moment, took in the scene and came to join them. The three of them stood in a silent huddle for several minutes.

The evening continued without news. Then, at seven o'clock, Stephanie telephoned. She had done all she could; she wanted to observe Laker's progress for another twenty-four hours and then she felt it would be more beneficial if he were to come home.

To die? Mary wanted to ask. They all wanted to ask but no one had the courage. Actually, Stephanie said later to Tom and Susan, it would take a miracle now for Laker to recover.

TWENTY-THREE

Next day, Laker came home. The large boot of Tom's estate car was padded out with thick blankets and cushions so that Mary could sit alongside and ensure that he didn't slide around.

His basket had been brought downstairs to the large utility room and a folding bed placed nearby so that she could sleep with him and tend to his needs. All that could be done for Laker in the Darling household had been done.

Stephanie had been explicit. 'We've done all we can,' she had announced. 'The bleeding from the liver has definitely slowed but still has to stop, and we can't do any more for that infected fracture until the cardiovascular side is stabilised. You will understand, I'm sure, that we can't operate simply to save his leg, and risk death under the anaesthetic due to his liver bleeding or his lung leaking. I know it may seem harsh but the leg is actually the least of Laker's worries. If it comes to the worst, he can survive with three legs. I'm so sorry, Mary, I can't do any more for him. It will require a miracle for the infection to clear up and the bleeding to stop – for us to save him, in fact. Just keep him comfortable… it may only be for a few hours, I'm afraid.'

Given that sombre prognosis, the Darlings had had no hesitation. There was no doubt whatsoever in their minds: Laker was coming home. On antibiotics and painkillers, with strict rest obligatory, Mary's companion was coming home to be with her, whatever the outcome.

But Mary was determined. *Laker is going to live, whatever it takes*, she told herself. *He* will *recover. That miracle* will *happen*. Her eyes closed tightly, tears oozing slowly from beneath her lids, she clenched her fists. Laker *would* recover. The only thing that mattered to her in this life was *not* going to die – not if *she* could help it. What good was this wretched gift she was supposed to possess if she could not use it to help her own dog!

The weather seemed to express the overall gloom. Rain hammered down and sheet lightning lit up the entire sky as Tom carried Laker to the car wrapped in a blanket. Susan and Mary hovered anxiously with a golf umbrella over the patient.

No one even hinted that it might be his last journey, that he might well be coming home to die, while Mary, herself, refused even to admit that possibility.

They arrived home to find Annie sheltering under the porch with a basket of herbs, plants and tisanes and a bundle of something in her arms that turned out to be an antique sleeping bag. 'Laker can do with all the 'elp 'e can get,' she announced. 'I'll stay as long as I can be of use and I've brought me own bed!' A compromise was agreed and a second camp bed to support the ancient sleeping bag was lodged in the utility room.

Laker may have been dopey but his eyes still retained a glimmer of the old vitality, a glint that became more of a gleam whenever Mary was near. When Annie approached, too, he was clearly aware of her and stirred weakly but it was only Mary who could bring about the faint glow. His hind leg in a large bandage, a shaved patch on his chest and underside, and his general frailty and debilitation were the only outward signs of a critically injured dog. Mary's anxiety was almost palpable. Round and round in her head ran the thought – *Without Laker, what point is there in anything?*

Annie was firm. 'You must try your hardest not to be like this; Laker will feel your distress and be unhappy for you. It will *not* help him, lass. Surely you know that.' Mary did know but it was all she could do to stop herself from crying endlessly at the sight of her beloved dog in so much danger. Just as bad, between her waves of grief, was the fury gathering, hard and corrosive, in her stomach. True, she knew the risks – the Source had told her in no uncertain terms – but it was so, so hard to resist the desire for revenge on those who had done this dreadful thing, put Laker in danger and caused all this agony. All cruelty to animals made her boil with fury but if Laker were to die, she would find it almost impossible to stop herself from seeking out and destroying whoever was behind this!

Annie and she tended Laker day and night. They arranged a shift system so that one of them was with him constantly and, when it was Mary's turn, Susan noticed that she was always either stroking him gently from head to tail, or holding her hands softly over the parts of his body that presented the problems.

From Mary's point of view, the situation remained desperate: there was just no sign of progress. She *would* save him, she *would*! If it were the last thing she ever did, she would save her beloved dog from a fate he didn't deserve. But, unlike the results of her efforts with the other creatures she had healed, this felt like climbing Everest blindfold.

'I'm just not getting any response at all from him, Annie. I can't feel any warmth in my arms and I know that's happened before when the healing *has* worked; but what's even worse is that he can't talk to me. Laker and me – we're just so close. We're always talking and even when we're not, we seem to know what the other is thinking! It must be really bad, Annie, if he can't even talk to me. And I'm not getting any response from him in my mind either. I'm so, so scared.'

Annie hugged her comfortingly in response and did her best to reassure Mary despite the worry clearly clinging to them both. Meanwhile, she could be seen either placing drops of one of her concoctions from a syringe carefully on Laker's tongue or crushing various plants and berries in her old-fashioned pestle and mortar before sprinkling them lightly on the scrambled egg or specially prepared tinned food that Stephanie had supplied. The fact that both foods sat by Laker's nose, untouched, as he lay unmoving with his eyes half closed, was immaterial. Nothing was too much trouble as they continued to administer Stephanie's medication and attend to all Laker's needs.

Neither of them cared about food for themselves and Susan gave up any attempt at mealtimes. Instead, she made sandwiches, leaving them covered, but they, too, were left half eaten or untouched. Lizzie called each day to visit the patient and bring goodwill messages from Mary's schoolmates. She sat patiently watching while Mary or Annie continued their ministrations, usually ending her visit by joining Susan Darling in the kitchen for tea.

On the second day, Susan asked the question that had been puzzling her. 'What is Mary doing exactly when she holds her hands over Laker? I know something is happening, Lizzie, but I don't know what – do you?'

Lizzie hesitated. 'I don't know much myself, Mrs Darling,' she said finally, 'but I think Annie could probably tell you more. She knows better than anyone, even possibly Mary herself, what Mary is capable of doing where animals are concerned.'

That evening when Mary was doing her shift and Annie happened to be passing through the kitchen, Susan stopped her. 'May I have a few words, please, Annie? I'd be grateful for some answers to one or two questions.'

At the end of the next half hour, Susan Darling had her answers and, incredulous though she was at first,

Annie's careful explanation and obvious knowledge of what had been happening in the last few months eventually convinced her.

'I think I'll keep this knowledge to myself a little longer,' Susan told the old woman after a long silence in which she considered what she had just heard. 'It's taken me all this time to understand and accept what you're saying. I don't disbelieve you, Annie, but there's still quite a bit of it that I need to come to terms with and I certainly don't think Tom is ready to handle any of it yet. I'll wait until the time feels right for that, but I'll be very happy to help you all I can. You just let me know whenever you need me.' And the two women smiled at each other in mutual complicity.

By the seventh day, both Mary and Annie were red-eyed with fatigue. Stephanie had just rung to check on Laker's progress, promising to telephone again the following day, astonished as she was at his continuing hold on life, and Tom, just home from work, was hanging up his coat when something unexpected happened: an unusual cry came from the utility room. Both of them dashed immediately to the interconnecting door.

'What's happened?' Susan demanded. 'Why did you cry out? Is he worse?'

As Mary, with joy and relief spilling out of her, turned slowly to face her mother and father, Annie was already bending over Laker. There was a silence before the old woman straightened up, her eyes full of wonder. 'I do believe 'e's turned the corner, Mrs D,' she said tremulously; 'this 'ere dog... 'e be on the mend!' And Mary and she clasped each other in a huge hug of joy before Susan went over to see for herself what Annie meant. As she peered past them down at Laker, she gasped in amazement.

Gone was the dejected, listless, frail animal they had brought home and in his place lay a dog exuding more life and energy than could have been imagined. The change was astounding. It was as if someone had waved a magic wand over Laker! Every line of his body signalled life. He struggled to get up, thumping his tail in excitement on his bed. His eyes were bright, his ears alert. His back bristled with energy.

'No, no, not yet, Laker,' Mary said firmly, holding him down. He lay still immediately, gazing at her adoringly.

'What happened? What did you do? How has this come about so suddenly?' Susan asked in astonishment.

'It hasn't actually been that sudden, Mum. I just didn't want to say anything too soon and this morning, when he seemed extra bright, I wanted to be sure before I raised any hopes. He's actually been making increasing progress with each hour since yesterday afternoon!'

'But you didn't say anything, didn't give us any indication!' said Tom.

'No, I couldn't be certain yesterday, and today I wanted to wait until it was beyond doubt.'

'Shall us take a look at that leg, Mary girl? Make sure, like, eh?'

'Oh yes, Annie, I was forgetting. We ought to do that straight away!'

'Oh, be careful. Do you really think you should?' asked Susan.

'Don't you worry, Mrs D. If young Mary 'ere has done as much as you can already see, it's odds on the leg is going to be absolutely A1!' And Annie patted her shoulder reassuringly.

Together, Mary and the old woman carefully unwound the bandage around Laker's fractured, infected hind leg, peeling away the crusted, bloodstained layers slowly and gently until they reached the final strip – to reveal a perfectly good limb with not the slightest sign of injury! There was a shocked silence.

'Good God! How has this happened?' demanded Tom in astonishment. 'What on earth did you do?'

Annie looked from one to the other of the Darlings, then placed a hand proudly on Mary's shoulder. 'I think it's time we explained one or two things ter your Dad 'ere, my duck.' Then, as Mary hesitated, she added, 'It's only right, Mary lass, 'e needs ter know. Come on… Can we all go and 'ave a cup o' tea, Mrs D, and then we can let Mr D in on all of it?'

As Susan nodded speechlessly, they all trooped into the kitchen and sat down at the large, wooden table. Minutes later, Tom and Susan were gazing at their daughter in silent awe. Mary, red-faced, was shuffling her feet in embarrassment as Annie talked about her gift and the journey she felt lay ahead of the young girl sitting next to her.

'And when that nice young vet lady calls you termorrer,' she ended, 'it'd be best if you didn't mention any o' this, 'cause this lass 'ere ain't ready yet. It'll be some time afore all this needs ter come out, Mr D, and it'd be for the best if you just let 'er think it's a miracle like. Is that okay?'

'Yes, oh yes. Of course,' replied Tom at once. 'I can speak for us both, can't I, Susan?' At his wife's nod of agreement, he continued, 'We can both understand how counter-productive it could be if this extraordinary gift of Mary's were to be exposed before it's appropriate, and we don't want to cause her any further problems. For heaven's sake, she's had enough in her young life and we need to protect her from anything unnecessary. You're quite right, Annie. It's far too early for this to come out in the open and, as you say, we must simply let Stephanie believe that it's the result of a miracle!' And he reached across to take the old lady's hands in his. 'We are grateful to you,' he said quietly, 'for being such a friend and mentor to our daughter. She is fortunate in that respect at least!' A small smile settled on Annie's face as she looked from Tom and Susan to their daughter.

Laker's progress continued. He simply went from strength to strength until by the time Mary returned to school two weeks later – she refused to leave him any earlier – he was almost back to the old Laker. The only small reminder of his ordeal was a barely perceptible, occasional limp on the leg that had sustained the fracture. In Mary's case, the only reminder of her own suffering was a tendency to be over-protective of her companion.

'That'll pass,' said Stephanie to the Darlings when they took Laker in for a check-up, 'it's early days.

Frankly, I'm utterly astounded by what has happened and so are my colleagues. We are all completely baffled; but I guess we must simply thank whoever is up there for the fact that miracles do happen!' And she regarded them thoughtfully as she spoke.

TWENTY-FOUR

'Have you thought about why that white van was there and possibly waiting for Laker to appear?' Lizzie suddenly asked.

'Yes, but we haven't any evidence to link it with you-know-who,' replied Mary, 'although I know you're thinking what I'm thinking.'

'I'm absolutely sure of it! It's too much of a coincidence to be an accident!'

'But we still have no evidence.'

'So you're saying there's nothing we can do about it!'

'Well, no one took the registration and no one could describe the driver so, yes, that's what I'm saying. There's nothing we can do.'

'Well, what a bummer!' said Lizzie. 'Comes from having brothers,' she added with a half apologetic grin as she saw the wry half smile that crossed Mary's face. Lizzie's language was becoming increasingly colourful and certainly gave vent to what they were both feeling.

'Nothing more from the Fellowes bunch? No more bits of conversation?'

Ah. This was probably as good a time as any to mention the bits of talk she'd picked up the same evening that Steph George had confirmed Laker's wonderful recovery. After all, Lizzie had to know sometime.

She relayed what she had picked up over the airwaves, how Lana Fellowes' voice had come through with force despite being so distorted with rage that it was barely recognisable – *The gippo's been too lucky this time but we'll get her yet. I've got other plans up my sleeve and the time'll come when she won't come out smiling! In fact, we get it right and she won't come out at all!*

'Hmm, well, Fellowes was obviously teed off about the outcome of something awful aimed at you but you didn't hear any mention of what it actually was, did you?'

'No, and even if I did, I couldn't use it as evidence, anyway. How much d'you think a court of law would accept what amounts to mental eavesdropping?'

'I know but you might have heard some useful info that would give us a lead.'

'At least whatever it was they planned didn't succeed.'

Mary smiled wryly. What a frightful month! No one could have foreseen that dreadful event or the outcome. How lucky she was that Laker was still with her, still had all his limbs, all his senses, could still enjoy life. Everything could have turned out so differently and then life, for her, wouldn't have been worth living. Laker was everything to her: the only creature that had managed – without even trying – to penetrate all her defences. He'd just slipped into her heart and soul and become part of her.

The frightful alternative that had loomed before her had, though, taught her that part of her life's work would be, somehow, to help anyone and any animal in that same dreadful position. She must do everything in her power, from now on, to save other creatures, wildlife or pets, feral or tame, whatever the situation.

'Still, what's more alarming is what they've got up their sleeves next! Doesn't that worry you?'

'I was more worried by my thirst for revenge, to start with. I can't afford to let that get the better of me, Lizzie, because I've been told that if I do give in to it, I'll lose my power to heal all animals and wildlife and I definitely can't risk that.'

'Right. You mentioned that after the business with the cat. I remember now. So who told you that, then?'

Oh damn! She'd have to expand on it now. Lizzie wouldn't let go until she did. 'There's a voice inside me that speaks up sometimes. It calls itself the "Source".'

'The source of what?'

'I just think of it as the Source of Life but I haven't asked. I just call it the "Voice".'

'Why not? Don't you want to know?'

'I don't feel it's necessary to ask everything – it's enough for me to know that it's chosen me to use whatever gifts it allows me to have.'

'So what about this revenge thing, then? Don't you feel you want that anymore?'

'Hell, I don't think I'll ever stop wanting it. That, funnily enough, is the hardest part for me. It probably sounds awful but I really want to destroy anyone who harms or injures animals and wildlife in any way. This hideous urge comes boiling up inside me every time but I can't afford to go down that road. Anyway, we don't know for sure it was the Fellowes bunch who targeted Laker, do we?'

'*I* do!' Lizzie was emphatic.

'Yes, but we still haven't got any evidence. Whatever we think, no one got the registration, even though one of our neighbours did say she'd seen the van crawling along our road twice earlier.'

'So it was obviously waiting for the chance to run him over. It was a definite plot!'

'I think so, too, but with no leads, how do we prove it?'

'Well, the bits of conversation you've already picked up indicate a plot and I bet if I do some sleuthing, I can come up with something in time.'

With that, the girls reached the end of the country lanes where the route to Milton Upper met a main road and so the subject was left hanging; but Lizzie remained determined to unearth whatever she could to nail the plotters.

❦

They had just crossed the main road when a loud screech of brakes behind and an unmistakable high-pitched scream made them spin round. The car that had braked so hard had stopped and, with traffic overtaking him, the driver was bending over something on the road. As they reached him, he straightened up, his face resigned, and Mary knew at once that it was too late. On its side lay a ginger cat, hardly breathing and with obviously serious injuries, judging by the blood flowing from its mouth and ears.

'It came running out in front of me. I had no time to avoid it,' said the man defensively. 'Look, I'm late for an appointment already; here's my card, call me if there's any expense – I'll pay!' And he shoved the card at Lizzie, spun round, jumped into his car and was gone.

Without hesitation, Mary took the cat gently in her arms and sat down at the side of the road. One or two passers-by looked at her curiously but continued walking. Mary was already in her own world.

There was no collar on the little creature so no one they could inform, no one to care about it in its hour of need. Well, if it were going to die, it would die with some love and compassion around it. She stroked it slowly, murmuring softly to it. Poor, poor little creature! She would never, never ask for a cat. Their independence, so great in some ways, was a double-edged sword: that love of freedom made it too difficult to ensure their safety, for it was impossible to keep them indoors and out of harm's way forever.

As she stroked, the warm sensation she was becoming used to, despite its absence at times, started spreading gradually down her arms and out through her hands. Slowly, it increased until it seemed to leave her arms and hands completely in order to surround and soothe the sad little body on her lap. She could feel the small animal's breathing easing more and more, until finally the intermittent rise and fall stopped altogether. She turned to Lizzie. 'Do you remember the sensation you had when I touched your broken wrist?' she said. 'When I couldn't feel anything but you snatched it away and gave me that strange look – as if I had descended from another planet?'

'Yes I do and it all makes sense now.'

'Well, I feel as if I'm in that same place again. I can't feel it now but something's obviously happening that I don't understand and I must talk to Annie, see if she can make sense of it.'

'I'm intrigued – can't you talk to me?' asked Lizzie.

'Sorry, but I really think it needs to be Annie. With all her experience, she'll know what's going on here or, at least, be able to work it out. This little one needs burying properly, too. We can't just leave her by the road and she doesn't have a collar so we can't find the owner – so I'd better go straight away and I'd rather do it alone, if that's okay?'

As Lizzie nodded understanding, she headed off to Annie's cottage. Still sad that she had arrived on the scene too late to help the cat, Mary was reflective. She must learn how to do something more positive in future situations like this. Her healing ability seemed to work with animals that were still alive, however bad the injuries, but it seemed there was nothing she could do once they had passed a certain point and were too close to death. She needed an outside opinion. This was just one more aspect of everything that had happened to her and it was too important to ignore. She had to talk to Annie now!

'This warmth spreading down my arm, Annie, it's the same warmth that became stronger every day and eventually let me heal Laker but it wouldn't allow me to save the cat. Why not? Do you know?'

The old woman looked at Mary's earnest face thoughtfully. 'The warmth is the sign of your ability ter heal, Mary girl,' she said simply, 'and maybe it has to stop there. You aren't the great Creator, lass, and although you've been given the gift of 'ealing, it's mebbe only up ter a certain point and it's not for you ter give or take life. Just leave it there for the moment. Be glad you can save the wildlife when you can. Don't ask ter make miracles. Take it easy. This little chap's time had come but at least you were able ter give 'im some comfort in 'is last minutes. And remember, lass – everything 'appens when the time is right. Be patient and let be.'

'D'you really think I'll be able to handle all this, Annie? I get so angry when there's cruelty involved. I know this was an accident but sometimes it isn't and I just want to destroy the people who cause the hurt. But the Voice inside me has already told me I mustn't or I'll lose the healing gift!'

'It *is* a gift, Mary, you don't need me ter tell you that, and it'll carry on growing in you bit by bit. You must expect ter feel different sensations and accept them as part of it all. Talk ter me, lass, and we'll 'andle it tergether 'til you get ter the stage where I can't keep up with you. Which will 'appen, lass, it will.'

'I'm very nervous about it all, Annie. I feel I can't do any of this without you.'

'You will, lass, you will. Just give it time. Stop trying ter run afore you can walk, like. There's big things ahead, Mary, much bigger than any of this. And the battles facing you will be 'uge, girl. You need ter grow into that skin afore you can 'andle such things. And, believe me, you will. Just give it time.'

'So you think the cat felt the warmth, Annie. Was I really able to help it?'

'You said the little critter seemed ter relax more? Its breathing slowly eased before it passed over?'

And when Mary nodded, she continued: 'That's because it were feeling love coming from you, Mary; the warmth was love, energy showing you cared. And it would 'ave felt easier in passing over. So yes, lass, you definitely did 'elp that poor wee creature some, even if you couldn't save it that time!'

'So, d'you want to come with me today? I want to get some more practice in on healing and Annie has a rabbit that needs it. You did say you wanted to watch.'

'Ha! Just try and stop me!' replied Lizzie.

Annie was waiting. 'Right, now this 'ere rabbit 'as an ugly wound in 'is 'aunch. Prob'ly barbed wire,

I'm thinkin'. Anyways, I've cleaned 'im up and there's some o' my special balm under this bandage but even so 'e'll take a few days ter 'eal, lass, as it were quite nasty. Now, we need ter practise your 'ealing so just concentrate on that for a bit, all right?' As Lizzie looked on in silence, Annie placed the rabbit on Mary's lap. She sat quietly and, within seconds, the creature was lying back peacefully.

The three of them sat in silence for a few minutes while Mary did as Annie had instructed. 'Now, Mary, you do exactly what you did to that cat. You stroke it gently an' slowly for a while and we'll see what 'appens.'

As Mary began her stroking, Annie watched keenly. 'You feel anything 'appening, lass?' Mary shook her head. Five minutes passed. Ten minutes. Fifteen. Forty minutes later, still nothing untoward had occurred. Nothing, that is, for Mary. The rabbit, however, was a different matter – it was sleeping soundly! Annie was about to comment on this when the small creature awoke, blinked lazily and then tried to move. Swiftly, Annie stopped it, picked it up and removed it to the table.

'Let's just take a look at this, shall we?' she said softly. 'See 'ow this 'ere wound is looking?' Minutes later, the bandage unrolled, the three of them stared down at an almost unblemished surface! There was the smallest hint of a disturbance to the fur on the haunch but that was it!

'An' you felt nothing, lass? Nothing at all? None o' that 'eat you said you felt spreadin' down your arm?'

Amazed and delighted though she was, Mary still continued to shake her head.

'It was just the same as it was with Laker to start with, Annie. I couldn't feel anything the first couple of times. D'you remember? When I was so upset about it because I didn't seem to be doing any good at all and he wasn't speaking to me either?'

Annie stared at her in silence, shaking her head in wonderment.

'There was a clear wound this morning. It were a bad one, an' all. I done the bandages meself. Another four or five days, I give it, afore 'e would be anything like fit enough ter go back ter the wild. Now 'ere we are, after forty minutes of your stroking, good and ready to go!'

'So does that mean that sometimes I'll feel it and sometimes I won't?'

'Yes, s'pose it do mean that, girl – for now. You'll just 'ave ter suck it an' see, as they do say!'

'But it doesn't stop them from dying, though, does it? That cat still died,' said Lizzie.

'Mary were too late that time, lass. The poor little mite were too far gone by that stage. We won't win 'em all, lass, not yet. Mebbe never. Just do your best, eh?'

Mary sat in silence. Hmm, so there were going to be times when, unless she could see the result, she just wouldn't know whether she was doing any good or not. She'd just have to trust. Hmm, one of the most difficult words in her vocabulary.

'Come on now, lass, it'll all be clear when the time is right! 'ave some patience, like. Take it bit by bit, eh?'

'Yes, take it easy,' said Lizzie, jubilant. 'Don't you realise what you're doing is already amazing? Just keep up the practice every time we get a chance and it's bound to get better and better!'

TWENTY-FIVE

On their way into Milton Upper the following morning, Lizzie was full of what had happened the day before. She hardly had time to draw breath for talking about it.

'Just like it was with Laker! Absolutely incredible! But yeah, I agree – we mustn't say anything about it to the others yet. They're only just getting used to the idea that you can hear cries for help from the animals. They'd go nuts if we gave them this to handle as well! Better wait a bit for that, eh?'

The two of them smiled conspiratorially, Mary with relief. At least she wasn't going nuts herself. At least she wasn't alone with this. Good job she had two people with whom she could share it and confirm it really was happening! If only she could get her hands on more animals that needed treatment – that'd be bound to help her get up speed!

On their way home that afternoon, the two girls were still discussing it.

'I suppose you can't ask the charities if you can

practise on any of their animals?' asked Lizzie.

'Well, no. How can I? For a start, how would I explain it? Then it would get out and think of the racket that would cause. No. I'll just have to wait for some more injured animals to turn up.'

'What about Annie? Doesn't she have any more in need of healing?'

'None in the last few days and we've dealt with the others she had. I want to get in more practice, too. Don't worry, I promise to include you whenever a chance comes up.'

Just then, a sudden flash of white accompanied by a mournful bleating interrupted them. Mary wheeled immediately, squinted then pointed. 'Over there, something's caught – look!' And she galloped off towards a fence bounding the fields to the right. With Lizzie in hot pursuit, she reached it and pointed again. 'Over there – lamb caught on wire – we'll have to free it. Have you got your penknife?' Without waiting for an answer, she hauled herself over the fence and set off across the field with Lizzie chasing behind. As they reached the wire in question, it was clear what had happened. A rather adventurous lamb, its mother standing by anxiously, had managed to get itself hung up in the wire fence topped by barbed wire and couldn't move.

'Think this is a job for the farmer, Mary,' panted Lizzie. 'It really looks too badly strung up in there!'

'Can you leave me your knife, then, and run to the farm? I'll soothe this poor creature and see what I can do in the meanwhile.'

As Lizzie ran for help, Mary knew she'd have

to talk with the animal. It might not be easy to get through all the distress waves around it but she'd have to make a solid effort. *Oh please, please help me with this,* she appealed to the unknown Source within her. *It won't be easy but I have to try.*

Please stay still, she pleaded with the lamb; *the more you struggle, the more you'll be caught up. If you can stay still, I'll do my best to get you free* and, slowly, she began to stroke it. Oh gosh, on closer inspection she could see that the barbed wire had penetrated the lamb's skin enough to cause bleeding. This would create infection if it were left. She must do something about it before Lizzie returned with the farmer.

Your lamb has a wound on its side, she said to the sheep. *I need to do something about that to stop any infection, so if you could help it to stay completely still, I can sort this out before the farmer gets here.* Immediately, the sheep moved closer to its youngster and nosed it gently, making small noises so that the animal became more peaceable, its movements slowing bit by bit until it was completely still.

Now she could examine it thoroughly and see the extent of the damage, it was definitely in need of healing; but first it would need to be removed from the barbed wire with care. She would deal with that first before doing any healing. As soon as she reached out with that intention, she could feel the familiar warmth beginning to spread along her arms and into her hands. Thank goodness!

In the twenty minutes that followed, she lifted the remaining trapped wool, sawing away with Lizzie's knife where she couldn't manage this, and talking away to the animal the whole time, keeping it calm and still. The mother, too, was now less agitated so she was getting through to both her and her youngster. With the lamb freed, she could work on the wound and, again, the flow of warmth guided her. It also seemed to be working faster now than on previous occasions. Ten minutes later, the wound closed and the wool flattened over the newly healed area. Almost finished, she heard voices approaching. Oh great, it was Lizzie with the farmer!

By the time they reached Mary, the lamb was free and in one piece. As she stroked its unblemished coat, the sheep raised its head and looked her in the eyes – *Thank you, thank you.* Mary could only smile with relief. *I am delighted we did it – don't let her make a habit of this!* she replied silently before turning to the farmer.

Frank Greaves cleared his throat. Normally a taciturn man, he wasn't used to talking to young girls. These two had undoubtedly done him a considerable favour. It was obvious immediately that the slight young girl with the unusual eyes had freed the lamb, seemingly on her own; her friend, the sporty looking one, had apparently chased round after him for ages, one of his farm hands had said.

'Thank you,' he said now, a little gruffly. 'I'm grateful. Most people would have carried on walking. Together, you two have taken the time – and trouble – to do what few others, in my experience, would have bothered to attempt. If there's anything I can do for you in the future, then you have only to ask!'

Mary cleared her throat. She'd been thinking

about this ever since they had rescued poor Mischief. Now here was the ideal opportunity!

By the time she had finished, the farmer was looking at her with something akin to respect. 'I have a number of fields that could be suitable,' he said, 'and I would certainly be prepared to stable him with my daughter's horses, but only if she thinks he's the right sort. We'll need to see him first. You make the necessary arrangements and I'll do the rest. Here's my number.' And off he went.

Lizzie was admiring. 'When did you think all that out?' she asked.

'I've been thinking about it ever since we managed to get Mischief away from that awful man. It was just a matter of waiting for the right opportunity and well, this was it, wasn't it? I couldn't let it go without trying, could I?'

The horse rescue centre was also admiring, if cautious. 'We'll have to do an inspection visit,' said Mike, their friendly inspector. 'We can't just let him have the horse.'

'He wants to see it first anyway,' retorted Mary.

'Then, he'll have to come here,' replied Mike. 'We can't take the horse to him, Mary. We don't have the resources to do that sort of thing – we are a charity, you know!'

Mary was immediately penitent. 'Sorry, Mike, of course you are and I should have thought of that. It might be difficult for him to come during a normal working day, that's all; he *is* a farmer and very busy, and – oh we *can't* lose this opportunity. Mischief would be so, so happy there; his daughter has horses too and she would stable him with them. Isn't there *any* way round this?'

'Hey – easy, easy. I didn't say it wasn't on. How about I go and see him as soon as I can, do the inspection visit first and take it from there?'

'Great! Thank you, thank you!'

I think I've found you a new permanent home, Mary told Mischief later that week. *It's somewhere you'll be very happy with other horses again and I can still come and visit, don't worry.* The horse snickered with pleasure as she stroked him and gave him his usual carrot. He nuzzled her shoulder affectionately and she stroked his nose and scrabbled his favourite spot behind his ear.

There was no need for anxiety. Mischief, glossy and happy now, was a changed animal from the sad, neglected creature that Mary had first seen and so adorable that Caroline, the farmer's daughter, fell in love with him on sight. As a result, three weeks after the incident with the sheep, Mischief was happily installed in his new, permanent home with Caroline's own two horses.

'That's Darling, isn't it?'

'Yeah. With her parents. Just a tramp behind that fancy front!'

'Can't hide her roots, however much she tries.'

'Look at her, preening herself; thinks she's so bloody marvellous just because she and that poodle, Paige, manage to haul some old bird out of a load of fishing line and the local rag trumpets about it!'

'But she can't be all bad. After all, she did free that lamb from barbed wire. That must have taken some doing!'

'Watch it, Paula, you're sounding like the rest of them. They're all practically licking her boots. You'd think she was some sort of goddess!'

'No, I'm just saying... she can't be all rotten. What about that dog of hers? That was some funny business. The animal should have been a goner! You said Jase was getting in a bloke with experience. If he was so frigging good, how come he messed up?'

'Yeah, that would have finished her off – which was what it was meant to do! She was dopey about him!'

'Was? Still *is*, isn't she? Because that bloke didn't do a good enough job of it! Either that or she's a witch! That animal should never have lived!'

'You're right. There could be something in that.'

'What? That she's a witch?'

'Well, what other reason could there be for the animal's recovery? Jase said the bloke told him it was a sure thing. He definitely hit it – threw it into the air – and he looked in the mirror as he shot away and it was just lying there dead still! And don't forget, we don't know anything about her background, do we? Her mother could have been one, too!'

'Yeah – and passed some of her tricks on, in the blood, before dumping her outside the hospital.'

'Well, we'd better be careful how we handle her if she is – could be risky!'

'Yes, well, *we* won't be handling her at all. We'll be keeping well away. No way are *we* going to be connected with what I've got planned. It's a much better scheme and she certainly won't come out of it smelling of roses. In fact, we get it right and she won't come out of it at all! Witch or not, her end is coming, you can bet your sweet life!'

'So when are you going to let us in on it?'

'Oh, not yet, not for some time. I'm not going to risk any chance of failure this time. It's going to be planned down to the last detail before I let you in – *if* I let you in – on what's involved. But it's a real winner – you'd better believe it!'

TWENTY-SIX

Mary was silent with disbelief. Annie's lessons this week had been on snares and Annie had just shown her the outcome for two animals: one, a fox, had tried to bite off its leg and had died in the attempt; the other, a cat, had been strangled by the noose around its neck.

'What sort of people do this?' she asked, miserably.

'It's cruel, barbaric bustards 'oo did oughta be snared themselves!' declared Annie.

'How can we stop this happening?'

'The government oughta ban 'em but they canna be fussed 'cos it be too much bother! They don't even keep a watch on 'em as they oughta!'

'So what do we do, Annie, if we see an animal caught in one of these dreadful things?'

'*You* don't do anythin', lass, 'cos you can get damaged yoursel'. The poor critter's scared an' damaged already an' needs gettin' out of there an' I've got those 'oo'll do it faster 'n' safer than you an' me. For now, you tell me, lass, quick as you can! When you move on a bit, I'll see you get ter know them, too.

Meanwhile, we 'ave ter put these poor souls to rest now. It's too late to do else for 'em.'

Mary walked home deep in thought. She would find out more about these contraptions. Instruments of torture for wildlife were barbaric. The law needed changing. If this was yet something more she'd need to challenge, then fine, she'd do it! Annie had said the road ahead would be rocky and the battles countless, so she was ready. In the meanwhile, she would save and heal as many animals and birds and other creatures as she could!

'What are you doing this weekend?'

'Actually, I'm going to start looking into snares.' Lizzie raised her eyebrows. 'Yes, Annie showed me how dangerous they are to wildlife and many are illegal. The law needs changing.'

'So what do you think *you* can do about it?'

'I don't know yet but I'm certainly going to start finding out!'

'Anyway, what about the Christmas hols? There's only a week to go now then it's two and a half weeks of not having to get togged up in uniform and slog ourselves stupid every night. I'm just going to veg for the first few days. You got any plans?'

'Er, sleep, eat, walk with Laker... and the same again. Oh – and see Annie, of course. Standard Christmas Day and then you and me could, maybe, manage some walks and bike rides with Laker, explore the common, take a look at the quarry possibly, help Bronwen out, visit the horse sanctuary, see Mischief?'

Lizzie laughed. 'There won't be much time left after all that. Do you realise how much you try and cram into every day? The time'll just flash by.'

And, in fact, the holidays did exactly that. Before the girls knew it, they were back at Milton Upper and well into the spring term. The pressure on both academic and sporting fronts was relentless and, to the chagrin of Lana Fellowes and her cohorts – still relegated to the fringes of every social circle at Milton Upper – Lizzie and Mary were gaining recognition in both areas.

'Couldn't give a toss about academic stuff,' Lana Fellowes fumed, 'but that gypsy's got a bloody cheek chasing sports fame too. That's always been my pitch!'

'Yeah! That's hockey and netball finals, track events for Sports Day, Regional Debate and now General Knowledge Tournament,' said Julia Cox, counting them off on her fingers.

'Yeah, but the tournament is the best. It'll be in all the local papers!'

'Are you sure? Darling and Paige have managed to get in on *that,* too?' fumed Lana Fellowes. 'Staddon can't be serious!'

'Lizzie's always been pretty smart on GK, though, and she and Darling did come out top in the trials,' said Paula.

'Since when have you been such a fan of those two?' snarled Lana.

'I'm just saying… they did earn their places, didn't they?'

Lana's eyes narrowed. 'Strange how you suddenly seem to be defending them, Paula. Wonder why?' A mean smile flitted across her face. 'Something we don't know?'

Paula was immediately defensive. 'All I meant was… they did win all the heats, after all. It wasn't as if they were given any special favours. That's all I was saying.'

Lana studied the other girl carefully. 'Hmm, wouldn't do to be too much of a fan, Paula. Be very careful you know exactly where your interests lie, won't you?'

Paula reddened and chewed a nail in silence.

'Anyway, what's this plan you've got to clip their wings?' said Julia quickly, in an attempt to defuse the tension.

Lana inspected her eyeliner in a small, gold compact. Snapping it shut, she thought for a few seconds. 'Think I'll leave that for now,' she said, smoothly. 'Time enough for all that later. Anyway, there are still some details I need to get sorted.'

'There's an old woman waiting for you at the gates, Mary!'

'Annie!' said Mary and Lizzie simultaneously.

'Quick, something's happened!' said Mary as she grabbed her bag and set off at a run, Lizzie galloping after her.

The figure at the gates was, indeed, Annie, who gestured impatiently at she caught sight of them. 'Hurry up – you're needed!'

Annie could move fast when she wanted and the girls found themselves panting to keep up with her, even whilst she seemed to be gliding over all the mixed terrains that they encountered.

Just as they were beginning to wonder how much further she was going, she darted off the side road they'd just taken, along a footpath through dense woodland. Several yards further on, she dived along a track leading through what looked like thick undergrowth until they reached a small clearing. Here, she stopped and fell on her knees beside what appeared to be, at first glance, a mound of leaves. Brushing them aside, she revealed a badger. Clearly injured, its neck oozing blood, it was barely conscious. The girls gasped.

Silently, Annie pointed a few feet away to the cause of the injury. A snare. Almost entirely concealed by foliage, it had been strategically placed to do calculated damage. Shocked, the girls stared at it.

'One o' them self-locking beggars,' fumed Annie.

'Didn't you say they were illegal?' said Mary, in horror.

'Certain sure, lass, but them bustards as own this 'ere land, and give a nod to this sort o' devilish torture, don't give no truck ter rules or laws! They know full well that those 'oo make 'em canna be forced ter chase 'em up, can they!'

'Hang on, I'm trying to understand this,' said Lizzie. 'Self-locking means the animal can't escape, doesn't it? Why is that illegal?'

'Because the bustards 'oo use these say the snare don't 'urt if the critter caught in it don't struggle. But they know full well that any poor beggars caught in the snare'll go on struggling to get out – it's only natral like, ain't it? – so they'll suffer agony as it gets tighter an' tighter and then die in the process!'

'I see. Well, it's more important right now, isn't it, that Mary gets down to helping this poor creature?' said Lizzie.

'I've actually already been trying to talk to him,' said Mary, 'but he's not replying.'

'Never mind chit-chat, lass, get on with some 'ealing. Poor beggar's not in any state to 'old a conversation!'

'Yes, he'll be dead before you've even got going!'

'Okay, okay – let me get started, then. And some quiet would help.'

Mary knelt beside the badger and extended her hands gently over him. Lizzie and Annie watched in silence. As the minutes went by, however, she began to worry. Nothing seemed to be happening. The poor animal was just not responding. The extent of the injury wasn't clear but the bleeding certainly was and, if she didn't stop it, the badger would bleed to death.

Even worse, none of the warmth she always wanted for reassurance that her gift was active, was evident. Damn! Perhaps it wasn't going to work for her today. Just when she really needed it!

Oh come on, come on. Please don't desert me now. This poor creature needs help. Don't let it die. Oh please don't let it die!

This wretched gift seemed to have a mind of its own. Well, it wasn't going to be much good if it only worked when it felt like it! She had to be able to rely on it one hundred per cent of the time!

More minutes passed without the faintest response. Then, just as she was beginning to despair, the Voice within her spoke – *You are trying too hard. Just as used to happen when you first started talking to wildlife. Remember what you discovered then. You just needed to relax and let it flow. You must remember the lessons you learn along the way, otherwise you're wasting your time – and mine!*

Oh yes, of course. Of course, of course. And she would certainly remember in future. The Voice was right. If she didn't remember what she learned along the way, she would, indeed, be wasting time for both of them – as well as all the wildlife lying there waiting for her to help them!

And, with that acknowledgement, the heat surfaced instantly and crept along her arms until it reached her hands. Just as swiftly, she sensed the waves travelling across to the badger and, seconds later, the blood began to disappear and the two jagged edges of the wound to knit. As the animal's hair closed over it, the badger stirred, stood up and shook itself.

Turning, it looked her full in the face, bewildered.

'Go on, lass, talk to it now, tell it wot's 'appened. Poor beggar's mind-boggled!'

Mary gazed at the creature with compassion. *I'm so sorry. I know you'll find it strange but I can talk with you and explain what's happened, if you're okay with that.*

Who are you? What happened? Something grabbed me around my neck!

Yes, you were caught by that frightful snare. You need to be extra careful in woodland like this and any dense undergrowth – and tell your friends and family, too. If Annie, my friend here, hadn't rescued you and called me in time, you could have died!

So I owe you both my life. Thank you, thank you.

And without further talk, it turned and vanished into the woodland on the opposite side.

'What can we do about this snare, Annie? Can we dismantle it, somehow?'

'All taken care of, Lizzie girl. I wanted ter show it ter you in summat like workin' order first. My friends in the forest'll be 'ere soon as we be off and they'll see it canna do no more 'arm.'

'So they've been watching us?'

'They know to keep their eyes an' ears open, lass, an' they look out for old Annie and the wildlife. An' they will for you, too, when you really get goin' and that time ain't too far off now, Mary. It'd be 'ere now 'cept you be 'olding matters up, girl. Seems when you relax and let it all flow, it works faster'n a lightning streak. You got mighty important work to do, lass. You mun quit messin' about and get on wi' it!'

TWENTY-SEVEN

It was a fine morning, cold with the crisp light of a still wintry sun across the fields and hedgerows. Mary and Lizzie were discussing the General Knowledge Tournament to be hosted by the school the following term. In mid-sentence, Lizzie stopped. They were passing a long drainage ditch overgrown with noxious weeds, nettles, brambles and other vegetation.

'There's something moving there. Look!' She pointed at what appeared to be a pile of newspaper and polythene. They moved nearer to the ditch to peer at it and she was right – it *was* moving, shuffling around slowly on the spot. Without hesitation, Mary jumped into the ditch.

'Hey – look out, you don't know what it is!'

'Well, whatever it is, it's obviously still alive so I will in a second, won't I?' And, without further ado, Mary took hold of the polythene and pulled it back, then recoiled as her hand came away smeared with blood.

'Aarrgghh! Whatever's in there is covered in blood!'

'Hang on – if you're going to look at it, we'll do it together!' Lizzie leaped into the ditch.

Gingerly, the girls inched back the polythene to reveal a dog – quite a large one – its face half covered with the blood dripping down from a deep head wound and its legs partially tied together, the cord hanging loosely where it had obviously been bitten through by the poor animal in its struggle to escape.

As the girls stared at it, horrified, a mental vision of the background to this dreadful scene entered Mary's head. Her eyes widened with incredulity then flooded as she shuddered in agonised disbelief at the vision she was being shown.

'What's happening? Why are you shaking? Tell me! Tell me!' said Lizzie, grasping her by the shoulders. 'Come on, you must tell me what you're seeing.' Then, frightened by the look on Mary's face as her shaking subsided, she stood back and looked at her, worried. Mary, fists clenched, teeth bared, was incapable of answering straight away. How on earth could she tell Lizzie what she had been shown? The scene had been too dreadful for words: the shovel rising and falling as the poor dog struggled, in vain, to avoid it, its legs tied so that it couldn't run; and then, when he thought the sad, defenceless animal was just a corpse, the newspaper and filthy old polythene into which the filthy scumbag had thrust the poor animal, leaving it to die in agony in that ditch.

Her fury had woken her worst demon and it had sprung forth to demand satisfaction. She swallowed hard, trying to stem the nausea she could feel rising. The hideous urge to destroy the human vermin responsible for this atrocity was becoming stronger and stronger and the usual rage-driven red mist was massing before her eyes. This vile scum, still out there, free to enjoy his existence, needed eliminating. Everything in her hungered to destroy him as painfully as her imagination would let her. Fire would be too quick. He must suffer!

A shame he couldn't be subjected to the same treatment he had dealt this poor, sad animal struggling in front of her to try and stand. The crimson vapour, filling her entire vision now, was gradually blocking out everything. She shook her head, trying – in vain – to clear it. And then the Voice gradually began to penetrate the mist…

Listen to me, listen, listen… You have been warned about this. There will be many, many incidents, like this and worse. If you cannot control your desire for revenge, if you continue to see that as justice, then your ability to heal, to rescue all the millions of animals that need you, will be taken from you.

She could not remain silent. The Voice must be told how defenceless these poor animals were against such persecution and of the need to punish such thugs as a warning against such atrocities!

But foul, vicious thugs like this one who persecute defenceless animals have to be punished fittingly, brought to proper justice as a deterrent to others who would carry out equally cruel, vile acts!

And it will be part of your task to see that they are brought to justice, but not *to dispense your own idea of that justice!*

But how will I be able to see that justice is done if I can't carry it out?

You are still making your way towards the time when all will be much clearer. Do not try to run before you are able to walk. Your mind and heart are young, so you respond with more passion than intellect. There is much still to learn and you will do so. For hear this: I shall not remain tolerant forever.

As the Voice faded, so did the red mist and, by degrees, Lizzie's anxious face came spinning back to replace it.

'Where are you, Mary? Come back. We're losing time. You need to get going on healing this poor animal if we want to save it.'

Oh God! She was right. The poor dog needed attention. Time enough, later on, to think about what could be done with the evil creature who had caused this frightful situation. Time now for healing while she still had the gift! The dog's eyes seemed to be pleading with her for help and she had lost valuable time on her own rage.

I'm going to help you now, she said to the injured animal. *Try and relax and you'll soon be better.* And without further delay, she extended her hands over its head and sent up a silent plea for forgiveness. She *would* control this rage, she would! She couldn't risk losing her most valuable gift. It was clear that she had it on loan for as long as she remembered the conditions attached to it. There must be a limit to the Source's patience and her continuing passion for revenge was evidently stretching that patience. She must be more careful in future, she must!

It was just so difficult *not* to rage at those who committed such atrocities on the animals and wildlife who shared this planet. After all, no one was forced to have a dog. It was a personal choice with responsibilities attached, as she'd found out when she'd wanted to adopt Laker, so why take on the responsibility if you didn't want it? And if you needed to get rid of the animal, why not take it to one of the many rescue shelters? There was absolutely no need to try and kill the poor creature, especially in such a vile way!

She must stop this, concentrate now, focus on the healing. All this mental wrestling was getting in the way. With that thought, immediately the heat began to spread down her arms and into her hands and – thank goodness – it seemed to be working even faster than the last time. Once again, her awareness of both Lizzie and their surroundings slowly receded until she was alone in her circle with the dog and the waves of heat enveloping them both. The dog's eyes closed, an expression of peace came over its face and its breathing gradually slowed. It was asleep! The blood issuing from the deep wound on the poor, stricken head, caused by that frightful beast with his vile shovel, was disappearing by degrees and the wound, itself, was beginning to look less angry. The dog was almost snoring, its flanks rising and falling as it fell into an even deeper sleep.

At that moment, other visions flashed into her head. Oh God! This pitiable, abused animal had not only been attacked with a shovel descending many times on its hapless head, it had been starved, kicked and beaten into submission first! No wonder it was so thin and broken.

Oh help me, help me! This is so bad. I never knew people could be so evil. I need to concentrate on the healing. Don't let me think of revenge – please! I must heal this poor, sad creature and I need your help. Please, please!

And minutes later the wounds closed, the hair covered them and the animal lay on the ground in front of her anguished eyes, in one piece but still sound asleep. Mary burst into tears as she related to Lizzie, between her sobs, the mental visions she'd had. Lizzie hugged her for comfort while she got the anguish out of her system.

'I can't let my passion for revenge take control, Lizzie. The Voice has told me I can't. If I do, I *will* lose this gift and he's losing patience with me, I know!'

'But your feelings are completely understandable. The filth who did this deserves the same treatment, worse even – I agree with you!' declared Lizzie in a voice vehement with loathing.

'Yes, but it's not for me to decide that, not yet anyway, he's made that clear. He says justice will be done but not by me. I am here to rescue, save and heal the animal world and that gift will be taken away if I don't stop dwelling on revenge.'

'So the gift's only on loan?'

'Sounds like it. And you must help me, please, because everything in me wants to destroy people like this. They don't deserve to share this planet with animals when they can't treat them with kindness and compassion!'

'Yes, well, I totally agree. But I hear what you're saying and I'll help all I can because you certainly don't want to lose this gift. Anyway, look at the dog – he's waking up and he seems completely healed!'

The animal now rising from its position on its side, its tail thumping slowly in the ditch as it licked Mary's hands, though still thin, was certainly a different creature from the one they had rescued from its unhappy state at the start.

'Yes, I may have been allowed to heal his physical wounds,' said Mary sadly, 'but the mental ones are a different matter, aren't they? I wish I could remove those awful memories from him as well but it'll be a long time, I think, before those scars go, if ever.'

'Give it time,' said ever-practical Lizzie. 'You don't know what lies ahead for you. You're still only in the early stages. Annie would tell you you're trying to run before you can walk!'

I don't know who you are but you're safe now, said Mary. *What's your name?*

The dog was silent. It hung its head.

You do have a name, don't you? What did the vile beast who did this call you?

You won't like it.

'What on earth's going on? What are you both saying?' asked Lizzie impatiently.

'I'm trying to find out his name and he won't tell me.'

'Why ever not?'

'I think he's embarrassed.'

'For heaven's sake! Tell him not to be silly; we're wasting time.'

Lizzie, my friend here, says we're wasting time. We won't judge you because of your name.

Rambo.

'He says it's Rambo.'

The girls looked at each other and at the dog. Then Mary had a thought. 'I think that was probably why the bloke wanted to be rid of him, Lizzie.'

'What? Why?'

'Because – look at him. Does he look or seem like a Rambo to you?'

The dog gave one bark then, as Mary looked at him, he spoke. *You're right. I wasn't what he wanted me to be.*

'I was right, Lizzie. He's just told me that the man wanted to be rid of him because he turned out to be different from what he wanted – a big, aggressive-type of dog, I imagine.'

'Well, I think he's a super dog, so gentle, and if I thought my mother would let us keep him I'd take him home right now. What are we going to do with him?'

'Take him to Annie, of course. She'll either know someone who will give him a great home or she'll keep him, herself, because she's been talking about wanting her own dog for some time. Anyway, he needs food, I know that, so we'd better get moving. But, before we start, what about another name for him?'

'Well, why don't we let Annie choose that?'

'Great idea!'

I'd like to take you to a great friend of ours who will certainly give you some good food. I think she may want you for herself but, if not, she'll find you a great home. Either way, you will definitely have a much more suitable name. I'm sorry

I can't keep you but I already have a dog and Lizzie's mum won't let her have one, or she would definitely take you home this minute. Will you come with us?

Oh yes, please, and thank you, thank you – for everything.

And the girls gathered up their bags and left what had started out as a truly dreadful scene, with the dog now a different animal, following them happily.

'I've been expecting you,' said Annie, 'and I knew you'd be bringing me some special company!'

'You did?' said Lizzie, in wonder.

'Oh, I should have told you, Lizzie,' said Mary. 'Annie does this sometimes. She often has a mental picture of what's been going on when it comes to animals.'

'So this is the young fella 'oo's going ter be living with me, then. And 'oo needs a better name, too, I gather!'

The dog seemed to be grinning as he gazed at the wise woman then moved forward and raised his head until he and Annie were both looking straight into each other's eyes. His tail started wagging, at first slowly then faster, until the whole of his body practically shook with pleasure.

'We'm goin' ter 'it it off just fine, lass. All he needs is a name, bags o' love and, right now I'm thinkin', a full belly!'

'He's yours to choose the name, Annie. And I think he knows already that he won't want for love or food here.'

'Well – 'e's goin' to be a welcome buddy for me, girl, so that's mebbe what I'll call 'im. So then, buddy, that's what we'm goin' to call you – Buddy!'

Mary grinned. She'd known Annie and this brave animal would take to each other on sight and now she had no need to worry about him anymore. His life with Annie would be everything he needed. He'd be happy for the rest of his time on this planet!

TWENTY-EIGHT

Where was she? What was this place? Africa? Yes. Surely, it was Africa. Wide sweeps of silent, shifting sand, vast grasslands, swooping mountain ranges, gullies and pinnacles, volcanoes, lush rainforest, alpine meadows. All of it ageless, timeless.

Borne aloft by unseen hands, she was being carried at great speed. Somehow, she didn't feel any fear or anxiety, only a sense of purpose. She was here for a reason. It would become clear if she was patient. Why was patience always so difficult?

Now, a mist-wreathed mountain peak was approaching and, without being told, she knew a stop was imminent. Another loomed, then another and another. Then, in a flash, a huge cushion of grassland appeared beneath her and she was lowered gently into its centre.

All around her, the views, scents and sounds, most completely foreign, mingled to fill her with awe. The size and the majesty of this land was truly breathtaking! For what seemed like minutes, she could only gaze in wonder.

And then, without warning, came a kaleidoscope of sights: lions, elephants, leopards, rhinos, buffalo, big game of all sorts, gorillas, chimpanzees – all the wild animals you could imagine – lumbered, plodded, prowled, slunk and stalked before her, followed by a cacophony of animal voices: trumpeting, bellowing, roaring, growling, chattering. A tumult that filled her ears.

As the clamour gradually became a background noise, the Voice made itself heard – *Your mandate in life, Mary, is to be an animal ambassador. You are to represent animal interests all over the world, looking out for them in all respects. You are in Africa at present but as time goes on you will visit other continents, be shown injustice and cruelty to animals in all countries.*

Humans everywhere need to become more caring and to acknowledge that their existence on this planet was intended to be shared with animals on an equal basis, not with humans as dictators and tyrants. At present, animals everywhere suffer at the hands of humans – exploited, tortured and killed in the interests of human greed. They hurt and bleed, mentally as well as physically, and the scars – if they survive – stay with them all their lives. At the moment, humans do not understand and this must change. Your mandate is to make them aware and to change attitudes – worldwide. Your peers and all young people worldwide will be key factors in this mission as they are the adults of tomorrow. They will help you to bring about the essential change.

You are tasked, too, with healing wildlife as well as domestic pets, from the smallest to the largest. They will not harm you once they recognise this, for the gift of communication has been given to you in order to make your mission clear.

The cruelty will be difficult for you to handle but remember, it is not for you to judge and dispatch your idea of justice. That is the task of those in positions of legitimate authority. It will be for you to make them aware of that need and to work together to eliminate cruelty through education.

This is a mighty task, said Mary. *Will I have any help?*

Your true friends will be few but those you do make will be steadfast in their support. You will also attract those already more advanced in knowledge but, as yet, without your present gifts – or those still to come. They will assist you in spreading the message as well as by providing support. But you will also have enemies on different levels of power. Those you have already encountered are of minor importance. In the future, they will be more powerful with scores of vested interests, chief amongst which will be greed – for status, power and wealth. They will seek to destroy you because you stand in their way. Make no mistake: the challenges will be immense and your battles mighty.

So… will you help me?

In situations of dire necessity, if you call upon me, I will answer. But remember, your gifts, still developing, will not be insignificant and you have two more to come – when the time is right. They are all, however, resources on loan to you specifically for this mission and must not be abused.

'Mary, Mary – where are you? Come back!'

As Lizzie's anxious face swam slowly back into her vision, her surroundings faded, as did the Voice.

'Where were you? I've been trying to make you hear me for ages!'

'Well, if you were whispering like that the whole time, it's no wonder I didn't hear you!'

'Well, you can't expect me to shout – Armstrong wouldn't take kindly to having *my* voice take over her lesson on irrigation in Africa! Anyway, that's not the point – where have you been all this time? You're lucky she didn't ask you a question!'

'Tell you later – too much to explain now.'

'Wow! You really saw all those animals? That's cool to the nth! And one hell of a task! Are you scared? Think I'd be just a tiny bit panic-stricken!'

'Can't afford to be, can I? That's the mission and I just have to get on with it. It certainly makes sense of everything that's happened, don't you think?'

'Well yes, but it's still a superhuman assignment for one person!'

'No one said I'd have to finish the job – just do what I can in my lifetime.'

'S'pose so. Seriously, how do you feel about it? Aren't you just a tad daunted?'

'Erm, sshh! I'm picking up something…'

Lizzie waited as Mary appeared to be listening. A minute or two passed before she spoke.

'That was a conversation Fellowes was having with someone and I joined it somewhere in the middle.'

'You don't seem very happy about it.'

'No. It sounded suspicious somehow.'

'How d'you mean, suspicious?'

Mary shook her head. 'Don't know. I couldn't make sense of it. They were talking about ropes when

I checked in and there was quite a bit of background noise. I just had a strong feeling something odd was going on. Anyway, we can't do anything at present. We'll just have to see how things pan out.'

'Going back to our previous conversation, I've had a thought,' said Lizzie. 'Do you remember what Staddon said in that assembly when he talked about things like commitment and determination and all that stuff?'

'Yeah. So?'

'The bit about leadership and delegation. Why don't you ask the Voice if it could be possible for you to assemble a team with some of your gifts, the really important ones like the animal communication and whatever else he might be willing to let them have, so that you'd have some real backup? At present, you're working completely alone and you're faced with one hell of a task. Old Hercules would have struggled!'

'Hmm, I think I might have to prove myself for a bit longer before I could approach that one. It's early days yet and he'll probably want to see what I can do, myself, first.'

'Well, being practical, a small team could handle some of the cases in each country if you're going to be going global!'

'Would you be willing to work with me? I'd feel a lot happier if you were there with me.'

'Hey, just try and stop me!'

Lizzie parted from Mary that evening with a fresh resolve. She'd have to do some serious sleuthing. Something was clearly afoot and sitting around waiting for the axe to fall wasn't her style. She'd begin with some discreet questioning of the Fellowes' hangers-on. If she chose the right people, there was a good chance of positive results! Yes, she'd start the very next day. But she wouldn't say a word to Mary until she had something concrete to report.

Mary, meanwhile, was solidly preoccupied with what she had learned during the Geography lesson. She'd have to bone up on the animal situation in Africa: clearly, a major part of her work was going to be concentrated there. And then there was India and the other Asian countries. The rest of Europe, too, wasn't free of cruelty towards animals: the bullfighting in Spain was only one example. And what about the States? She'd heard quite a bit, too, about the dog-meat trade around the world, much of it illegal. Hell's teeth! All this and she'd not even thought about marine life! Lizzie was right – she really would need a team of helpers. Would there be any chance? Would the Voice allow it? Only time would tell. Meanwhile, she had to make a start here, on her own country.

That night, dreams scudded through her sleep, some bizarre like the one in which all sorts of animals were parading through the streets of Milton with placards threatening strike action; and others which, though farcical, enchanted her, like the winged elephants trumpeting with exhilaration as they took off into space!

As the last elephant faded into the distance, she became aware of increasing wetness and woke to find Laker, roused by her small chuckles and murmurs of delight, lying alongside her on the bed, licking her face.

Before she could do more than give him an absent-minded pat, the same mental screen that had clicked into place unexpectedly during the Geography lesson did so now. As Laker and her bedroom receded, a succession of familiar wildlife creatures began to move across her vision. Further instruction from the Voice must be imminent! In turn, foxes, badgers, rabbits, squirrels, otters, domestic pets, including horses and donkeys and then a variety of farm animals, trotted into view, accompanied this time by their voices.

Then, as before, all of it became a backcloth for the Voice itself. *Listen carefully, Mary. It will be part of your mandate to represent and care, also, for all these creatures, here and wherever else they seek your help. The same rules as before will apply.*

But this time Mary was ready with questions.

This is a mighty mission and I am completely up for it. But I have been thinking and wondering if – when I've proved myself – I could have a team of skilled helpers who would tackle the needs of animals in other countries so that we could spread the word more quickly. There must be people the world over with as much love for animals as I have and they could also recruit even more helpers. With a global taskforce, we would have much greater success and *more quickly. Is this your intention?*

You have predicted correctly but you must convince me, first, that you have the courage, spirit and resolution for this mission. You must prove yourself before the rest follows.

What will satisfy you?

A definite commitment from you after you have handled more cases. You will encounter a variety of situations in which aspects of cruelty will confront you. The way in which you react will show me what I am looking for. Already, you have identified your demons. There will be situations in the future that will challenge your self-control and discipline. I will need to see how you conduct yourself throughout. That will show me how you are progressing.

I am bound to make mistakes.

You will possibly never achieve perfection but a level of self-control is required that you have not shown so far. You need to show me that you will simply get on with the job in hand and leave the punishment side to those responsible for it.

I can promise that I will work really hard at that.

Your enemies, as you grow in knowledge and experience, will include bullies of various types, on different levels of worldly power and sophistication. They will require appropriate handling. The ways in which you choose to overcome all forces of opposition will determine your success with this mission.

You mentioned more powers still to come?

Your two remaining powers will be given to you as and when the situations arise. Only then will you be fully equipped to fulfil your mandate. In the meanwhile, you must use your existing resources wisely. Should you abuse any of them, you will lose the use of that resource for a period of time. Naturally, this will mean that, if a situation arises that requires the use of that resource, you will be at a disadvantage which may, on occasion, be grave.

Only when I am satisfied that you genuinely understand the concept of justice and where you stand in relation to its execution, will I consider any future aid. As yet, you are relatively "young" in your responses to animal cruelty and your reaction to the perpetrators is somewhat crude. You will receive help in understanding and opportunities to show me that you have achieved the growth necessary to ensure that the punishment is in the hands of those properly charged with this duty. If you have no more questions, I shall leave you to think about all this.

And if I think of any others that are important?

I will always know and – rest assured, Mary – you will always receive an answer.

Mary remained silent and the Voice was gone.

TWENTY-NINE

As Mary walked to meet Lizzie the next morning, she was deeper in thought than ever. The Voice had given her plenty to be going on with. This was an almighty task and no mistake. Far, far greater than anything she had realised could be involved. Did she really want it? After all, she could still turn it down; she hadn't committed herself totally yet, had she?

'So I was right, wasn't I?' Lizzie said triumphantly. 'If this work is going to be needed all over the world, you're going to *have* to have a team of helpers, aren't you?'

'Yes, but I was told I'd have to prove myself first, show I can use the resources I have properly – and, especially, control this urge for revenge that's my worst demon. I have to get that under control, Lizzie, I really do – otherwise, I'm not only *not* going to get through the vetting process but I can say goodbye to any idea of *Mission Successful,* as well as having any sort of global team. And all those poor animals will not get the help they need!'

She stopped and scuffed the ground in frustration.

'The thing that's worrying me now is, can I really go forward with this?'

'What d'you mean? Go forward with what? You can't mean you're thinking of giving it all up now, surely!'

Lizzie's voice rose in almost a squeak of disbelief.

'Well, it's such a mammoth task. Never mind *Mission Successful*, it's looking more and more like *Mission Impossible*! I don't know if *I* am up to it. It would be mighty enough with a team of helpers; starting off alone is a hundred times worse. I mean, I know I have you and Annie but the bulk of it is going to come down to me, isn't it? Not only that, this business of controlling my urge for revenge is humungous. Some of these people who torture and kill animals, Lizzie, are just so incredibly vile that my natural urge is to do something like it to them! The poor animals are so defenceless. Pets, farm animals, animals in the wild, whatever – they are so dependent on us and they don't deserve such cruelty. And these foul characters need to realise it and pay for what they've done!'

'Mmm, I know, and I feel the same, but what the Voice is saying is true – you can't be judge and jury as well as do the healing. The punishment bit has to come from people whose job it is to dish it out – and that's not you! You're here to help the animals, aren't you?'

'Yeah, that's all very logical but it doesn't take into account any feelings, which is what's so difficult.'

'Well, I'm just being practical. Look, I know it's difficult for you but I think your position is quite clear: you either do what you can to help the animals –

or you don't. That's your choice. You probably won't achieve everything but if your gift is taken away, you won't be able to help them at all because, if I've got this right, the Voice or the Source or whatever you call him, will remove the other gifts pretty damn quick!'

'Oh Lizzie, you're so practical and logical, aren't you? And, inside, I know you're right.'

'Glad I have some uses!'

They both grinned.

'So? What are you going to do? I'm astonished – shocked, too – that you're even considering giving up. You've hardly got started! And even if you can't solve all their problems, you know the huge difference you *can* make to the animals. You have a really vital job to do and you wouldn't have been given these gifts only to hand them back and pull out of it. They need someone on their side, Mary – and that's you! I know if it were me, I couldn't possibly quit. We Paiges *don't* quit. My dad has always told us that from when we all started school. And you know something? I didn't have you down for a quitter, either!'

That did it. Lizzie was right. She couldn't possibly give up on this. She *wouldn't* give up on it. Massive though the task ahead was, she'd been chosen, given this mighty chance to do what she could for the animals, for all wildlife, and, whatever it would take, she was going to do it!

She squared her shoulders and turned to face Lizzie who could see immediately that her remarks had hit home. 'Okay, let's go for it, shall we?'

And they both punched the air simultaneously.

Absorbed in conversation on their way home that afternoon, they were delighted to spot a familiar figure sitting a short distance ahead in the middle of their path. Redcoat! And behind him, a sight even more heartening – a vixen and three small cubs frolicking around their mother.

Hello, Mary, I thought it was you and your friend. How's life?

Great, Redcoat, and it's good to see you well and happy too. Is that your family?

Yes, Mary, I thought you'd like to see them. Come and meet them – but then there's a friend of ours that needs your help. Can I take you there? It's not far – just a few fields away.

I'll just ask Lizzie if she wants to come, Redcoat, in case I need her help.

'Lead on, Macduff!' was Lizzie's robust reply as the rest of the family vanished into the undergrowth. Fifteen minutes later, after a run through unfamiliar countryside, the need for help was obvious.

Huddled in the far corner of the last field, with little grass and no shelter, was a small, skewbald donkey looking extremely sorry for himself. As the trio came nearer, they could see that his bones were obvious and he had a weeping, inflamed eye. When they were about twenty feet away from him, the donkey made an unsuccessful attempt to struggle to his feet. He fell back on the ground and looked at them piteously. Looking over his shoulder at Mary, Redcoat made to move forward – *Could you wait there a moment, Mary? I just want to let him know there's nothing to be afraid of.*

Fine, Redcoat. Tell him we're here to help him, won't you?

Replying with what looked suspiciously like a nod and a grin, the fox moved forward slowly and lay down on the ground near the donkey. A strange sort of communion seemed to pass between them before Redcoat stood up and turned. Looking Mary straight in the eyes, he spoke – *His name is Scooter, Mary, and he's been here for some weeks, he thinks, but he's lost track of time. All he knows is that his owner just dumped him here and hasn't been back. Before that, though, he had little food or care and felt completely unwanted. Still does. He's very sad, starving and scared. He's also horribly lonely. I've told him you'll make things right. You will, won't you – just as you did for me?*

Of course we will, Redcoat. He has nothing more to fear now. He will be loved and taken care of, I promise you.

As Mary moved closer and fell to her knees, Lizzie did the same until they were close enough to stroke the small animal who was clearly unsure how to react. He flinched as Mary reached out to stroke him gently and, as she did so, her mind immediately began to pick up his background. She shook her head in sorrow.

Without hesitating, Lizzie jumped in. 'There's no time to lose, Mary. We have to get on with sorting him out so we can take him to the *Horse and Pony* sanctuary. He can't walk at the moment and there are obviously other things wrong. Come on – he's been like this long enough. Get going with the healing!'

Lizzie was absolutely right. She must start immediately – before the demon surfaced. Wasting time on emotion would simply get in the way again.

Are you taking him to Annie, Mary? said Redcoat.

No, Redcoat, we've moved on a bit since we last saw you and I can tackle this bit before we take him to some other friends where he can live happily with horses and ponies, and maybe even another donkey friend or two.

Then, looking Scooter in the eyes, she addressed him directly. *I think Redcoat has told you, Scooter, that we're friends and we're going to do our level best to help you. The bad times are over. Please just lie back and relax and, I promise you, very soon, you'll be much better.*

And, with Lizzie and Redcoat looking on in silence, she held out her hands over the small donkey. As if in acknowledgement that she had kept her word in getting on with the job undistracted by emotion, the familiar energy flow began in earnest and, within seconds, the power increased, reaching her hands and enveloping them both. Now that she had started, Scooter's other maladies were being shown to her: his hooves were badly overgrown and couldn't have been trimmed in months; he had intestinal worms in abundance; his poor ears were painfully full of infection; and, of course, he was starving. There was certainly no time to lose! As usual, everything around them disappeared. All her awareness of time vanished and, once again, she was alone with the small donkey in a warm bubble of white light as she poured healing energy into him with all her might, until Lizzie's voice in her ear and hand on her shoulder told her that the healing was complete.

Coming back to her surroundings as the energy drained away, she felt completely exhausted but could see instantly that the donkey was standing straight, his hooves trim and with no bones or other sign of weakness in evidence. Best of all, he was gazing at her with something very like gratitude in his eyes.

You look so different. Are you feeling better? she said.

Oh yes, so much. Thank you, thank you. But please don't leave me here – it's so lonely.

'He's asking us not to leave him here, Lizzie.'

'I should think so, too – you can't be surprised at that. Just look at this awful field. Broken-down fences, barbed wire, mud everywhere. And he must be scared as well. Plenty of yobs around, I'd imagine, who'd get tons of amusement from chasing the poor thing around and tormenting him. Hurry up and tell him he's coming with us. Can we make the sanctuary, d'you reckon? Or is it Annie's overnight?'

'Oh, Annie, I think – she won't mind having a donkey in her back garden for the night, especially one as appealing as Scooter. And we can walk him to the sanctuary tomorrow.'

Redcoat, who had been looking on, thought it time he took part in this conversation.

Hey – that's some power you've got there, Mary. Scooter's looking a completely different animal. I hardly recognise him. And he's so much happier. I know where to come in future if any other friends of mine need your help. Is that okay?

We'll always be happy to help you and all your friends, Redcoat. Any time, day or night, feel free to call on me.

'I think he might just be that tiny bit more popular if he could manage to wait until the morning at least, Mary,' Lizzie added. 'Your mum and dad might be a bit happier with that instead of being dragged out of bed in the dead of night!'

THIRTY

Mike and Maureen at the *Horse and Pony Sanctuary* were delighted to have Scooter who would be one of only two donkeys there. Scooter would have an older female donkey companion, Lucy, who, given her initial reaction, would be only too happy to mother him. Introduced to her as soon as he arrived, he met with a royal welcome and the girls left on a "high" having promised to visit as often as they could, as well as to keep their ears open for potential new owners who would welcome – preferably – both of the animals.

'Are you going to try and find Scooter's present owner?' asked Lizzie, curiously.

'No. This is my first attempt to steer clear of wishing punishment on this wretched person, Lizzie, and I must stick to it. It would be pretty difficult to track him down, anyway, I think, and I've got so many other things to think about. At least we've saved Scooter which is what matters. It'd be great if we could find him and Lucy a really good owner but until then he's happy where he is. So, please kick me if I look as if I'm weakening. I've got to beat this demon and here's my first chance to have a serious go at it!'

It was a busy Saturday morning in the Darling household and Susan needed more sugar for her latest batch of charity fair contributions. With Tom busy in his study, Mary cycled off to pick it up, leaving Laker at home in order to avoid the Saturday traffic and shopper crowds. She was preoccupied. So much to think about: her lessons with Annie and her progress on that front; the research she wanted to do into snares and what could be done legally to make them less damaging to wildlife; volunteer work at the animal shelters with possible secretive healing opportunities; and, of course, the looming regional GK tournament in which she and Lizzie would be representing Milton Upper. Consequently, she was taken by surprise when, on her return with the sugar safely in her rucksack, a dark-haired woman stepped into the road and signalled her to stop.

'Aren't you one of the girls who helped that swan not so long ago?' she asked. And, when Mary nodded, she continued, 'I read about it in the local paper and how much you care for animals.'

'Is there something you need?' asked Mary.

'Well, I've heard there's a poor dog been abandoned, tied up in the local quarry. Expecting pups she is, too. I'm no good with dogs – bitten when I was young – so wondered if you could help. You being good with wildlife an' all…'

'Oh, of course,' said Mary. 'Poor thing. How awful. I'll go and get her straight away!'

The quarry wasn't far. If she got a move on, she could make it in fifteen minutes. Hmm, she'd have to walk the dog back to Annie's so that could take longer – unless she took it home. Then she could persuade her mother to run them both to Annie's, couldn't she? What about the sugar? Maybe she should go home first… For a minute or two, she stood undecided, then her heart won. Her mother would understand and she'd been okay for sugar for the current batch of baking. She'd cycle like mad to the quarry, collect the dog and, with a bit of luck, be home within the hour. She turned in the direction of the quarry.

People who abandoned dogs made her sick. They shouldn't get dogs in the first place if they couldn't handle the responsibilities! Hey – she must get off her personal soapbox. If she carried on, she'd rouse the hideous demon and that wouldn't do. Right, then, she'd think about the dog and ways of finding homes for its puppies. What breed would it be? Large dogs needed more food and exercise than small ones. Even if the shelter took it, they didn't have unlimited funds and, if she was landing them with an animal about to have puppies, with more food needed when they were weaned, she should do her best to help. Oh, that was a point – she didn't have a spare lead with her. Never mind, she'd probably have the rope the morons who'd dumped her had used to tie up the poor animal. Yes, she'd start making enquiries about homes for all of them, immediately. Annie and Lizzie would help her.

She was nearing the quarry now. She'd better start keeping an eye out for the dog. Fortunately, there was only the one main approach road but, bordered by trees, bushes and minor tracks penetrating thick undergrowth, it offered plenty of scope for leaving a poor animal that could be hidden away easily and not discovered until it was too late. Then there was the disused quarry, itself. Oh heck! That could offer masses of hiding places. She might have quite a search on her hands. Then again, the dog might be barking which would lead her straight to it – unless it had been left there for some time and was too weak from lack of food. Damn! After all this, she might not be in time to save it!

Sunk in thought as she cycled, she was oblivious to her surroundings until – too late – the wire across the path did its work. Without warning, her bike went flying and she was hurtling through the air to land, sprawled, in a thick bush. Before she could gather herself together to discover what had happened and whether or not she had any injuries, everything went black as what felt like a rough sack was thrown over her head. Beefy arms grabbed and lifted her and a sweet, sickly smell assaulted her nostrils.

'Tom, could you go and look for Mary? I'm getting worried. She went out on her bike, only to the local shops, to pick up some sugar for me, well over an hour ago and should have been back by now. Even if some animal crossed her path, she knew I needed that sugar and wouldn't have taken as long as this. And Laker's very disturbed. He's been running back and forth between the kitchen and the side gate for the last half hour. Something *must* have happened!'

Another hour passed before Tom Darling returned – without Mary. His face troubled, he looked at Susan and shook his head. 'No sign of her or the bike anywhere. I drove as far as the town which you said she wouldn't have gone near. I don't know where else to look!'

'Did you try Annie?'

He nodded. Then, seeing the worry on Susan's face, he added, 'I shouldn't worry unduly. There's possibly a perfectly reasonable explanation for this. She'll probably turn up soon, full of apologies about some cat or bird she's been helping! You know what she's like, Susan.'

At that moment, the doorbell sounded, Laker barked twice, and there, on the doorstep, stood Annie. Her expression serious, she didn't wait to be invited in but moved past them into the kitchen. As they gathered round the kitchen table, the reason for her visit became obvious.

'I'm come to say that, since you left, I've 'ad some bad vibes,' she said gravely. 'I think our Mary's in trouble, big trouble.'

At that, Laker barked again. Everyone looked at him.

'What sort of trouble?' said Tom and Susan together.

There was silence while Annie hesitated. Then, 'I'm feelin' some bad people 'ave got her,' she said.

'Where? Who would do such a thing?' asked Susan. 'And why?'

Annie was silent while she thought for a few seconds. 'Mary's got some bad enemies an' it feels like they've organised a way ter put 'er out of action,' she said, slowly.

'Oh no! Enemies? What enemies? What has she done to make enemies?' Again, Tom and Susan spoke together.

'We've only been here fifteen months. How could she make enemies? She's still a child – only just fifteen in a few weeks! What has she done?' Susan's voice was unusually high-pitched.

Tom squeezed her arm for comfort. 'Calm down, love,' he said.

'Lizzie told me 'bout the trouble she's been 'aving at that school and there were the business with Laker too. She's convinced that were a plot ter get at Mary. That there dog, 'e be 'er life, so Lizzie thinks they tried ter knock 'im off 'cause they knew it'd destroy 'er.'

'But that's shocking! Why, for heaven's sake?'

'There do be some as can't live with people like Mary. She be too straight, too much for 'em and 'cos they don't understand 'er, they see 'er as, like, alien. These perticlar girls be jealous an' vicious. They want 'er outa the frame, like.'

'My God, that's terrible. You mean that awful Fellowes girl, don't you?' Susan's voice was faint.

And, as Annie explained about the white van and how it had been seen patrolling the area in the hours before Laker's accident, both Tom and Susan paled. This was more serious than they had realised.

'Why didn't anyone say anything about this at the time?' said Susan, shakily.

Annie simply shook her head. 'Pulling Laker out o' the pit 'e were in took top place, din't it?' She shrugged, her voice cracking. 'There weren't no time for getting those 'oo did it, were there?'

'These girls…' said Tom impatiently. 'Are they the same ones she had trouble with last year?'

'I think so,' said Annie, 'but Lizzie could prob'ly tell you more.'

'Well, let's get her here fast,' said Tom, firmly. 'The police, too, immediately. Is there anything else you can tell us, Annie? Anything about anything that Mary's involved in? It seems there are certain things, important things, we don't know about our daughter and you never know how it could be helpful.'

'Yes, and any other feelings you get, Annie, that might also have to do with this?' added Susan.

'Feelings? What feelings?' said Tom with a touch of acerbity.

'Oh, Tom, be quiet; you wouldn't understand, anyway,' said Susan. 'These are intangibles – like Mary's healing gift – and beyond our rational, engineering mind. Let it be. It's enough that Annie is close enough to Mary to let us know whatever she can pick up!' And the two women exchanged an understanding look.

'Thank you, Annie,' she added as the old woman rose to leave the room.

'I be on me way now,' said Annie. 'Best ter be on me own in case somethin' else comes through. I can get 'ere quite fast by the back way if anything comes ter me.'

The police, when they arrived, were understanding and thorough in their questioning and gathering of information, although there seemed to be little that Tom or Susan could tell them. Lizzie, however, was a different matter. Angry and upset as she was at hearing what had happened, her voluble input told them all more in twenty minutes than either Tom or Susan had gleaned from Mary in the entire thirteen months of her time at Milton Upper.

The more she heard, the more Susan was horrified. How little she had known about her daughter's difficulties! Not much of a mother who didn't know her own daughter had been a target for such vicious bullies. Mary must have been so unhappy! If only she had suspected half of what she was hearing now for the first time, her daughter's life could have been so different, so much easier and happier. Her guilt was intensified when the police asked why no one had reported Laker's accident and the activity of the white van.

'We were just so preoccupied with Laker's recovery,' she protested weakly, as the policeman who had asked the question studied her carefully before putting his notebook away.

'I'm afraid I have to ask if you have any objections to us searching your home.' And as Susan looked taken aback and Lizzie snorted in disbelief, he continued, 'It's just part of our standard procedure in any missing person enquiry, which this is. We have to establish the fact that she hasn't gone to sleep in a cupboard or whatever.'

While the two constables carried out the search, Tom comforted Susan. 'They have to dot all the i's and cross the t's, Susan. It really is just standard procedure.'

The search over, the policeman who had taken the lead headed for the front door. 'I understand your anxiety, Mr and Mrs Darling,' he said, 'and yours too, Lizzie, but try not to worry. We will be starting our own house-to-house enquiries immediately and if nothing turns up tomorrow, there will be more extensive searches of the various areas around here, perhaps bringing in police dogs and volunteer members of the public.'

'Well, I'm doing some of my own sleuthing at school,' declared Lizzie, 'and I'm definitely going to find out more. I won't give up until I do!'

The policeman looked at her with respect. 'Well, it would be particularly useful if you could find out anything about that white van. Even some of the registration number would be more helpful than you may realise, as we do have various ways of tracking down vehicles even with only minimal information. And, of course, it goes without saying but I'll say it anyway – whatever you do find out, please keep us informed.' And he handed them all cards as he turned to go.

All this while, Laker had been running back and forth, unable to settle.

'He's our daughter's dog and they're extremely close,' said Susan. 'It's almost as if he knows what's happened and, of course, he's agitated. He's wondering where Mary is. She spends practically every minute of her spare time with him and, all of a sudden, she isn't here.'

'Well, maybe he'll be able to lead us to her,' the policeman replied, raising a quizzical eyebrow as he left.

'You know, that could even be a possibility at some point, you never know,' said Tom.

'Don't joke, Tom, I'm so worried.'

'Actually, I wasn't joking, Susan. Laker and Mary are so close that it wouldn't surprise me if he did end up leading us to her! They'll find her, I'm sure, and we'll have her back here soon. As the man said, you must try very hard not to worry. It won't help.'

'I'll keep you informed about whatever I discover,' said Lizzie as she, too, left, 'and I know where to start. I'll also keep the police informed. I won't rest until we find Mary, I promise.'

THIRTY-ONE

Blackness. Silence. Her head ached and she couldn't open her eyes. There was something tied across them. Tightly. A blindfold! That explained the blackness. She couldn't see. She couldn't scream either. Something was tied across her mouth. A gag!

Just as bad – she couldn't move. Panic! Her wrists were tied, painfully, behind her back and her legs at the ankles. It felt like she was lying on something rough. Fingers reaching out, she fumbled to feel it. Coarse, gritty, slightly hairy and smelly, too. Yes, a sack. And the feeling of cold under her told her she was definitely on the ground. That sickly sweet smell was still faintly around, too. What was it?

She must fight off this panic. It was threatening to swamp her and that wouldn't do at all. Stay cool. Think about this calmly.

Where was she? How long had she been here? Who had done this? And *why*? The last thing she remembered was cycling towards the quarry, then suddenly flying through the air as her bike took off somewhere else.

Was anything broken? Hard to tell, trussed up like a chicken. But her head was throbbing like mad. Bloody hell! Lizzie would have grinned at hearing her swear. But this was no laughing matter. It was gross. How on earth was she going to get out of it?

She strained against the rope binding her wrists. Useless – too tight. Her legs? The same. Someone had done a damn good job with these ropes. Wait a minute! Ropes. Where had she heard talk of ropes? Her mind still felt fuddled. She couldn't think. Just take it easy now, no rush. After all, there wasn't a deadline, was there? Hang on! How long had it been since she went out for that sugar? Her mum and dad would definitely be worrying by now. Oh nooo, the sugar. Where was that? Bit of a useless trip all round, it had turned out. Her mother had needed that sugar and here she was, tied up and lying on an old sack if her nose wasn't deceiving her, imprisoned in the middle of nowhere, cold as hell, and – minus her bike – with a long hike to get home!

And what about that dog? Huh! What dog? That must have been another trick to get her here. Oh, what an idiot she'd been, falling for that. Hmm, if she kept this up, the Voice would be completely justified in taking away every gift she had and getting someone else to do the job. Some animal ambassador she was turning out to be!

Hang about! Gifts! She'd completely forgotten her gifts. Think now, Mary, think hard. Holy cow! Had her mind gone completely? What gift did she have that could help in this situation? Speed. Yeah, well, not a lot of good that one since she couldn't even move! She had to get out of the ropes first. So? Strength – ah! That was what she needed! She hadn't really tried it out since she'd bashed those yobs who'd been tormenting Laker and then hurled them into the lake. Plenty of it then. Oh, and the swan, too. She and Lizzie had lifted it in getting it to the bank still tangled up in fishing twine. Yes, the swan had been a fair old weight. And she wouldn't have managed that without the help of added strength! She hadn't tried out any strength since then, had she? So, maybe it was time to have a go now. Hold it! Belief. She had to believe. Hadn't she discovered that an important part of these powers was self-belief? Whenever she had doubted the healing would work, it hadn't. Yes. That was it. She had to believe. And she also mustn't force it – she'd learned that, too. Let it flow naturally.

Right, then. Rest for a few minutes, relax, then count to ten and go for it! Aaarrgghh! Aaarrgghh! Aaarrgghh! Minutes later, she fell back, exhausted. No good. She didn't have enough strength. Either she hadn't been able to summon up enough self-belief or the power hadn't developed enough. Either way, it hadn't worked. No good griping. She just didn't have it and even if it was going to develop, it wasn't here now. She'd have to think of something else.

Hang on – voices! Someone – people – were coming! Footsteps approaching. A key grinding away – must be rusty – in the door. Then it opened and slammed shut. Heavy steps came towards her and stopped.

'So, we going to give her anything to eat?' A man's voice. Then a mumbled reply. She couldn't make out all the words.

'They want her to starve? You kidding?' Again the mumbled response.

'Well, no one's going to find her, it's completely deserted. Workings ended years ago. But she's got to have water. We can't deny her that.'

So she was in the quarry.

The sound of a bottle being opened, the gag removed and the bottle held to her lips. She'd like to have spat it at them but good sense told her that wouldn't go down too well – and she was parched. Good sense won. She drank thirstily. Then she decided on boldness. She swallowed hard.

'Who are you? Where am I?' It came out in a croak.

A sharp intake of breath, then an agitated mumble before the gag was replaced, though not quite as tightly.

'She must have done something pretty bad to deserve this. I thought it was just to scare her!' More mumbling.

Beside herself with fear and anger, in spite of the gag, she made mumbling noises as loudly as she could.

'She can hear us; come outside and we can talk about it.' Another mumble.

'Look, it's the second day with no food. We've got to keep giving her water 'til this is sorted. And it better be sorted fast. If she dies, it's murder, mate. No one said murder would be involved. I didn't bargain for this. I thought it was supposed to be a warning.

This isn't for me – I'm off!' There was the sound of footsteps going away from her, the door opening and shutting again, key turning and the voices arguing outside.

Oh no! Whoever had planned this wanted her dead! She was going to die in this place – like this! Oh no, oh no! She wouldn't see Laker again, or her parents, Annie, Lizzie! Oh no, no! Despite her efforts to stay calm, hot, angry tears welled up beneath the blindfold and she felt herself beginning to sob with fear and growing panic. This wouldn't do. She'd choke if she wasn't careful. A stabbing pain shot across her chest. She must stop this, calm down, think carefully. This awful plan would *not* succeed. She wouldn't let it! There was too much hanging on her ability to stay alive. Her mission in life, the animals, Laker… No, no, no!

Lizzie was not at all satisfied with this conversation. She looked hard at Paula.

'There's more to this than you're letting on, Paula!' she said firmly. 'There's something you're not telling me and I'm going to say this only once – if you don't spit it out in the next two minutes, I might just make you regret you ever met me!' And she moved closer to Paula, bunching her fists.

The other girl shifted uncomfortably. 'I've told you the truth, Lizzie. I honestly don't know. The others don't let me in on everything nowadays.'

'Why not? Others may have been hangers-on but the three of you, at least, have always been as close as worms and dirt!' said Lizzie contemptuously. 'What's changed?'

Paula flushed at the comparison. 'I happened to say I thought you and Mary deserved all the recognition you'd got recently. And I meant it. They didn't like it...' she ended, lamely.

Ah, so that was it! Lana certainly wouldn't have liked even the slightest hint of approval of Mary and Lizzie's success from one of her inner core. Paula would certainly have been left out of whatever machinations the other two had got up to after that, relegated to the sidelines immediately, thought Lizzie. Hmm, there really wasn't anything useful to be gained from the girl. She turned to go.

As she did so, Paula added, 'I had no idea there was anything awful planned. I'm just as shocked about what's happened to Mary as everyone else. If Mary has been kidnapped, though, she'll have been taken somewhere no one would think of looking, don't you think?'

In the Darlings' kitchen, Susan, Tom, Lizzie's parents and her older brother Matthew sat in silence. Matthew, two years ahead of Lizzie and Mary, with university in his sights, was particularly frustrated. 'The police haven't come up with anything yet and it's been three days since Mary went missing! There must be something else we can do!'

'We haven't any leads, Matthew. No one seems to have seen anything. I called on every house I could along both the routes Mary could have taken to the local shops and no one even remembered seeing her! The police have done another even more thorough house-to-house enquiry – and nothing. They said after that, they'd be making more extensive searches of the various open areas around here and even using police dogs. How about Lizzie? Has she come up with anything?'

'She'll be here soon – she's taking Laker out this afternoon. Where is Laker, anyway?' said Ellen Paige.

'He was here a minute ago. Laker! Laker! Here boy!'

'He's not been himself, at all, since Mary went missing. Been flying back and forth, looking for her constantly, hasn't eaten, won't settle. It's quite incredible how close they are. No one else can take her place, you know.'

'Ah, here's Lizzie… Uhh!'

Lizzie had appeared at the back door whereupon Laker, without warning, flew past her to the side gate. As they all watched, he stood at the gate with his head on one side, as if listening intently.

'What's he doing?' said Ellen.

'When he does that, it's usually because Mary's talking to him,' said Lizzie.

'How d'you mean – talking to him? She's not here,' said her father somewhat testily.

As Susan opened her mouth to reply, Tom held up a hand to stop her.

'I've learnt a bit about this lately,' he said. 'I know you'll find this a bit weird – I did at first – but Mary has a peculiar ability to communicate with animals somehow and, of course, she and Laker are extremely close. So I guess what Lizzie's trying to tell us doubting Thomases is that it's entirely possible that Laker is possibly hearing from Mary right at this moment!'

'No! Really?' said Ellen and Nigel Paige simultaneously.

'Are you serious?' added Nigel.

'Yes, really,' said Tom, 'and, don't ask me how, but, from being a complete sceptic, I've come to accept that sometimes things like this can actually happen.'

As Nigel Paige continued to look sceptical, Tom continued, 'Well, anyway, Lizzie, I was just explaining to Matthew that no one seems to have seen Mary cycling to the local shops. It's a complete mystery – you'd have thought someone would have noticed her somewhere along those roads.'

'What about the non-residential part?' said Matthew. 'Has anyone taken a look there?'

'Which part? What for? What are you suggesting?' said Susan, her voice higher than usual.

'There's a stretch of country road after the residential part and, if anything had happened there, no one would have known,' said Lizzie, slowly.

'What d'you mean "if anything had happened"?' asked Susan Darling desperately. 'What are you thinking could have happened, Lizzie? Have you found out something we should know?'

'Not really… The thing is… Oh, I don't know…' said Lizzie, scratching her head, uncertainly.

'Just tell us what you're thinking,' said her father, 'then we can decide whether you may have discovered something or not – and, for heaven's sake, get on with it!'

'Well, everyone at school is anxious for news and most of them are now friendly towards Mary so they do care about her. Those aren't the ones I've been targeting. I've been going after others more likely to know something. I promised confidentiality, even said a reward could come their way for any help etc, but they're tight-lipped. Someone's put the fear up them, for sure. Then one of the girls who hangs around on the edge of the bunch I'm interested in made a chance remark that was interesting.'

'What? Why was it interesting?' asked Matthew. 'What did she say?'

They all looked at her expectantly.

'Well?' said her father impatiently. 'Spit it out, Elizabeth – we haven't got all week!'

'I know, I know. I'm trying to remember exactly what it was,' said Lizzie, slowly. She tapped her nails on the table, reflectively. Then suddenly she snapped her fingers. 'Got it! I'd mentioned places we'd thought of searching for Mary or her bike and, as I was going, she said something like "Well, if she's been kidnapped, she's probably been taken somewhere they were sure no one would ever think of looking"!'

There was silence while everyone digested this.

'I hadn't said anything about kidnapping,' Lizzie continued, 'so why would she think of that as a possibility?'

'And where would we not think of looking?' said Ellen.

THIRTY-TWO

Time had lost all meaning. Her hands were aching from the constraints, her legs immobile for so long she could hardly feel them, and her stomach, well, her stomach just felt non-existent, food a mere memory. Two more visits from someone bringing water – in silence this time – had kept her going on the thirst front but there was no attempt at conversation of any sort. The blindfold still in place, night and day were just concepts and she was no nearer knowing what was going to happen to her.

Mary, however, was far from beaten. How long she'd been in this ghastly situation, she still had no idea, but what she did know was that she had by no means exhausted all her options. There were still unexplored possibilities. When she calmed herself and stopped swinging between rage and misery, she recalled how Lizzie had asked more than once whether or not she could initiate contact with other people by telepathy and she hadn't pursued it; but she knew that she could communicate with animals, although she hadn't yet tried it without the animal present. So? So there was always a first time, wasn't there? And who knew her better than anyone, human or animal? Why, Laker of course! And he was certainly used to her talking to him when they were together, so why would it not work when they were apart?

She was famished, and thirsty, too, now. Weak and exhausted from both lack of food and sleep and freezing cold too, she bit her lip. Hmm. They may have been able to tie her down and silence her physically but she wasn't beaten! Not yet! Her mind was still free, wasn't it? And, now that she had gathered herself together sufficiently, she was going to attempt something she'd never tried before. She was going to try to talk telepathically with her dog miles away! No human would do. No. It had to be Laker.

Laker knew her better than anyone else in the world. When they were together, he knew what she was thinking and feeling almost better than she did, herself. He knew all her moods from one minute to the next. So why wouldn't he know when she needed him? And why couldn't she tell him enough, even at a distance, to make it possible for him to guide a rescue operation? Laker had only been to the old quarry once and that was when she had first had him. Would he remember where it was? Was his sense of direction strong enough for him to find her? Well, she could always guide him. Anyway, there was only one way to find out. She had nothing to lose, after all.

The minutes went by as she strove for control of her feelings. If her mind wasn't calm and controlled, if her fears were in charge, then she had no hope. This was all part of her battle for the upper hand, essential if she were to attempt the sort of telepathy she was contemplating. And it wasn't easy because despair was hovering close by all the time: she was terrified she was going to die here alone, without her dog or anyone else who cared for her. For the umpteenth time, she asked herself who could hate her so much as to devise a plot like this which would end in her death? There was an evil hand at work here.

And again she shivered in spite of her bonds.

Laker was unable to settle. He ran back and forth to try and find his beloved owner. His Mary. Where was she? He could feel, somehow, that she needed him, but how? Where? What could he do to get her back? He lay disconsolately near the side gate. She would appear soon. She must. Why didn't she speak to him? She usually did when they were together. Why not now? Another hour passed as he lay there. Susan appeared with some food.

'He's still not in the least bit interested,' she reported back to everyone. 'He's just lying there with his nose to the gate. It's as if, without Mary, nothing matters. He didn't even look at me.'

'He'll eat when he needs it,' said Tom, and Lizzie, pragmatic as ever, nodded her agreement.

Had they all looked out at Laker half an hour later, they might have gained fresh hope, for he was sitting bolt upright. The fragments of whispers that had been filtering through the gloom in his mind for the past hour had suddenly become more than that: he had heard his name, and not just once. Four times it had sounded with increasing clarity and then, following hard on the heels of that source of exhilaration, had come a definite plea for help from the girl he worshipped. *Help me, Laker! Help me!*

He bounded to his feet and stood, bristling with excitement. Mary was calling him! His Mary was actually speaking to him. She needed him. At last! He would reply!

Is it really you, Mary? Where are you?

And then, amidst considerable muffled noise, there were further fragments. What sounded like shuffling, mumbling, voices arguing, a door banging, footsteps, mingled with blackness, then snatches of Mary's voice talking to him, calling his name repeatedly and that "quarry" word again and again! Quarry! Mary had taken him to a quarry soon after his arrival here, hadn't she? She and Lizzie had heard some birds had been seen in the quarry. So they'd all gone there. The quarry... The quarry... Could he remember where it was? How to get there? He must, he must! Mary needed him!

Agitated almost beyond any feeling he'd ever known, except the terror when those yobs had been trying to drown him, he rushed back and forth in a frenzy between the kitchen door and the gate. Then, beside himself with frustration, he sprang through the door into the kitchen, slid along the tiles and ended up spread-eagled in the doorway to the hall.

'Laker! What on earth?' said Susan in astonishment. In response, he leaped up and put his paws on her shoulders, looking earnestly into her eyes and barking.

'Something's happened. He knows something!' Susan said excitedly. And as Lizzie stood up, Laker jumped down, turned round and did the same to her, before bounding off through the kitchen door to the side gate where he remained, barking loudly.

'He's trying to tell us something, Mrs D! I'm sure of it! Look, he's standing out there now, by the gate, just barking.'

Drawn by the commotion, the others crowded into the kitchen.

'Well, looks like he wants us to follow him,' suggested Tom. 'Let's try it, anyway. Come on, grab his lead and let's go!'

'We'll all go!' said Nigel Paige. 'Come on, let's get on with it!'

'We'd better take the car,' said Susan. 'We don't know how far he's going to lead us.'

'Hadn't we better tell the police what's happening first?' said Lizzie. 'We might need help!'

'Yes, sensible move,' said her father approvingly.

'Quick, then,' said Tom, 'but we don't know where we're going, do we? Oh, go on, tell them anyway, but fast! Leave a message with someone if you have to.'

And, as everyone gathered themselves together and headed towards the front door, Tom clicked the lead on Laker, now practically taking off vertically in his agitation.

'They've said to hold on a few minutes,' said Susan. 'They're sending a car to accompany us and, Tom, that makes sense. As Lizzie said, we might need help and they'll have personal protection equipment in case we hit trouble. We have no idea what we're letting ourselves in for and a few minutes more won't hurt.'

'Wait a minute, everyone!' Lizzie, ever-practical, had had a thought.

Everyone stopped and looked at her. Lizzie held out her hand to Tom. 'Mr D, Mary and I have done a lot of walking with Laker and, with all respect to you, I think he'd probably let me handle him more easily, especially if he's going to lead us to Mary as we think he might be doing.'

As Tom hesitated, Susan nodded emphatically. 'Lizzie's right, Tom. She's been with Mary and Laker on walks much more than we have. Let her lead the way with him. You drive instead and we can follow them slowly.'

At that moment, the police car, with two policemen and a policewoman, pulled up outside the front gate. The discussion that ensued ended in the two cars following Lizzie and Laker in close convoy.

The small cavalcade headed off through the estate until they reached the junction with the stretch of country road that Lizzie had mentioned earlier. Here, Laker stopped and hesitated before turning away from the direction of town and towards open country. As they prepared to set out in that direction, Lizzie decided to have a quick word with Laker. She bent down towards his ear and spoke quietly so that only Laker could hear her.

'I know you can understand me, Laker,' she said. 'And I know how important this is to you. But Mary is my friend, too, and we need to make sure we can rescue her without putting her in any danger. So please don't bark or make any noise at all. We mustn't warn anyone of our arrival. Do you understand?' The dog looked at her with intelligence in his eyes and Lizzie insisted, later on, that she was certain he had understood.

And so girl and dog set off at a pace that seemed to indicate that Laker had a fair idea of his destination. The cars followed. A mile later, at another junction, once again, Laker seemed in no doubt of his direction. The cavalcade continued on its way until they all arrived at a third junction and, when Laker turned without hesitating, once more, Lizzie began to feel certain where they were heading. A few yards along the road, she stopped and held up her hand to the two cars following her.

'I think I know where we're heading,' she said to them all. 'The old disused quarry lies in this direction so that's where Laker seems to think Mary is being held. I think we only took him there once, when Mary first had him, so it's a miracle he remembers where to go, but there are masses of places she could be hidden so we're going to have to search.'

'Isn't it possible that Laker will be able to lead us to her?' asked the policeman driving the police car, pulled up close behind.

'Oh possibly, but we don't know who might be watching and we don't want to put Mary in any danger so we'll have to go carefully and quietly,' said Lizzie.

'Have you thought of a career in the police force?' replied the policeman with a wry smile.

'She's thought of so many she'll never live long enough to decide!' said her father. 'Lead on, Macduff. We need to get there sometime this year if possible!'

The procession continued, with Laker becoming increasingly eager as they continued. At the sign pointing to the quarry, he began to run, Lizzie keeping pace. The cars picked up speed until the road narrowed to a track which gradually petered out. All around them was scrub falling away beyond clumps of gorse and scattered, stunted bushes with minor tracks here and there. Lizzie held a finger to her lips for silence and did similarly to Laker who wagged his tail as if in understanding.

'Let's get the cars off the track and into the bushes,' the police sergeant in charge instructed quietly. 'The less notice we attract, the better.'

That done, with Laker and Lizzie leading the way, they stood silently in a clutch looking down into the quarry. It was clear that, with so little cover there, Mary could not be secreted in the basin itself.

'What now?' said the policewoman. They all looked at Laker who, ears cocked, appeared to be listening intently to something. A minute or two later, he began to whine softly whilst straining eagerly straight ahead across the basin.

'Whatever he's after must be on the opposite side,' said Lizzie.

'Well, we can't cross in the open. We'd better go round the edge,' said the policeman and, with Laker leading, the party followed slowly and silently in single file around the edge of the excavation towards the opposite side. Once there, Laker stopped and sat down. Minutes passed while everyone waited.

In the same moment that Tom opened his mouth to speak, Lizzie held up her hand to stop him as Laker suddenly stood and listened intently before setting off through the shrubs and gorse, his head held high and nose pointing ahead.

It had tired her out. The constant effort of projecting her thoughts to Laker for heaven knows how long – time had lost all meaning – had exhausted her. She was sure he was coming because she'd managed to discern, through the mist of muffled noises in her head, just one word – *coming!* But nothing else had come through since then and the pain in her head had increased. She needed a rest.

It seemed as if hours had gone by since those footsteps had sounded and there'd been no further visits. But Laker was on his way, she knew. She could feel it. In a minute, she'd make another effort to free her wrists. Her earlier attempts must have had some effect because the ropes seemed less tight and, to her surprise, her wrists seemed less sore. She could feel Laker coming closer now and, in a minute, she'd call him again before having another go at the ropes.

Laker! Laker! I'm in a shed, I think! she repeated several times.

Then, taking a deep breath, she exerted all her strength against the ropes around her wrists. Was it her imagination or were the ropes giving? Yes. No. Yes. She could definitely feel a slackening. She'd wait, call Laker again and then give it another go. *Laker! Laker! I can feel you coming closer! Keep going, Laker!*

Now for the ropes again. A deep breath first, then... Aargghh! Yes! They were! It wasn't her imagination! She could feel them parting bit by bit! And just as exhilaration was flooding through her veins, she heard a noise outside. Heart in mouth, she stopped what she was doing and listened. Oh no! Surely those people hadn't returned. Not now, please, not just as she was certain help was on its way! Silence. Then the noise again. Not a key in the door but a snuffling. A definite snuffling. Laker! She could feel his presence. He'd found her!

Laker! she shouted mentally. *I'm in here!* And in that same moment, the ropes parted completely and her wrists were free. A minute or two of rubbing and shaking them to restore circulation before she could tear off the blindfold and gag and see her surroundings for the first time. Minutes in which the snuffling had become a series of increasingly robust nudges at the door while she swallowed and cleared her throat.

A long swallow again and then another attempt to do more than croak. 'Laker!' she managed to call out, 'I'm here!' And the next minute, someone charged the door and it flew open amidst a shower of splinters. After that, everything seemed to happen at once as bodies piled through the doorway: uniformed police, her parents, Lizzie and her parents and, in front of them all, moving like lightning, her beloved Laker! He got to her before anyone else and, in a flash, was all over her, licking her anywhere he could!

Feet still tied together, she could hardly move for Laker everywhere and it was only when the policewoman, kneeling, was able to get between her and Laker and remove the ties that she could try and stumble to her feet with hugs from everyone. Hardly able to stand and with Laker still wound around her legs and refusing to be dislodged, she was held up by her parents who hugged her again and again. Then Lizzie took over and she smiled weakly at her and everyone else through tears of relief as she gazed around her at the walls of the disused workmen's hut that had been her prison.

THIRTY-THREE

The police interview was not going well. Lana Fellowes, her father sitting to one side of her, was looking mutinous. Her father, openly annoyed, looked at his watch impatiently.

'How much longer does this have to go on, officer?' he demanded. 'We've been here for almost two hours now and, as far as I can see, we're still none the wiser. My daughter insists that she can't help you with your enquiries.' He looked fiercely at his daughter. 'And that had better be the truth, Lana, or, I promise you, you will live to regret your failure to speak up!'

Lana reddened and studied her feet.

'Now,' he continued, as he stood up to go, 'if you wish to call her in again, officer, I shall need at least a day's notice as I intend to be accompanied by our solicitor!'

The policeman shrugged, exchanging glances with his policewoman colleague, before snapping shut his notebook with a sigh of resignation, standing up and indicating the door.

'There's more to this than that young madam's letting on,' he said later, 'but as long as she continues denying any knowledge, we can do nothing – unless, of course, we manage to nail one of the other two.'

To the Darlings, the police said little except that their enquiries had proved fruitless so far but they hadn't abandoned hope that a single, key development could still turn the investigation on its head.

'Okay, Paula, you and I need to talk! And fast. Somewhere private where no one'll see us together so we can thrash this out properly. Because if anyone can help me get to the bottom of what happened to Mary, and why, it'll be you – and I'm not going to leave you alone until you do!'

Lizzie, on form, was a force to be reckoned with and Paula knew she was beaten. More than that, the former Fellowes camp follower had become disenchanted with dancing attendance on the other two and, in the process, being ostracised by the majority of their classmates. Now, however, Lizzie wanted her to "grass" on them and that was a completely different ballgame.

Few knew Lana Fellowes' capacity for malevolence better than Paula. Still in their entry year at Milton Upper, at a birthday party for Lana, Paula had inadvertently come upon the girl holding down a pet kitten – a birthday gift from her godmother – struggling for its life in a bucket of water until the very last moment before it would have drowned. Its crime? A playful paw on Lana's freshly-painted toenails!

It was not her only source of fear where Fellowes was concerned. Unknown to her parents, Lana had recently begun to display – in Paula's opinion – an unhealthy interest in certain dubious local circles. Having exhausted the resources of the school library, she had somehow made contact with members of a local coven. Consequently, Paula had a clear priority – self-preservation.

'Even if I did want to help you,' she protested, in a far corner of the sports field after school, 'I don't know anything of any use. Lana didn't tell us any names – or didn't tell me, anyway. After I said you and Mary deserved your success, she cut me out of all her plans. So I can't tell you what I don't know, can I?'

Lizzie was unrelenting. 'No, but if you think hard, I bet you could come up with something, some detail, however small, that could give us a lead. You must have seen the white van, surely... No?' as Paula shook her head emphatically. 'What about the bloke I saw her meeting after school? The one with the flashy sports car? Who's he? Where did he come from? Surely she mentioned his name sometime? How did she meet him? What did she say he did for work? Do her parents know about him? Think, Paula, think!'

'She didn't tell her parents about Ja— Oh, I remember now, she did say his name – Jason. She called him "Jase". Said she met him in a local pub one lunch hour, when she sneaked out for a quick drink!'

Oh right, thought Lizzie, *add that to the list of Fellowes' capers on the sly!* 'So what d'you know about him? Did he drive the white van? Or did he find someone else to do the dirty work?'

'I don't know anything, really I don't,' said Paula. 'You'd have to ask him that, Lizzie. Honestly, I can't tell you what I don't know. But even if I did, I still wouldn't tell you. You don't know what Lana's capable of – she's evil!'

'I'll tell you what,' said Lizzie, 'if you think Lana's evil, "you ain't seen nuthin' yet!", as my brothers tell me often enough! So come on, Paula, we can do this one of two ways: you can co-operate, come quietly and save your miserable hide; or I can drag you howling round every pub car park in Milton so everyone knows what's going on. One thing's for sure: I am definitely going to find that flashy car, with "Jase" propping up the bar inside, no doubt, because I just know he's involved somehow. Either way, Paula, you are definitely going to give me what I need, so it's decision time, kiddo!'

She was back there. In the blackness. Unable to move. Her wrists and legs tied. That sickly smell again. Almost gagging with something tied across her mouth. Unable to scream. Panic! Oh! She *could* scream – *was* screaming… Aaaargh! Aaaargh! Aaaargh! Struggling, fighting the bonds. Then, wetness. Arms round her, holding her, soothing her. Laker, licking her all over, devoted, protective. Her mother's arms, comforting, easing, calming.

The same nightmare over and over.

'It's got to stop sometime,' said Tom to Susan the next evening. 'Just go with the flow for now. If we find it continuing for too long, we'll get her some help, don't worry.'

She had a dread of bedtime, of falling asleep, even with Laker near her. Then, without warning, the Voice intervened. The healing, Mary, the healing. *You are forgetting your mission in which your primary task, for now, is the healing. Get back to the healing and your other worries will disappear!*

To her astonishment, she shared this, all of it, with both Annie and Lizzie. With not a second's hesitation, either.

'He'm on the ball, lass. That there 'ealing is the nitty gritty, 'tis that what gives you the upper 'and. 'Cos you ain't thought, girl; by and by, 'tis the animals wot'll be there ter 'elp you in times o' need. You mun get goin' again, lass – and fast. Use the rest o' this recovery time you got ter start back in there pronto. Then the 'ealing an' the animals will stop you stressin' soon enough 'bout these past 'orrers, you'll see!'

'Annie's spot on, Mary. Get going again with the healing. It'll take your mind off what's happened. Then, before you know it, you'll be back on the right road, with no time for rubbish in your life. And, let's be practical about it, after all: you've learned some valuable lessons from this little jaunt and you won't be taken in like that again, will you?'

They were right of course. She'd had weeks not using her most important gift and it was time she got started again and – Lizzie, true to form, also had a point – she *had* learned important lessons from the experience. She'd been naïve and silly to be taken in by that woman, a stranger she'd never seen in her life before that day. And – face it – she'd also felt a bit flattered that the woman had recognised her from that piece in the paper. That wasn't her usual form – she'd have to watch that. If she was going to let newspaper articles go to her head like that, she'd turn into another Lana Fellowes, full of herself before too long.

'No time like the present,' declared Lizzie as she and Annie both turned up the very next day, each bearing a cardboard box containing casualties: a small blackbird with an infected eye and three newborn kittens, one clearly at the end of its tether, in need of immediate strength and sustenance.

'Tossed away in a blasted litter bin by some beggar 'oo couldn't be bothered even to turn 'em over to a shelter!' said Annie, trying hard to watch her language in front of Susan Darling. They were the first in a succession of patients delivered by both her friends in the week that followed, all needing attention in varying degrees. Healing was back on the agenda with force so that, by the end of the week, the impact of the nightmare had diminished significantly and Mary was well on the road to recovery.

'And so,' said Lizzie to the police sergeant whose card she had guarded so carefully, 'Paula did come quietly and we did all the pubs in Milton Cross to see if this bloke's car was in any of the car parks, and it wasn't. So we did the rounds again the next day and the next – because I knew he'd have to turn up in one of them at some point.'

'Bet you're flavour of the month,' said the police sergeant with a grin. 'At what point did you get a result?'

'Oh, day three – she was getting a bit bolshie by that time but I wouldn't have quit and she knew it. We finally spotted it in the add-on car park behind the *Pig & Whistle*.'

'Then what?'

'Oh, Paula legged it, said she'd deny knowing anything if you questioned her – she's petrified of Lana, you know.'

'And you? What did you do then?'

'Oh, I haven't got brothers for nothing. Just tackled it head-on. Went in, said I knew he was Lana's latest and would know about the white van, and I'd shop him to you lot if he didn't give me the name of the driver and where he could be found. At first, he denied everything but then I decided to bluff and told him I had an informant who'd seen him with the bloke. Just as I thought, he's a bit of a wimp – he cracked straight away. Turned out he was just the middleman. Lana supplied the dosh and he paid white van man to hang around and find an opportunity to finish off Laker. Said he met the bloke only once and that was through someone else. He only knew him as Pete. Didn't know where he hung out and couldn't remember the complete number plate but he did give me the first bit. He denied any other plot. So here's what he remembered – and it's all yours now!' And she handed over the piece of paper bearing the details in question. 'You *are* going to follow it up, aren't you?'

'Straight away, Lizzie, straight away,' said the sergeant, with a respectful smile. 'And this time, *we'll* keep *you* informed!' And, as Lizzie turned to go, he added with a small grin, 'Let us know when you're ready to consider the police force, won't you?'

🦋

'And so that was that!' said Ellen Paige as she and Nigel relayed to the Darlings, over a drink that evening, what Lizzie had done. 'Now we must wait to see what happens. I do feel sorry for Graeme and Liz Fellowes, I must say. He's a decent chap and she's okay, too, even if she does tend to be too easy-going with Lana. They've been too lavish with her but they don't deserve this and they're going to be shell-shocked if Lana emerges as the mastermind behind it all.'

There was silence while Tom and Susan digested all that had been said.

'Hmm, well, the girl's got problems, no doubt there,' said Tom, 'and I don't know how much that comes from her mother's leniency and father's workaholism. Graeme's probably never around to see what Lana's getting up to!'

'Well, he *is* Financial Director of *Maynard's* and they've just opened a branch in the States, haven't they? That's a huge responsibility for anyone!'

'Whatever the reason, it's still shocking if she did set out to damage Mary so seriously,' said Susan, 'but all that will surely be taken into consideration when they eventually decide what's going to happen to her.'

'Hmm, when they get her to confess, you mean,' said Nigel. 'Without more evidence, it's only the word of those two blokes against hers, when all's said and done. And she'll just go on denying everything, you wait and see!'

'Yes, you're too generous, Susan; the girl's evil,' said Tom. 'It's a damn good job Lizzie's managed to get anywhere with this. Mary's lucky to have her as a friend and I'm sure she knows it.'

'Well, the reverse is also true, of course,' said Ellen.

'So, what's the state of play now?' said Lizzie, pacing up and down. 'How can everything be taking so long? It's been five days since I gave them those van details. What on earth are they doing? Honestly, the criminals in this country must be having a field day!'

Mary, with Laker still glued to her side, smiled sympathetically. No one understood better than she how much her friend was afflicted with impatience. For Lizzie, nothing happened fast enough and, with no report of progress, her boredom threshold was being sorely tested. 'Dad says Fellowes is still denying everything and the other two seem to be scared of her, for some reason, so no one wants to spill the beans.'

'You're joking! Scared of Fellowes? Why, for heaven's sake? Oh, wait a sec, though – Paula did mutter something about Fellowes and some strange local circles. That could have something to do with it, I suppose. Have to say, no one's missing her at school, though. In fact, the longer she's away, the better. It's much healthier without the nasty cow. And, strangely, even her cronies seem quite relieved.'

'Hmm…' said Mary, thoughtfully.

'What does that mean – hmm?' said Lizzie. 'What do you know that you're not telling me? You've got that look on your face again. Come on, spit it out!'

'Not much, but something unexpected did happen. I picked up some snatches of something going on last night, something involving Fellowes and, believe it or not, Lasher!'

'You're kidding! Fellowes and Lasher? What?'

'I'm not sure but it seemed to be something they didn't want made public. The snatches of talk I heard contained one or two bits that gave that distinct impression – things like "for your ears only" and "remember, nothing about the meetings!" '

'Well, there's nothing we can do at present until the police let us know what they've found out about the van. If this bloke that Jason paid to nobble Laker does turn out to be the driver and they can nail him, then we've made a start and we're in with a chance of getting them all to cough.'

'Have you been reading some more of those crime thrillers? I recognise some of the terms I'm hearing,' said Mary, amused.

Lizzie's only response was a broad grin.

'You are not obliged to say anything. Anything you do say will be put in writing and given in evidence. My colleague here will be taking notes.'

The interview room was so still that even a breath might have been heard. Detective Sergeant Cross, who'd been doing this for longer than he cared to remember and had heard it all, stared, expressionless, at the man opposite him, as the solicitor he'd requested to advise him settled himself in. Like most twenty-three-year-old men in this situation, Jason stared back defiantly. It contained an element of bravado, of course, and Detective Sergeant Cross was unaffected by bravado – in his job, he'd seen it all and bravado was just that. Under clever questioning, it usually broke down at some point.

Of average height with unremarkable features, Jason would have passed by in the street, unnoticed. Slim and wiry with longish dark hair just brushing his collar, the only noticeable feature about him now was what seemed like an inborn restlessness: fidgeting about in his seat, he seemed almost as if he could take off at any minute. As the silence continued, he shifted uneasily yet again.

His solicitor sighed impatiently just as DS Cross reached for his notebook to commence the questioning. His colleague, taking the notes, waited. Both officers were prepared for the inevitable series of 'No comment' replies.

THIRTY-FOUR

'So, what will happen next?' asked Tom Darling of Superintendent Miller who had come to update the Darlings on progress.

'Well, our forensic people are turning the vehicle inside out, so we have great hopes of coming up with unshakable evidence on that front.'

'What's the position on the abduction?'

'They're all denying any knowledge of it,' said Superintendent Miller, 'and, until we can break one of them, we're temporarily stumped. But we've got other cards to play. One of them was worried enough to bring you water two or three times and you heard his voice, didn't you, Mary? Think you'd recognise it if you heard it again?'

As Mary nodded, Superintendent Miller looked thoughtful. 'Well, that'll certainly help. The ID parade is on for tomorrow and a voice ID will now be on the agenda as well. There are other ways and means, too, so one way or another, we'll nail them. Bit too long in the tooth to let small-time crooks like this beat us, don't you worry!'

'So, an ID parade tomorrow and possibly a voice ID as well? They're not cracking easily, then?'

'No, they're all denying any involvement apart from the hit-and-run and, of course, almost killing Laker probably won't carry as harsh a sentence as the abduction,' said Mary bitterly. 'I don't see much evidence of justice at work there!'

'Hey, don't start getting wound up about that now,' said Lizzie. 'I know how you feel but, for the moment, it's more important we collar them for what they were trying to do to you. And then the punishment for that will probably cover Laker's side of things. What about forensic examination of the back of the van? You were bundled into a vehicle and carted off. How about evidence in the back?'

'You're right and he said his forensics people are working on it. Anyway, we'll find out if and when, you can be sure of that. They're not going to give up. He seemed pretty determined.'

'Wonder what he meant by "other cards to play" and what "other ways and means" he was referring to?' said Lizzie, thoughtfully.

'Are you absolutely sure?' said Superintendent Miller into the handset. 'Great! And the other? Right. No way it could be mistaken? How soon will you know? Hmm, no faster? Oh no, I certainly want you to be sure of it. Well, ideally, yesterday! Okay, okay, tomorrow it'll have to be – as early as you can make it.'

He replaced the receiver and grinned at his sergeant. 'It's looking good. We'll have that confirmed tomorrow and then we'll get the two of them in and put the screws on! Enough pressure and one or both will cough. We can always dangle the other carrot as well to make sure of it.'

His sergeant, usually poker-faced, permitted himself a fleeting smile of satisfaction. 'Tomorrow could be quite entertaining, sir,' he said.

Another couple of days off school, then. Couldn't be bad!

The Head's telephone call had been definitive. 'The police have been in contact. They'll be calling you, of course, but wanted me to know, from the education point of view, that they think it advisable for Mary to remain at home for another couple of days, perhaps even a week. They feel the situation is critical and her co-operation in the case is of immense importance at this stage. They need to be able to call on her at any time so, if that's acceptable to you? Oh, of course… Her results to date show that she's well able to cope with most of her subjects and any extra help needed won't be a problem, I'm sure.'

The voice ID had been everything he could have hoped for. Fifteen voices with Mary listening intently to each, and two of them twice. It had helped, of course, that one phrase Superintendent Miller had selected for them to repeat had been the one where the bloke had baulked at being involved in a murder. He'd known that the right chap would protest at that with genuine conviction and that, try as he might, it would be impossible for him to hide the surviving trace of his regional accent. So she'd been certain in the end and – funny thing that – she'd seemed almost sorry for him. It was the right choice, of course, and when her friend had reminded her, for the second time, that he'd been the driver who'd almost killed her dog, she'd fallen silent.

Yes, Superintendent Miller was well satisfied. His other piece of evidence had also been confirmed; he only had to up the pressure now on the two he'd pulled in for questioning in order to nail the third and, boy, was he going to apply those screws! Calling her in again, though, would have to mean a charge. And it would have to stick next time. Her father would not take less. He was difficult enough last time and he'd make sure he had the top solicitor with them that he'd threatened last time. The girl was a wily one, mind. Very cool customer. The makings of a professional criminal. Would need watching.

'So they've all been charged? I have to say, we never thought you'd do it!' Almost speechless with astonishment, Tom Darling had, nevertheless, recovered himself sufficiently to smile broadly and shake Superintendent Miller's hand, with feeling. Susan and Mary were clearly relieved, while the entire Paige family – invited over for the police visit – were openly jubilant, Lizzie punching the air repeatedly.

'What are the charges?'

'All three jointly charged with Kidnap, Conspiracy to Murder and Attempted Murder.'

'Phew! Bet that knocked Graeme Fellowes for six!' said Nigel Paige. 'What about the bigshot lawyer he said he'd bring in? How did he react?'

'Well, neither of them was happy, of course, but they couldn't dispute the evidence. He made it clear, though, that we should expect a top barrister from London for his girl when it comes to the trial, but that won't be for six months and *sub judice*, of course, as they've been charged and the matter's awaiting trial. Meanwhile, the men will be remanded to prison and the girl to the care of the local authority.'

'Which means?' asked Lizzie.

'To a secure children's home, as she's still a minor.'

'Hmm,' said Tom Darling, 'Graeme and Liz will be knocked back by that.'

'And Lana will throw a total wobbly. Wouldn't be surprised, in fact, if she didn't try and do a runner!'

'Well, the magistrates were quite clear about it: these are very serious crimes and they're not going to get off lightly.'

'How did you get them in the end, then?' asked Lizzie. 'I've been wondering what those "other cards" were that you said you still had, as well as the "other ways and means" you mentioned!'

Superintendent Miller smiled. 'Apart from hints at a lighter sentence for co-operation with us, you mean?' he said.

'Oh, right,' said Lizzie. 'Yes, apart from those. What else? I've been flogging my brains out to try and think what else you could have had to threaten them with and, unless you came up with some evidence we didn't know about, I'm beaten!'

'There is definitely a place for you, young woman, in the force,' said Superintendent Miller admiringly. 'Just let us know when you're ready to consider it.'

Lizzie grinned, as did Mary who knew her friend well enough to know that this would be only one of a hundred options on Lizzie's list, when the time came.

'So, go on then,' said Lizzie, determined not to give up. 'What else did you have on them? What did I miss?'

'The footprint. Or rather, heel print,' he replied. And as they all looked mystified, he went on to explain. 'Pete, your kind bloke with the water, Mary, had stepped – without noticing – in the black ash remains of a fire near the shed where they held you, and left us a beautiful partial print of the heel of his boot on the concrete floor of the shed. It had an unmistakable pattern and was a perfect match for one of the boots amongst others in the back of his van where, incidentally, we also found traces of limestone particles. Those alone, though, might not have been enough to do the trick. We needed to pin him down to the shed.'

'Wow!' said Lizzie. 'Who spotted the print, then?'

'Oh, we have one or two eagle-eyed people in our forensics bunch. In fact, we could so easily have missed it because it was partially obscured by a bag of old tools that had toppled over on it behind the door that was, before we broke it down, but our man spied it on a subsequent visit and took a chance on his theory.'

'Cool!' said Lizzie. 'Real cool. Didn't think to search the shed for anything incriminating.' And she fell silent while she digested this.

'What about the fact that he did bring me some water?' said Mary. 'Won't that stand in his favour at all?'

'Oh yes, and a good word will certainly be put in for him on that score bu—'

'And he definitely said that he didn't know murder was involved and he didn't want any part of it,' she added. 'As you know, I identified his voice. Surely that must say something for him?'

'I'll add it to my notes and mention it in court, I promise,' said Superintendent Miller. 'But don't *you* forget that they are being jointly charged because they're all equally criminally liable. It will be for this man's defence to persuade the jury that he was not aware of the intention behind Lana Fellowes' scheme and that won't be easy. I've an idea that that young woman won't let him off easily – she seems like a hard nut and, unless her boyfriend confirms it, could argue that it's just his word against theirs and they're all in it together.'

'Anyway, why do you care, Mary?' said Lizzie. 'I've already reminded you once. He's the same thug who was paid to knock off Laker. Surely you want him to pay a high price to cover that? You don't want him to get off lightly, surely!' At that, Mary was silent.

'So, what happens next?' asked Tom.

'Well, Lana's father asked for bail but the magistrates weren't convinced that the family would be able to satisfy the conditions so, as I said earlier, she's been remanded to the care of the local authority until the trial.'

'Wow! Bet that'll go down like a lead balloon,' said Lizzie.

'Yes. Mr Fellowes is definitely not a happy man,' said Superintendent Miller. 'He's furious with his daughter; seemed to take it very personally, as something of an open rebellion against him and everything he represents. He also appeared highly concerned about his reputation locally.'

'Oh yes, that he would be,' said Tom. '*Maynard's* CEO is not going to be at all impressed by this: his top finance man has a daughter who's placed her father, and therefore the firm, in disrepute, and this at a time of critical expansion overseas. Oh yes, Graeme will certainly not be a happy man. Right now, I imagine he'll be worrying about possible effects on his future with the company!'

'And what about Lana's mother?' asked Susan. 'Poor woman; she's going to come in for a bucketful of criticism.'

'Hmm, she didn't look too happy at the court, I must say. Think her husband had already made his feelings very plain.'

'How long will Lana be in care?'

'Well, in about six months, it'll be a trial at the county assizes for all of them. As I said, these are very serious crimes and all the sentences are likely to be stiff. Probably life imprisonment for the two men. It will then be for the Home Secretary to decide, many years down the line probably, when it's safe to release them.'

'And Lana?'

'I think the phrase is "detained at Her Majesty's pleasure", which means she could be locked up for quite a few years. Again, the Home Secretary will decide when she can be released.'

'Bloody hell!' said Lizzie, before she could stop herself and, as her parents shook their heads disapprovingly, she blushed.

'Hmm, poor Liz and Graeme – they're going to be shell-shocked.'

'Should have thought of that when they were busy buying her glitzy baubles and letting her think she was superior to everyone else!' said Lizzie. 'It's no more than the evil cow deserves! Good riddance to bad rubbish, I say! Hope they lock her up and lose the key!'

Everyone was silent, reflecting on the truth of Lizzie's words even while recognising the harsh reality behind them.

'Have you informed Keith Staddon?' asked Tom.

'I'm on my way to see him now. I wanted you to be the first to know. I hope young Mary here is well on the road to recovery and I assume she's going to be returning to her studies now?' And he smiled as Mary nodded her thanks.

'So, that's everything I wanted to report, I think,' said Superintendent Miller.

'Thank you,' said everyone, as he rose to leave.

'Hope to hear from you when you're ready, young Lizzie,' he said. 'We won't forget your input. Well done!' Lizzie flushed as both families joined in the sentiment.

As relieved as the Darlings and Paiges were, so were their opposite numbers incensed. The Fellowes' household that evening was a grim place indeed. Lana's parents, shocked and furious at the position in which their daughter had placed them, as well as the blot on her own future, were finding it difficult to absolve each other from blame, each seeing the other as being entirely responsible for Lana's criminal activity and malevolent intentions. Both were incredulous that this could have come about from a daughter showered, in their opinion, with blessings beyond compare. And just as ghastly – if this were to be believed – how such a nightmarish individual could have resulted from either of their genes!

Their daughter, meanwhile, was seething at the indignity of her surroundings. The lack of luxury was bad enough; now her lips curled in distaste as she surveyed the "rejects" forced upon her as inmates and what passed for food at the communal meal that evening. That hotshot London barrister had better justify the fee her father was intending to pay him! He'd have to get her out of this rat-hole pretty damn quick or she'd make more waves than any of them anticipated!

THIRTY-FIVE

Mary's face was the colour of beetroot. Standing just inside the door of the classroom, astonished and bashfully misty-eyed, she twisted and untwisted her fingers, unable to think what to do next. Lizzie, at her side, smiled understandingly but happily. The reason – without precedent and completely unexpected – was the sight still confronting them. As Mary had pushed open the door and entered, all her classmates, already assembled, had risen to their feet, beaming, cheering and clapping with gusto.

Eventually, as Mrs Hunt moved forward to greet her, the cheering died away and, with Lizzie grinning broadly and clapping her on the back, she moved towards her seat, smiling uncertainly.

Reflecting on the day later, she could hardly believe how miserable she had once been in this very same place. How different it was now! Everyone was so friendly and welcoming and, in the warmth of their camaraderie, she was beginning to find it easier to be more relaxed and sociable. The atmosphere in all the lessons was so easy and good-natured, it was difficult to remember the tension that had existed.

The one person towards whom she still had misgivings was Lasher. Since her return to Milton Upper, she seemed to have avoided crossing his path. A relief – but somehow strange! It wasn't as if the school was a vast multi-storey complex occupying multiple acres of land. In a routine day, she would normally have expected to see him at least once in the distance, if not a direct encounter. She must be receiving help by an intuitive awareness of his approach long before he even came into view. Bizarre!

'Have you seen Lasher this week?' she asked Lizzie as they walked home at the end of her first week back.

'Mmm, once or twice, I think. Why?'

'Well, I know you'll think this weird—'

'More than usual, you mean?' cut in Lizzie, with a grin.

'No, seriously... I haven't, not even once, and I have this strange feeling that I've been helped to avoid him in some way.'

'How d'you mean?'

'Well, somehow I seem to know when he's coming or is somewhere near and I think I must take a different route, without realising it.'

Lizzie looked at her sideways. 'All for the best, I'd say. The bloke's a nasty piece of work and "evil" isn't too strong a word for him, if you ask me. The less everyone sees of him, the better. You especially – he hates your guts!'

'Yes, I realised that soon after I got here and I've often wondered why.'

'Hmm, there's something about you – and I can say this now because we know each other much better. And you won't fly off the handle as you would have done at the beginning, now you know I'm well and truly on your side. You do, don't you?' And, as Mary nodded, Lizzie went on, 'I don't think you're conscious of it but there's a directness, a sort of honesty, about you that makes some people uncomfortable. Because you're quite rigid, you know. You won't compromise. Something's either black or it's white. For you, there aren't any shades of grey and even if you don't say anything, your face shows it. That's difficult for lots of people, especially at our age. They don't know how to handle it. Fellowes and her cronies pretended to be what they're not and I guess they always will, because that's them. They could fool a lot of people – or thought they could – but not you. And you showed it from the start. So they hated you. It's the same with Lasher. He knows you see straight through him, to the dirt, and he can't hide it. Remember the French expression we learned – "bête noir"? Well, you're his black beast!'

'Well, thanks a bunch; makes me sound horrific. But you're right, I really don't know I'm doing it. I certainly don't set out to do it. So, what about you? How have you managed to handle it – this awful thing about me that I didn't even know I was and certainly don't know I'm doing?'

'Well, it took even me some time and I like to think I'm smarter than most!' Lizzie grinned. 'It was a bit uncomfortable to start with but once I understood what you were about, I was fine. And then, of course, I found out you were even more weird than I thought!' And she threw Mary a humorous shoulder punch.

'I'm beginning to feel I hardly dare go out with this awful burden. People must see me coming and run for cover!'

'Well, you can't do anything about it,' said Lizzie, cheerfully. 'That's you and you're stuck with it, so we'll just have to live with it, won't we? If you could be a tad less serious, lighten up a little, it could help – larking about a bit, joking, always makes life more enjoyable for everyone. You'd have to practise that, mind you; it doesn't seem to come naturally for you. But I wouldn't worry about it, you've managed okay so far, and I suppose I could always walk in front of you, apologising in advance for what's coming, couldn't I?'

Even Mary grinned at this.

'Oh, and by the way,' Lizzie added, 'I should have said, obviously Lasher doesn't come into the bracket of those you want to like you. Think we'd rather have red hot pins stuck in our eyes, wouldn't we?'

As the girls approached Annie's cottage that Saturday morning, Mary could feel her arms and hands tingling in anticipation. Annie had promised a morning of healing practice for Mary and so Lizzie had asked to join her. For Mary, this was great: the more Lizzie came along to these sessions, the better. This was to be her future and Lizzie wanted to be involved so it made sense for her to see and know as much as possible. Being honest with herself, it was, also, really good to have her friend with her – she no longer felt alone.

Annie met them at the side gate, as was usual with healing cases in the kitchen or garden. Accompanied by Buddy who sat quietly, she beckoned them towards the cage in the garden where a small spaniel puppy sat looking sorry for itself.

'Afore you get going, lass, you need ter know something we didn't expect. I don't say as it'll stop you but you still oughta know.' As the girls looked questioning, she continued, 'One o' yourn mates from school 'as been 'ere and it's 'er pet,' she said, nodding in the direction of the puppy. 'Now, she didn't mention you or Lizzie, just the school, and I ain't seen 'er afore but the pup's a sweet'eart and she seemed a nice lass, so I took it in, like, and told 'er I'd do me best for it.'

'What's the girl's name, Annie?' asked Lizzie, practical as ever. 'It'll help us to know for future reference, Mary,' she added.

'I got it written down 'ere, girls,' said Annie fumbling in the pocket of her ancient smock for the scrap of paper on which she'd scribbled. 'Yes, 'ere we are... Caroline Arry?'

'Caroline Merry,' Lizzie corrected her gently. 'So, Mary, we must be careful if Caroline ever brings up the subject. Have you mentioned Mary at all to her, Annie?'

'You think there's a screw loose in me 'ead, girl? Course not!'

There was silence as all three digested the possible repercussions of this news. Mary was the first to speak. 'We all know this gift of mine can't be allowed to go public yet, Annie, but there is a way around this and I'm sure Lizzie will agree with me.' She looked at Lizzie as she continued. 'I'll simply do the healing for this little puppy and we can let her believe *you* did it. How about that? Lizzie?' She looked Lizzie in the eyes as she asked the question. Her friend was unfailingly practical and objective, seeing arguments for and against anything dispassionately, where she, herself, was often too emotionally involved. Lizzie would tell her straight away if this suggestion wouldn't work. And so it was. After the briefest silence, Lizzie nodded emphatically.

'Good idea. The only way round it, in fact. You okay with that, Annie?'

The old woman smiled in agreement. 'As long as you'm sure you don't mind me takin' the credit, like, lass?'

'I haven't got a problem with that, Annie. The most important thing is always the welfare of the patient. You taught me that, remember?'

The three of them smiled in mutual complicity, after which Mary simply got on with the healing of the puppy's muscle sprain.

'Hmm, active little soul, ain't 'e?' commented Annie, as the puppy bounded around at the end of the session.

'Think Caroline needs a bit of advice on how much exercise to give this puppy,' said Mary. 'It's very tempting to think puppies can do more than they should when they're as active as this but you can do a lot of lasting damage if you let them run around too much, too early. Could you advise her, Annie, please? Because we're not supposed to know she has a puppy; she certainly hasn't mentioned it at school.'

'Yeah, and the other danger now,' said Lizzie, 'is that Caroline is popular and bound to mention this experience to others, so word is definitely going to get around that Annie's is *the place* for any pets in need of healing. That means we must be careful she and others don't see us coming here, Mary. Maybe it would be sensible practice, Annie, for us to use one door and all the others coming for healing use the other way into the garden?'

'You are just sooo practical, Lizzie,' said Mary gratefully to her friend.

'Hmm, not goin' ter be easy, any o' this,' said Annie, 'but we'll do our best. It may be we ain't goin' ter 'ave much choice in this, girl,' she added looking keenly at Mary. 'You may just 'ave ter live with what 'appens, suck it an' see, as I've said many times afore now. Things'll come out, lass, when they be meant ter come out and that's as may be!'

'Annie's right, Mary, and we need to think how we're going to handle it, in advance, so that we're prepared. They all like you now and maybe we should start preparing them for the fact that you have this other gift. How about we remind them again that you can talk with animals and wildlife? Then, when they're all quite used to that and the time is right, we can move on to the healing bit?'

'You'm a sensible lass,' said Annie approvingly and, as Mary looked doubtful, she added, 'Take heed o' what Lizzie says, girl, take it in stages and, always remember, everything 'appens when the time is right!'

The nightmare of the abduction and imprisonment in the shed had all but ceased and she'd been so relieved. But now this! This was horrendous. Twenty times worse. The room was closing in, the walls and ceiling moving, inexorably, towards her. She couldn't breathe. Her chest was tightening. The stench of something foul, rotten, was all around. Dense, invasive, overwhelming. Coming for her! Oh God!

And then, in the next moment, there was barking. Loud, fierce barking. Again and again and again. And something was upon her, barking and growling, snapping and snarling! But not at *her* – at whoever, whatever, was attacking her. For attack it certainly was – and not human. Undeterred, her knight in shining armour – Laker – was on the job, defending her for all he was worth. What a champion! And, instantly, she was awake and struggling to sit up, battling for breath, panting, gasping, wheezing and, all the time, fighting not to vomit from the stench.

Fumbling for the bedside light, she managed to find it, switch it on. And, as she did so, the room, flooded with light, revealed a thick, fetid, black mist slowly receding, together with the walls and ceiling. And Laker standing astride her, his neck and body rigid and his hair everywhere standing up, continued to snarl, growl and bark at the unknown assailant. The next moment, the bedroom door was thrown open as her parents rushed in.

'Are you all right?'

'What's happened?'

'Why is Laker barking like that?'

They both spoke at once and Mary, petrified and shocked as she was, had to think fast. Quietening and soothing Laker, she was mindful of the fact that her father had never been keen on a dog in the bedroom, even less so on her bed! So now she had to stop him from ordering Laker out. For her own happiness, peace of mind and protection, this had to be the priority. Her secondary consideration was to stop them worrying. So, on both counts, it would be best to stick with territory already familiar to them. The usual nightmare would make sense of it. Yes, she'd fall back on that and then they'd understand.

'I'm so sorry,' she ended. 'I haven't had one for some days now and I thought I'd got over them but it seems I haven't quite seen the end of it, so poor Laker was only trying to defend me. It's honestly not his fault; please don't blame him. At least you know I'm being protected, don't you?' And she looked pleadingly at her mother. A short silence ensued but it worked. Shaking his head, her father allowed himself to be ushered gently out of the room by her mother who looked back at Mary with only the smallest hint of disbelief.

THIRTY-SIX

For once, while Lizzie burbled away happily, Mary was almost completely silent on the Monday morning walk to Milton Upper. The events of Saturday night had left her drained and she'd been astonished that her parents had not wanted to know more about the row in her room. Clearly, they had not heard any of the tumult surrounding the attack but Laker's noise alone had been enough to wake the dead, and yet neither of them had asked what had provoked such a mighty defence from her dog. There had been no questions at all. Very odd! And she still had to share it with Lizzie and Annie.

To make matters worse, she'd seen Lasher at the school gates. Lizzie, deep in conversation with one of the other girls, had been looking the other way, so she hadn't witnessed what had happened. And Mary had only caught it by chance. Turning his head as he heard the sound of a car behind him, Lasher had spotted her and, instantly, his face had distorted in an expression of pure ugliness, an evil beyond anything she'd ever encountered. She could hardly believe what she'd seen. Oh, if only Lizzie could have seen it, too! It had disappeared in a flash as Keith Staddon appeared round the corner, but too late – the damage had been done and Mary was shaken.

She would tell Lizzie everything at some point but she wanted to discuss it all with Annie first and so, at the end of school that day, she pleaded a herb lesson and headed off for *Freedom Fields*.

As she pushed open the garden gate, her troubled face spoke for her and Annie needed no explanation. Her response was simple and direct. 'You been under attack, girl, bain't you?' the old woman said. 'Come, sit and tell Annie wot 'appened, start to finish. This'll 'elp you, too.' And she pressed a cup of one of her herbal concoctions into Mary's hand.

When Mary had finished, the old woman was silent, her face unusually serious. 'You'm going ter need 'elp, lass,' she said at last. 'Fast, too, if I'm right in where this is 'eading.'

'So it's as bad as I thought, Annie? Can *you* help me?'

'This be out o' my reach, lass. The only one can sort it, I'm thinking, is the Voice. You mun go inside yoursel' and talk to 'im. No time like now. Go and sit by the river, bottom o' the garden, where you won't be worrited by anyone. Sit with your back to the willow by the water there 'cos the willow be known for its 'ealing and growth, so it'll give you strength for this. You take as long as you need, lass, but go – now!'

'What do I say, though? I've never called him up before.'

'Certain sure 'e knows some o' this already and 'e's waitin' for you to ask for 'elp. Times when some 'umbleness be called for, lass…'

The water seemed to shimmer with an intensity that Mary had not noticed before and there was an unnatural silence as she sank to her knees on the riverbank alongside the willow tree. Unusually, there was no birdsong and no movement of any sort, not even the odd plop of a small fish in the water or the hum of any insects. As her back made contact with the willow's trunk, she felt an immediate welcoming warmth almost as if it was offering some much-needed comfort and, seconds later, she felt something stirring deep inside her. The urge to speak was pronounced but the instinct that was telling her to wait, to bide her time, was even greater and so she did.

Minutes passed as she sat in silence. It was not difficult; in fact, it was becoming quite comfortable and there was even an odd sense of communion with the willow tree while she waited for the right moment to speak with the Voice. Then, just as she felt that moment was approaching, a current of energy rippled up her spine and along both arms and the decision was made for her. The Voice spoke, so clearly it almost felt as if it was in her ear – *You need help. I am here. Speak as you feel. Do not try to hide anything because there is no point and you will be wasting time. I demand total honesty even if it reveals weakness. I know what I know. I need to hear what you are feeling.*

And so Mary told it all, from start to finish, without attempting to conceal her fear and feelings of vulnerability. *I don't know what to do,* she ended, *or where to go for help. This is way beyond my experience and seems so menacing and unreal. What is it? What's happening to me? Whatever it is, I haven't any way of fighting it and I'm terrified. Can you – will you – help me?*

This is just one of the many attacks, replied the Voice, *that you will sustain during your involvement in this mission. It has come slightly sooner than expected but that is all to the good as we can prepare you, by degrees, for this and worse.*

Worse? What a dire prospect! This had been dreadful enough. Now she was being told that worse was to come. She really didn't know if she was up to handling it!

And I know that you are petrified by the prospect of something even worse but, once you are armed and know that you are protected, you will find that prospect much less harrowing because you will be equipped to deal with it. It must be done by degrees, in order that you grow into your future skin at a realistic and comfortable rate. You have mighty work ahead and will face powerful adversaries, so must be prepared accordingly. We shall make a start immediately so that you are armed against forces of the type that have already attacked you. Be assured that your defences will match – and ultimately exceed – the strength of your assailants. You will, however, have to experience each new attack first in order for the power of your defence to increase to match and, eventually, overpower it.

And my dog? He defended me stoutly last night but he has no defences of the type that you are going to give me. Please, would you arm him equally? You must know how much he means to me and, for as long as I can have him, he will be with me wherever I go. Without him, I might not wish to remain on this planet.

I do know what he means to you and will do as you have requested.

Thank you, thank you! Can I also ask about Lizzie and Annie, my only friends, who are committed to helping me in this mission? Annie has certain healing gifts and I need her. Lizzie has important practical skills and gives me incredible support. They are the only two friends that I trust and will be accompanying me whenever and wherever they can. They are bound to come under attacks of some sort in future, as a means of getting at me. Will you consider giving them some protection?

I will need to observe these friends at work for a time before I can decide what would be an appropriate level of protection. We shall return to this subject when I feel sufficient time has passed, or before that if events make it necessary, and I will give you my decision. For the moment, we must focus on you and your dog. Sit back now as you were and close your eyes. You will sleep for some time, as will your dog at home. When you both wake, you will be armed against attacks similar to the one that you have already experienced. The armour for both of you will match each increase in force from future attacks.

Mary woke to find Annie and Buddy sitting alongside her on the riverbank.

'You look very peaceful, my bird,' said the old woman. 'Everything okay?'

'Oh yes, yes, Annie. You were right. The Voice knew everything – and understood it all perfectly. And yes, I'm fine now.'

And she recounted what had happened.

The hero's welcome she received from Laker and his confirmation that his "treatment" had taken place, was all that she could have wished. Now it was only Lizzie she owed an explanation.

With the weekend approaching, this explanation was still hanging over her.

'There just aren't enough hours in the day,' she complained to Lizzie as they walked home on the Friday afternoon.

'I don't think the twenty-four day was planned with people like you in mind,' replied Lizzie, grinning. 'You really need fifty-two and then some!'

Sitting with Laker and Lizzie behind *Freedom Fields* overlooking the river that weekend, while waiting for Annie and Buddy to return from one of their foraging sorties, Mary was almost at peace. For the time being, anyway, her only concerns were the remaining backlog of school work – and the account of the attack and follow-up that she still owed Lizzie.

'I know you're probably thinking about what you still have to catch up with,' said Lizzie, digging in her bag. 'Here are some more handouts and notes and I'll help you copy them out if you want. You know that, don't you?'

'Oh, I know, it's just that trying to keep up with everything else, too, is heavy. Still, tough – it just has to be done. Thanks anyway.'

'Well, the offer's there; you helped me when I broke my wrist, don't forget.'

As Mary opened her mouth to reply, Laker bounded to his feet and growled, the hair on his neck bristling. And suddenly she had the distinct sense of being watched – by something ugly. The hairs on her arms prickled and her throat tightened. She froze. And then, in the next second, she felt... nothing. It was as if nothing had happened!

'What's up? You've gone completely white – like you've seen a ghost! What is it?' Lizzie was shaking her by the arm.

She took a deep breath. 'I just felt strange. I don't know why.'

'What d'you mean, strange? What sort of strange?'

This was ridiculous. Was she being paranoid? But she'd definitely sensed something weird again. Something sinister. It was almost like the other night; only, in the wonderful open air with nature all around, there were no walls to close in on her. Once again, though, it was just as if something foul, something noxious, had been hovering, menacing her. And – fleetingly – she'd felt as if a gigantic weight had descended on her chest. Then, as swiftly as it had come, it was gone. Ah! She'd got it! That was probably the protection kicking in, for Laker had also settled equally swiftly.

Well, she could use it to broach the subject with Lizzie. Her friend would have to know sometime so, as Annie would say, no time like the present. Taking a deep breath, she launched and, by the time she'd finished, Lizzie was gazing at her in awe.

'And you've been dealing with all this yourself and not telling me?'

'Well, there's been so much going on and I didn't know what to say. It was all so dreadful and I thought you'd get fed-up and bin the friendship – think it was all too much to bother with. And I was too scared to risk that.'

'You really do take the biscuit at times, you know that, don't you?'

'Meaning?'

'Well, we've known each other properly now for almost a year and you still don't have a shred of faith in me. You really think I'd let something as poisonous as that kibosh a friendship that's way more valuable?'

'But you don't realise how dangerous it could be.'

'Well, you've just told me that you now have protection against it; is that what kicked in just now, d'you think?' And, as Mary nodded, she continued. 'So that'll be increasing gradually. You've also asked for protection for Annie and me which may not be there at present but your chap, the Voice, will be sizing us up and he'll dish it out when he's good and ready. So what's the problem, then?'

Mary had to smile at some of Lizzie's expressions even whilst recognising the sense behind what she'd said.

'I'll tell you what the problem is, shall I?' Lizzie continued. 'It's *you*, Mary Darling. You still have no faith, really, in anyone except yourself and your dog. You even doubt Annie at times, don't you?' And, when Mary remained silent, she went on, 'And that's incredible when she's stood by you from the start and given you so much!' As Mary still said nothing, she went on, 'It's time you had a huge attitude change, that's what. You need to do something fast about your understanding of friendship and your attitude, in general, towards other people. There are some really nice girls in our lot and you're still suspicious and wary of them when they don't deserve it. You need to examine yourself and do some life-changing work on that person in the mirror! And I shall give you 'til tomorrow to make a start!' And she gave Mary a good-natured but exasperated thump.

'Now, back to the main issue. We'll handle it, right? Don't tackle things before you have to. We've got an idea what's coming, so let's just get on with the Now!'

Lizzie was right, of course. She *was* still wary, still untrusting – even of Lizzie, who didn't deserve it. Lizzie was a true friend and she'd have only herself to blame if she messed up this friendship. Okay, she'd got the message. There was too much hanging on this. She would make that effort and she'd start this very minute!

It was July now and the summer holidays were upon them once again. After that would follow their all-important exam year with serious work to be done. For a while, at least then, the animals and wildlife would have to take a back seat. Before that, though, six glorious weeks were approaching, weeks in which they could roam, free from routines and the pressures of study and homework. Six great weeks in which long walks with Laker and Buddy beckoned and their animal interests could take top place in the list of priorities. For the time being, too, life was tranquil with no battles to fight.

The annual prize-giving at the end of term held few surprises. Mary's unavoidable lengthy absence had, unfortunately, lost her the Year Prize for English, but there was one award that made up completely for this disappointment. It was an award that caught everyone off guard – particularly its first recipient. This particular prize was Keith Staddon's brainchild, highlighting his personal belief in the meaning of true friendship. Unprecedented as well as unique, the award for the most loyal and supportive friend went to a completely astonished Elizabeth Paige!

Lizzie was, in her own words, "gobsmacked" – a somewhat "yobbish" term as her parents expressed it. But Lizzie, true to form, chose to ignore this and, beaming from ear to ear, she made her way to the stage to be presented by Keith Staddon with a substantial book token and a plaque which she carried back proudly. And no one clapped and cheered more vigorously than the friend who had put her name forward!

Mary couldn't have been happier. Sitting next to Lizzie with their families around them felt so, so good. She was free – even if only temporarily – of both her major enemies. So much had changed in the last eighteen months, she felt a completely different girl from the one who had joined Milton Upper sixteen months earlier.

Life in general was much easier and happier all round now – because she was no longer alone. She had so much; it was almost beyond belief that she could now count on *two* and a half real friends. Annie and Lizzie had made all the difference in the world to her, especially Lizzie, who had made it possible for her to feel – and be – more relaxed with everyone. And Laker was her soulmate. She could boast great parents who were coming to understand her and – best of all – her mission in life would always have the power of the Voice behind it. Not all of it would be pleasurable, much would be heavy-going and some of it positively Herculean, it seemed. It was, however, a challenge of the heart and she couldn't wait to get on with it!

EPILOGUE

Alone in her room at the secure children's home – comfortable by most standards but bare and austere by comparison with the luxury of her own – Lana Fellowes scrutinised the object in her hand carefully, smoothing the small scrap of denim and pressing the hair firmly in place.

'You may think you've won this time, Darling,' she raged, 'but the war isn't over, bitch. Oh no, not by a long, long way… And you have no idea what a weapon I'm holding! You'll pay – and how! – for this humiliation. Children's home indeed! Locked in with a bunch of losers! Oh boy, are you going to pay! Yes, oh yes, gipsy trash. You don't realise just how much…'

And, thirty miles away, a man was driving to a gathering of his brotherhood – with blackness in his soul.

ACKNOWLEDGEMENTS

My grateful thanks to:

My husband, Robin, for his support and powers of endurance.

Jim Parsons, my mentor, who gave me the valuable benefit of his knowledge and experience, enabling me to regain self-belief and continue writing.

Susan Bird, my vet, without whose veterinary knowledge and advice, a key episode in this book would not have had the authenticity necessary to give it legs. Similarly, retired police officers Fred J L Davey MBE, Simon Dell MBE Policing Historian and Superintendent Rick Walker BA(Hons) whose help ensured that representation of police procedure of the time was authentic.

Rebecca Muttlebury, forensic scientist, for essential information.

My computer engineer, Julian Mildren, *The Computer Doctor,* for whom no problem was ever too big or too much of an effort to solve.

My good friend, Dorothy Horswell, who, from the moment she discovered I was writing this novel, supplied faith, humour and moral support. She also read *Mary Darling*, offering valuable feedback.

Mia Ward-Edwards, aged 14 at the time, and Wendy Hocking, both extremely helpful readers whose feedback and opinions were invaluable.

Peter Beere, author, Ruth Muttlebury, artist/poet, Paul Taylor and various members of my writing groups for their belief and encouragement.

Finally, a special thank you to a very dear lady, Joan Marsh, whose unceasing belief and confidence in me, from the reading of my first short story, supplied more impetus than she will ever know.

And not forgetting - of course - my wonderful dogs,
Coco and Jessie, whose unconditional support and
enthusiasm was inspirational.